FINDING REDEMPTION

A SLAYING LOVE NOVEL
BOOK 5

AMANDA SIEGRIST

A Special Note…

First, reminder that this series used to be titled the *One Taste Series*. If you started the *One Taste series* at the beginning, you know that this series was supposed to end with *One Taste of Sin*. I had no intention of writing Newman's story. I honestly didn't like him by the end of book 4. I love when readers fall in love with my characters. You never know when writing a story if a reader will love them as much as you do. So, when one reader reached out to me asking if Newman was getting his story, I felt bad saying no, but I just couldn't do it. I was super mad at him for his actions—for his cheating. But she strongly felt he needed his story told. She wanted to understand why he acted the way he did. In my mind, once a cheater, always a cheater. But, over time, she convinced me Newman DID need his story told. Although, I was scared to write him. And I'm totally scared to share his story because he's a different kind of hero for me because of his past. If you didn't notice *awkward grin*, I don't like cheaters. *chuckles* But I hope I did his story justice, that you fall in love with Newman as much as I surprisingly did by the end. Am I still mad at him sometimes when I think about what he did? Um, yeah. But I understand his pain more…and well, Amelia doesn't like it when someone doesn't understand him, doesn't try to see the person he is underneath all his rough parts, and I don't want to upset her! Lol

I want to dedicate this book to Buffie Gier. If it wasn't for you nudging me to write this story, it would've never been written. And you picked the perfect title for it as well. Newman thanks you very much.

♥ Much love, Amanda Siegrist

A DISGRACED EX-DETECTIVE. A WOMAN WHO WON'T GIVE UP.
A CASE THAT COULD SAVE THEM BOTH.

1

His grandfather once told him, "The best things in life require the most patience." He had been teaching him how to hunt. Newman thought it meant he should take his time aiming so he'd have a perfect shot, but he always took too long and missed. He was a terrible hunter. Plus, he wasn't a fan of sitting outside for hours on end in the freezing cold waiting for a deer to cross his path. He didn't like hunting and told his grandfather it wasn't the best thing for him.

"How hard did you try? You barely gave it a chance. Patience. It's always about patience and taking your time," his grandfather had replied in a sad, disappointed tone of voice.

That was his one and only year he went hunting. It didn't matter he *had* tried. He sat the entire weekend in the tree stand alone, shivering from the freezing temperatures, even with hand and foot warmers to help keep the chill away. And a deer had crossed his path. He lifted his shotgun, took aim, and...and well, he couldn't pull the trigger. The deer had looked him in the eye and froze, daring him to shoot. But he couldn't do it.

Maybe he hadn't tried as hard as he could've.

Newman stretched out, sitting on the same couch his grandfather had owned when he lived in the tiny cabin.

He owned it now.

Even though he disappointed his grandfather—not the only time in his life he had—his grandfather left him his cabin when he passed away five years ago. Now it was his safe haven. His home. His escape.

Three months ago, his life disappeared. His livelihood. Everything he worked for...gone. One quick blink, and it all vanished.

Great job. Good friends. Almost a great relationship. Unfortunately, he damaged that months ago by cheating on a good woman.

Three long months ruminating, dissecting every part of his life, how it all went wrong.

There was so much he should've done differently, starting with Chrissy and his feelings for her.

Snapping his legs together, he stood up abruptly.

Nope. He didn't want to think about her. Because every time his mind conjured her, it conjured the dangerous feelings he wasn't ready to face.

Glancing at the punching bag hanging in the corner near the fireplace, he decided he needed to release some tension. A daily occurrence. So much tension. So much shame. So much rage consumed him. He liked to use sex and lies for an outlet, blaming others for his problems. These days, he used the punching bag instead. He rarely had contact with anyone, unless he made a trip to the grocery store, which meant he didn't have many chances to lie. Or have sex. Not that he didn't run across a beautiful woman or two when he went shopping. He usually smiled.

They smiled back. Before it could turn into anything flirtatious, he hightailed it out of there as fast as he could.

He was done with sex.

For the time being, anyway. He wasn't sure he could completely give it up. He was a guy, after all.

He'd have to join the real world soon. He couldn't live off his savings forever. He needed to find a job soon.

Tossing his shirt off, he stretched his arms, rotating and removing the kinks before he demolished the bag. He never used gloves while punching. Sometimes, his hands hurt so intensely, he knew he should stop. He didn't. Other times, he bruised his skin or even started bleeding. He still didn't stop. The pain was part of his penance for his actions.

Throwing a punch, he let the thrill, the power in his hands fill him up. Every time he hit the bag, a part of his damaged soul released. He figured as soon as he freed all the bad parts, the good part of his soul would be free to live a normal life.

He only had to be patient like his grandfather told him.

Some days he didn't think he'd ever live a nice, normal, carefree life. Honestly, he didn't deserve one.

Punch after punch released. He moved around hitting different spots on the bag. The muscles in his shoulders and arms started to ache, his hands throbbed, but he kept hitting.

The bag, not swinging too much, almost connected with him when a loud knock sounded on his door.

Holding the bag to stop its motion, he glanced at the door. Nobody visited him. The only person who knew the location of his cabin, besides his family, was Sauer, his old partner and best friend. He hadn't answered Sauer's phone calls since he left, and he didn't expect him to visit. His wife probably wouldn't let him. She hated him as vehemently as everyone else did.

Whoever it was could leave. He didn't want company.

Heading for the bathroom to grab a towel, another loud knock echoed in the small confines of the cabin.

And another knock.

And another.

Snagging a towel from the hallway closet, he wiped his face, removing most of the sweat, then slung the towel across his shoulders and headed for the door. If this person insisted on bothering him, then they could deal with his wrath. He didn't punch long enough to release the tension boiling like a hot volcano inside.

He flung open the door.

The woman standing on the other side gasped, her eyes trailing around his chest as if mesmerized.

At one time, her blatant approval would've started his libido and so many fantasies he would love to perform with a beautiful woman. Now, it just further notched up his irritation.

He wouldn't call himself a ladies man, but he had his fair share of women. He liked women. They liked him. Simple as that.

"I'm not buying, donating, or know directions to anything around here. Go away."

He didn't give her a full-on appraisal of her slim figure, something he had always done in his old life. Instead, he started to close the door. Her hand slammed against it, stopping him. He could've easily shoved the door shut, most likely with enough force to cause her to fall on her ass. He could be a dick. An extreme dick that said he had no conscience.

But he did have a conscience. He cared about people. He truly did.

He had to start acting like it.

Opening the door wider, he cocked a brow. He might not slam the door in her face, but it didn't mean he had to be completely nice. She was bothering him at a bad time.

"Are you Detective Newman?"

Detective Newman...

He hadn't heard those words in over three months. He didn't think he'd ever hear them again. Because he wasn't a detective. He would *never* be a detective again. He sabotaged his own job. Ruined his life. Destroyed relationships that meant something to him.

"Who the hell are you?"

This time he took a moment to look at the woman. She had bright-pink hair with a few light strands of purple mixed in. He had never seen such colorful hair...well, on such a beautiful woman. The color suited her complexion—light, pale skin with a few freckles sprinkled around. Sweet red lips. No lipstick. Natural red lips that looked perfect for kissing.

Which he wouldn't be doing. No more kissing. No more touching. No more sex.

"My name is Amelia Benedict, and I need your help."

"Not interested." His hand tightened on the door, needing to close it. The urge was so strong, his hand clenched harder to stop it from shaking.

"My brother is missing. He's only thirteen. I need your help."

"Call the police. I'm..." He swallowed. "I'm not the police."

She brushed her hair behind her ear, rolling her eyes. The gesture reminded him of Dee, Sauer's wife. He wasn't always a fan of her, but he always respected her. Now she hated him. Thought he was a douche. And he was. He wouldn't deny it.

"I did call them. They said they needed to wait forty-eight hours."

"For a kid? Highly doubtful."

She rolled her eyes again, huffing. "Well, it's not the first time he's..." She shrugged. "That he's..."

He cracked a smile, knowing exactly what she wasn't saying. "He's what?"

"That he's missing, in a sense."

"The only thing that makes sense right now is you're bothering me." He tilted his head as his smile grew. "And he likes to run away, am I right? Which is why the police told you to wait forty-eight hours. He's done this before and they're sick of it."

"I'm sick of people not taking me seriously. Okay, so he's left home before on his own accord. I won't deny it. But not this time. He's in danger. I need to find him."

"I still can't help you."

Putting her hands on her hips, another gesture that reminded him of Dee, she narrowed her eyes. "Billy from the gas station said you're a detective."

Damn. Small towns could be annoying at times.

He had never lived in a small town before. He only ever visited Napleton when he was a young boy to see his grandfather. He never realized how much people enjoyed getting into each other's business until he came to lick his wounds.

"Billy's wrong."

"Rebecca Sue from the grocery store said you would help a person without blinking an eye."

"Rebecca Sue's wrong."

Shifting her hips, a little too enticing to his deprived eye, she stared at him with the sadness bleeding from her gaze. "Mary from the post office said you're a lying, cheating bastard who I shouldn't trust for a second."

Frowning, his hand fell away from the door. "Mary's the only one right."

Amelia suddenly clapped her hands, a beautiful smile adorning her exquisite face. "Great. You're the perfect guy, then."

Furrowing his brows even more, he tried to understand what she was saying. Perfect guy? He agreed he was a lying, cheating bastard. How did that make him the perfect guy?

"Look, Amelia—"

"Most people call me Mel." She shrugged, swiping a strand of hair behind her ear. "But call me whatever."

"I'm not a detective anymore. I'll never be a detective again." A sharp pain struck him in the chest. "I don't help people. I lied to my friends. To my boss. I cheated on my girlfriend for no damn reason. I'm not perfect. I'm far from perfect. In fact, I'm the last person you should be asking for help." He put his hand on the door again, ready to slam it in her face. "I wish you luck on finding your brother."

This time, he did slam the door in her face.

MEL STARED at the closed door, pondering her choices.

Choice A. She could turn around and get back in her car and find her brother on her own. And fail miserably.

Choice B. She could knock on the door until the rude asshole—super hot rude asshole—answered and she pleaded her case. She wasn't opposed to begging on her knees either.

Choice C. She could open the door and invite herself in.

Then proceed to plead her case and possibly get down on her knees and beg.

Nodding, she made her decision quickly. She grabbed the handle and pushed open the door. Detective Newman—

Wait. He said he wasn't a detective anymore. What did she call him, then? Just...Newman?

She'd ask him after she got him to agree to find her brother.

He was in the corner farthest from the door punching hard at a bag hanging from the ceiling. He hadn't heard her open the door yet, so instead of making her presence known, she stared.

Intensely.

He might be an asshole, corroborated by Mary at the post office and a few other whispers around town, but he was a mighty fine-looking asshole. Sweat glistened on his back, his muscles bunching as he swung hard at the bag, not stopping for even a quick break. A defined chest, chiseled in all the right places. When he first opened the door, she had wanted to run her hands up and down to see what it felt like. She had never dated a man so ripped before.

And she probably never would. She didn't attract the sexy muscular men who made it their life's mission to look good at all times.

Although, with the way he was attacking the bag, he wasn't doing it to keep in shape. More like, release the demons inside building and festering. She knew a little about demons sucking your soul away.

His unkempt black hair that could use a comb—not that she was judging—was slick with sweat. He paused in his attack, turning to grab the towel lying on a small circular table, and ran it over his face and across his head, which made his hair even more unruly.

She inhaled sharply as he twisted her way.

He caught her gaze. His jaw tightened. His royal-blue eyes, so fascinatingly beautiful, eyed her with such a fierce expression, she was afraid she picked the wrong choice.

She didn't know this guy. She didn't know what he might do to her.

Although, in his defense, he admitted to cheating on his girlfriend, but he didn't beat her. So that meant he wasn't violent. Right?

Mary seemed under the impression he couldn't be trusted. That he was a loose cannon.

Rebecca Sue, who had a caring, trusting heart for most people, had said his grandfather, Pappa Roy, said he was a good man, which made him a good man. Honestly, for most people in this town, Newman's grandfather's word held a lot of weight. Not that she ever met the guy. But people loved to regale stories about him all the time like she cared or something. To be polite, she normally listened. Or, more like, made it appear like she was listening.

Neither said a word as they stared at each other. Since she didn't know how he'd react, she waited for him to say the first word.

"Do you always barge into someone's home when you're not welcome?"

She could work with that. He wasn't telling her to get the hell out.

"I don't visit many people."

A brow rose. "That didn't answer my question."

"Being a detective, I guess you'd interpret it that way."

His eyes cast down to the floor. "I told you I'm not a detective anymore. I can't help you, Amelia."

Her full name slid out of his mouth in a silky smooth tone, yet filled with desolation. People rarely called her

Amelia, and it sent a rush of something unfamiliar through her. She wasn't sure how to decipher it.

But she wasn't here to get googly eyes over a man, especially a man-cheating whore. Another thing Mary called him.

She was here to elicit his help to find her brother.

"Okay. You're not a detective. I won't say it again, but you *were* a detective. You have a skill set I need." She took a step closer, praying he'd look at her again.

Her mother used to say she had the eyes of a temptress. One look in her eyes and people would never disobey anything she said. So far, that was a lie dealing with this guy. He slammed the door in her face.

"My brother...he has issues. I won't deny it. But he's only thirteen. He's all I got left." Her voice broke. "I don't care what you might've done in the past. Right now, I need you."

His eyes met hers. "Nobody needs me."

She wanted to wrap her arms around him and hold him. He sounded so lost and alone. And feeling his hard, muscular chest wouldn't hurt either. She never let an opportunity pass her by, something her mother always drilled into her, too. *You see an opportunity, take it, honey.*

But again, she wasn't here to get laid or feel sorry for this guy. She was here to find her brother. By any means necessary.

Groveling commence.

She started to take a step forward, figuring she should get closer to beg on her knees, when he held his hand up.

"Stop." His jaw clenched. "Don't come near me."

Okay.

She was back to thinking maybe she shouldn't have walked in here. Was he violent? Should she be worried?

Well, she wasn't too worried. She knew how to hold her

own. Fighting, defending herself, had been a top priority the minute she moved out of her parents' house. Escaped, more like it.

But she didn't want to get distracted and go down that particular memory lane. She needed to grovel to this annoying man, so she'd do it from where she stood.

"I'm not leaving until you say you'll help me. Please." Her knees shook, terrified she'd have to get down and beg. His expression still looked fierce and unyielding. "Please, Newman. I need you."

A muscle ticked in his jaw, his eyes narrowing. But he didn't say a word. Instead of speaking, he ran the towel over his face again and turned away from her, then walked out of the room.

Not exactly how she expected this to go, but she didn't lie. She wasn't leaving. He'd have to call the cops on her or physically pick her up and remove her. Then lock the door so she couldn't walk in again, because she would. She also knew how to pick locks, so really, that wouldn't keep her out either. Nothing would stop her from finding her brother.

And sadly, he was her only option in this rinky-dink town. The cops didn't believe her that her brother didn't run away again. He was in serious trouble. She could feel it in her bones.

She didn't move from her spot. Glancing around the small cabin, eyeing the tiny kitchen to the left, the living room where she stood, and his workout station on the right near the fireplace, she didn't have many options where to go. She could take a seat on the couch. That might be better.

But her feet wouldn't move.

She wouldn't exactly classify it as fear, but she couldn't move.

What was he doing?

Grabbing a gun? He might not be a detective now, but he had been in the past. And he lived in a small cabin in the middle of the woods. He probably had a hunting rifle or shotgun somewhere.

He didn't look happy when he walked out of the room. She should be nervous. Extremely nervous, especially since she didn't know the guy. Just because he was good-looking didn't mean he was a good guy. Most times, at least in her experience, it meant pure evil hid underneath the handsome facade.

Looking at the lonely bag hanging in the corner, she wondered what it would feel like to throw a solid punch at it. Since her brother went missing last night, the anger and fear bottling up inside refused to settle down. She needed to release it. Except, she didn't know how. Scrubbing the house from top to bottom only took so long, and it didn't work to unleash the tension coiling deep inside.

"You're tenacious. I'll give you that."

She jumped, startled she didn't hear him walk back into the room. He stood near the old couch she had pondered sitting on. Now she was glad she didn't. It would've put her closer to him. It looked like he had taken a shower, his hair freshly wet and combed. She wasn't sure which look she preferred now, seeing it combed and styled in a spiked, classy way. The messy look was just as sexy and alluring as this style was. Although he hadn't bothered to shave, still sporting a rough, scruffy jaw—about two days' worth, if she had to guess. She didn't mind. It enhanced his handsome features. He, unfortunately, put on a black T-shirt and a pair of jeans. How long had she been standing here?

"You're not going to leave, are you?" His brow rose. "Do I have to call the—" He swallowed. "Police."

So interesting he had a difficult time saying such a

simple word, especially when he used to work for the police department. She didn't know the entire story of why he quit, but she was suddenly dying to know. Why did it pain him to say the word? His eyes shattered with agony.

People loved to talk in this town, sharing stories, spreading rumors. Yet they never said why Newman left his job and moved to the small cabin in the middle of nowhere.

Maybe they didn't know the real reason.

Crossing her arms, she shrugged. "You can do whatever you like. If you call them, they'll have to drag me out of here kicking and screaming. I'll do whatever I have to if it helps me find my brother."

Glancing at the floor, he shoved his hands inside his pockets. "I'm not the right person for this."

"You're my only option." Her mind begged him to look at her. "Whether or not either of us likes it. I need you because my brother needs you. And you need me."

His gaze jerked in her direction, puzzlement lighting his eyes. "Excuse me? I don't need a damn thing from you." His eyes grazed up and down her body. "Except maybe one thing."

She shivered at his perusal. He was obviously attempting to make her feel uncomfortable. His gaze screamed loud and clear he wanted sex. Maybe later when she found her brother, she'd take him up on the offer. It had been a while. Sex was sex. She wanted some. And he definitely made her horny for lots of sex.

He was trying to scare her off. *News flash, buster.* She didn't scare that easily.

"You do need me." A slow grin formed. "You might say you're not a detective, but you miss it. You miss the thrill. The chase. You miss being a part of something. So yeah, I'd say you need me just as much as I need you."

His eyes flashed with pained torture, then narrowed. "You don't know me."

She swallowed. Well, he was right about that. She didn't.

But she knew herself pretty damn well.

And every time she looked into his eyes, she saw a bit of herself. Swimming and floating in misery with no chance of survival.

2

HE DIDN'T WANT this woman in his cabin, his domain, begging him for help. He didn't want anyone here or even near him.

He was a virus. A disease. Bad luck. No matter where or what he did in life, things always went to shit. And if he tried to help her find her brother, nothing good would happen.

You might say you're not a detective, but you miss it. You miss the thrill. The chase. You miss being a part of something.

He hated how what she said was true. Too damn much. He missed his old life. His friends. His job. That feeling he was making a difference one case at a time.

So maybe he didn't always infect and destroy things. He and Sauer closed quite a few cases—some tough ones they almost gave up on.

But damn it. She didn't know him. She might've hit a sensitive spot, a few things ringing true, but she didn't know him.

Nobody did.

"I'm not leaving." She crossed her arms in defiance.

A corner of his lip curled up before he realized what he was doing, immediately turning his smile into a frown. He would not let this woman get under his defenses with her bold attitude. He didn't care how much he admired her assertiveness. Not simply admired it either. It turned him on. It was hot as hell.

And her pink hair... He liked it. She reminded him of a fairy. But not a sweet, docile fairy flying around spreading pixie dust and happiness. More like a warrior fairy, soaring through the world with one thing on their mind. Fortitude. To make the world a better, safer place.

What the hell was he thinking?

Was there such a thing as a warrior fairy?

He was losing his goddamn mind.

"I'll toss you out if I have to. I can't help you." Then he crossed his arms in mockery.

Her eyes narrowed, two tiny slits piercing him with a death glare worthy of skewering him with one touch. "You can. You're just refusing to. There's a difference. Go ahead and touch me. I dare you."

He snickered. "Sweetheart, you don't want me touching you. You won't like it."

Neither would he. Not because he was afraid he'd hurt her, but because he was terrified he'd pick her up and carry her to his bedroom. He hadn't touched a woman in three months. It was like a drug. A sweet, sickening drug that needed to be fueled at all times. He hadn't had a dose of anything in forever. He needed a fix. With her enticing, defiant attitude, she made it easy to want, to crave a touch of her sweet, delectable body.

A sassy smile spread across her juicy red lips as if she knew exactly what he was thinking. "I might like it." Then her smile disappeared. "But my name is Mel, not sweetheart."

Whoa. Whiplash. One second teasing, then firm about what he should be calling her.

He didn't need this irritation in his life. Letting his arms drop to his sides, fisting his hands tightly, he nodded at the door. "Get out. I'm not helping you."

She shifted, planting her feet firmly in a defensive position in case he decided to charge at her. Oh, he had no intention of touching her. He didn't trust himself. He'd been deprived of sex for too long, and it didn't matter who she was. He wanted to screw her ten ways to Sunday. Any woman would do at this point. That's what her presence in his safe haven had done to him. The carefully built wall he fortified started to crumble into pieces. All because of a visit from one sassy, brash woman with pink hair.

"He's only thirteen. Please. You have to help me. Nobody else will."

He laughed with no humor behind it. "You must be out of your mind to think I'd be your only hope."

"Half the time I am out of my mind. The only good decision I ever made in life was to take care of my brother, and I'm failing at it. You know what it's like to fail. I want him back safe and sound, and I want a second chance. Don't you?"

Again, thinking she knew him or something. She didn't know shit. Turning away from her, he stalked to the kitchen a few feet away, ignoring everything she said.

A second chance?

He didn't deserve a second chance. He took a good relationship and flushed it down the toilet with one wrong decision. A decision he went into with his eyes wide open. He knew exactly what would happen when he slept with Tonya. Because he set it up that way.

Like the true bastard he was.

"Detective Newman—"

"Don't call me that!" he shouted as his arm swung across the kitchen table, sending the empty plate and glass cup from his lunch shattering to the floor.

Breathing heavily, his fists clenched by his sides, he couldn't look at her. To react in such a way to a simple title. A title he couldn't claim ever again. Every time she called him detective, a piece of him died a little more.

Squeezing his eyes shut, he counted to ten, trying to calm the rage sizzling like an inferno deep inside. He rarely lost control. At least, not in such a blatant manner. His loss of control usually entailed overt behavior. Lying, quick sex, snapping and yelling, but he definitely never threw or broke things.

When he heard tiny sounds near him, small clinks of ceramic hitting together, his eyes popped open. Amelia was crouched down picking up pieces of glass from the plate and cup that broke.

"Stop. Leave it."

She shrugged, continuing in her quest to clean up his erratic mess. "It's not my first rodeo. I caused the mess, I'll clean it up."

Oh, hell no. She didn't cause a damn thing except make him take a deeper look at the mess of his life. Something he'd been avoiding since the moment he arrived at his cabin. With three long strides, he was by her side, gripping her arms in a strong but not painful grip.

She shivered, cowering away from him. Her reaction told him enough, as had her words about cleaning up the mess. She'd been abused before.

He might be a lot of things, but he had never laid a hand on a woman, and he wasn't about to start now. He would never hit her.

But he wasn't ready to let her go. He couldn't even feel her soft skin—not with her thick winter coat on. Even knowing he was frightening her, making her wonder whether he was going to hurt her, he couldn't let go.

She was a strange woman. Refusing to leave, insisting he had to help her. Yet cowering and showing fear with the slightest touch.

She fascinated him a little too much for his liking.

Urging her to her feet with a gentle tug, he let go of one arm and held out his hand. "Give me the glass."

He could feel her body trembling, yet the strength in her eyes said she would not go down without a fight. Just one more reason to respect this woman. Even as scared as she was, she would defend herself. Good for her. Not that she needed to against him. But still.

Slowly, her hand reached out and placed the shards of glass into his palm. Her fingers grazed his skin. It sent a bolt of electricity straight to his cock. Damn, he wanted to wipe her fear away with a kiss. Something sweet and simple. Something to calm her down and let her know he wouldn't hurt her.

Maybe it would help calm him down some, too.

He knew he should've never touched her. Now, he couldn't let go.

"Who hurt you?"

She glanced at his hand still wrapped around her bicep, then back to him. "What makes you think anyone ever has?"

"I'm a—" He caught himself before uttering the word that sent him into a violent tailspin a minute ago. "I'm a smart man. It's not hard to see."

A smile touched her lips. "Which makes you perfect to find my brother."

So tenacious. She saw an opening, she jumped in with both arms swinging.

He pulled her closer. Her smile died as his mouth stood mere inches from hers. It wouldn't take much to lean even more and kiss her.

"I'm not perfect, Amelia. And I have no patience. You shouldn't trust me for one second."

"But I do," she whispered, her sweet breath hitting his face, enticing him to close the distance.

The intensity in her gaze said she wasn't lying. That she honestly trusted him.

Well, to find her brother.

If he was good at one thing in life, it was his job as a detective.

Dropping her arm, her soft, sweet tone scorching him to the bone, he took a step back, squeezing his fists shut. A wince crossed his face as the pieces of glass cut into his skin, yet he didn't loosen his fist. He needed to feel the pain, anything to keep away from her. From devouring her, from showing her pleasure instead of pain.

"Have a seat on the couch while I clean up this mess." He stared hard at her so she understood perfectly clear. "I made the mess. So I'll clean it up."

There was no way in hell he wanted her to think, for even one second, she made the mess. He made the decision to toss the plate and cup to the floor. Not her. It didn't matter she said something to upset him. He still made the decision to fling his arm across the table in rage.

She nodded. "You're going to help me?"

"We'll talk." His hand tightened around the glass some

more. "But this in no way means I'm saying yes. We're only going to talk."

A sweet, delicate smile graced her luscious red lips.

If she kept looking at him like that, he wouldn't be able to refuse her a damn thing.

What kind of mess was he getting himself into?

———

MEL SAT ON THE COUCH, her knee bouncing off and on as she waited for him to clean up the mess in the kitchen. After throwing away the glass, he washed his hands with soap and water, then grabbed a paper towel, wrapping it around his right hand.

He swiped a broom from a tiny closet in the kitchen.

Her knee started bouncing like crazy.

He cut himself.

He was cleaning up the mess.

The bouncing wouldn't stop as she watched him sweep up the glass. Then it stopped when she glanced away, realizing she was staring. Back and forth she went, watching, stopping, watching, stopping. Not once in her crazy, erratic glances did he look at her.

She still couldn't understand why he insisted on cleaning up the mess. She created it. She made him upset enough to throw it on the floor. Her father always said it was her fault when things like that happened.

And he cut himself. That was her fault, too. She saw him squeeze his fists. A slight wince crossed his face. But not once did he cry out in pain.

Neither did she.

Not that he hurt her. His hand on her arm wasn't even

near painful. He had a firm grip on her, but with one quick move, she would've been able to get him off. Except, she didn't sense he was going to hurt her. He was all talk and bluster, no action. It was all the anguish building up inside him that made him act like a complete jackass. If he simply dealt with his issues, he probably wouldn't be such an asshole.

Not her problem, of course. Only her brother was her concern, and she would do anything to get him back, to save him, including allowing this guy to lay a hand on her. When he first grabbed her, she wanted to scream in terror, something she used to do in her old life. Her old shell of a life. No matter how many times she told herself don't cry, don't show fear, she usually did.

He was right. Someone had hurt her in the past. Her father. Day in and day out, the man made her life a living hell. The second she walked out of the house and moved away, she learned how to defend herself. No man would ever make her feel weak and useless ever again.

So Newman could put his hands on her all he wanted, but he would never control her. Never hurt her. Unless she allowed it.

Soft clinking sounds echoed in the tiny confines. Glancing toward the kitchen, she saw Newman shut the cupboard underneath the sink, then he put the broom away.

He washed his hands once again, using two pumps of soap from the dispenser, then swiped another paper towel, wrapping it around his hand. Taking his time, he walked into the living room and stood near the couch but didn't sit down. It was the only available space to sit. Apparently, he didn't want to get too close to her. She was fine with that.

They stared at each other.

Neither said a word. She didn't know where to start or what to say.

Then she saw him press on the paper towel. He was still bleeding.

She stood up. He flinched. Not enough where a normal person would've noticed. But for someone who had grown up flinching every time her father walked into the room, she saw. She noticed everything.

"Come on." She nodded toward his hand. "We should bandage that."

"I'm fine." He didn't look down at his hand. His expression didn't change, still displaying annoyance that she was in his home.

"You're bleeding."

"You need to stop thinking you know me. I said I was fine."

A soft chuckle floated out. "You really live up to the lying bastard part."

His eyes clouded with agony before he glanced away. She instantly felt bad for saying anything. She was trying to lighten the mood, not make him feel bad. But it was true. He was lying to her face. He wasn't fine—not with his hand bleeding.

Making a decision, probably a bad one, not anything new, she walked right up to him and grabbed his uninjured hand. This time he visibly flinched, his vivid blue eyes widening in surprise.

"Don't be such a baby. Men are such whiners when they're hurt or sick. Come on." She started to drag him toward the hallway to the bathroom.

Surprisingly, he didn't say a word or fight her. She didn't want to fight him either. She would attempt to hold her own, but the way he attacked the punching bag, she didn't think she'd come out the winner. It didn't mean she wouldn't fight with every last breath in her body.

Stopping at the first door she came upon, she flipped the light switch and smiled. The bathroom. Dragging him inside, she knocked the toilet seat lid down with her boot and then nodded at it as she let go of his hand. "Have a seat."

"Who made you the boss around here?"

Rolling her eyes, laughing, she opened the cupboard below the sink. "Clearly someone has to boss you around. You're a hot mess."

Very hot.

She would never deny how handsome and yummy the man was. But she didn't mean that kind of hot in this instance. He was an utter mess.

She totally wasn't taking the job to fix the issues he had, but until she found her brother, she'd do what was necessary.

Finding a medicine kit, she grabbed it, then turned toward him where he continued to stand in the same spot. Arching a brow with the best glare she owned, she nodded at the toilet seat again. "I said sit."

He looked ready to lash out. With a fist? With tainted words? With tears? She wasn't exactly sure, but the look of torture on his face said he wanted to do something. Finally, after they stared at each other for what felt like minutes, he took a seat.

Not seeing a closet in the bathroom or any washcloths underneath the sink, she stepped into the hallway. She found what she was looking for in a small closet right outside the door, then walked back into the bathroom. Newman still had the same annoyed look on his face. She wet the cloth with warm water, then held out her hand. "Let me see your hand."

He eyed her, his expression oddly blank, except for the

annoyance. He still hadn't masked his annoyance at her presence. Tough. She wasn't leaving.

"Now."

Nor was she going to be ignored.

He slowly reached out his hand, palm open. A few nicks and scratches coated his palm, along with two deep cuts. He cringed when she lightly dabbed at them, but he didn't say a word.

"Does it make you feel better to hurt yourself? You're such an idiot."

"For someone who wants my help, you have a funny way of endearing yourself to me."

She pressed harder on his hand to stop the bleeding. He grimaced, his lips tightening into a straight line, yet he didn't say anything. Well, she might've pressed harder to show him she wasn't afraid of him. She would say and do anything she wanted, unafraid of the consequences.

Her father showed her she could survive anything. She survived eighteen years of hell. She could survive this.

He looked down at his hand. "Tell me about your brother."

Finally, she was getting somewhere with him. He was actually going to hear her out.

"Look. I'm not going to lie. My brother has not been a saint. But who is these days?"

He flickered a glance at her with a hint of a smile curling his lips.

She couldn't help but press on his wound to staunch the bleeding as she continued. "I moved out as soon as I turned eighteen. My father was an asshole. I begged my mom to come with me. My brother was only five at the time. I should've never left him."

She paused to rinse out the rag and to give herself a

moment. Talking about her past was normal for her. It made her who she was today. She embraced it instead of hiding from it.

But with Newman...

Oddly, for some reason, she cared what he thought about her.

Why did she care? He was a means to an end. She needed his help to find her brother. That was it. Who cared what he thought of her.

Most people took one look at her pink hair and flamboyant mouth and made an immediate opinion that she was nothing but trouble. Whatever. She never cared what those people thought, so she wouldn't care what he thought either.

Placing the washcloth back onto his wound, she was grateful he didn't fill the silence with words that wouldn't mean anything. She heard it all. She was thankful he didn't try to placate her.

"About a year ago, my mom called and said she needed me. She left my dad and moved here with my brother Adam. I heard the desperation in her voice. And I always told her if she needed me, I'd be there. No hesitation. So I packed up my shit and I came. She handed me custody papers for Adam and said she was sorry and left."

Taking the washcloth off, she saw the bleeding had stopped. Grabbing a dry washcloth, she dried the area before taking a piece of gauze filled with antiseptic and placed it over his wound.

What a smart man still not saying a word. She could kiss him for understanding she needed to tell her story at her own pace. Most people loved to stop, add their sympathies and unwanted advice. It always drove her nuts. Some people didn't realize she didn't always need to hear something in return; she just needed them to listen.

"It's been a year from hell for me and my brother. I saw him here and there over the years, but not much. We barely knew each other when I came. He has not made a moment of this easy on me. But I love him. I will do anything for him." She grabbed the gauze tape and started to wrap it around his hand. "He's run away a few times. Typical teenager defiance. He has a lot of shit he's dealing with. I get it. I'm never mad at him. We had a heart-to-heart the last time he did it. Let me tell you, the asshole chief around here made it pretty clear he wasn't going to take any more of his shit. So I made sure my brother understood what could happen if he kept this kind of behavior up."

Finished wrapping his hand, she stood up and threw away her garbage and then washed her hands. They shook as she dried them on the hand towel hanging near the sink.

Newman still didn't say a word.

She stared at the wall as she continued. "We stopped by the store yesterday afternoon to get a few groceries. There was a pickup truck in the parking lot when we were leaving. The guy creeped me out. I didn't see much of his face because he was wearing a black hoodie with the hood up, but he was just...off, you know. He watched us the whole time. I didn't see him follow us, though." She turned toward him. "Shortly after we got home, Adam said he was going to ride his bike back to the store, about a mile from our house. He didn't really ask. He just left." She shrugged. "Not that he would've taken my no very well. Probably would've still biked anyway. When it got dark out, and he still wasn't back, I knew something was wrong. I knew that man did something. He was off. Seriously off. There was something..." Inhaling a deep breath, she blew it out in slow increments, remembering how the chief of police laughed in her face. "He has my brother. I know it. Adam did not run away again. He didn't."

Newman stood up.

She took a step back, hating herself for retreating. *Never show fear.* Something her defense instructor drilled into her.

"You said you didn't see much of his face, but can you describe anything about him? Anything distinctive?"

Heart racing a mile a minute, she tilted her head. "You believe me?"

He shrugged. "I believe that you think something terrible happened to your brother. Whether something really did, I don't have enough evidence to say. I look at everything in front of me and go from there. It's not about believing you. It's all about following the evidence."

Reaching into her jacket pocket, she pulled out a slip of paper and held it toward him. "Then here's your first lead. I wrote down his license plate number. I told you. He creeped me out. That's the only explanation I have for writing it down."

Newman eyed the piece of paper, then took it from her. A small smile touched his lips. "I'd say it's gut instinct. Let me make a call." His smile died. "I can't promise anything. Don't expect a miracle from me."

Oh, she didn't. She knew it had been a long shot when she came here, especially with the rumors around town about him.

But, at the moment, he was her savior. Her only hope. And she'd take it.

3
———————

TAKING A DEEP BREATH, displaying his best smile, he gently grabbed his wife's hand from plugging in the Christmas tree.

"I think it's time we take down the tree, not plug it in."

Dee flashed him a maniacal look, then tried to force her hand closer to the socket. "Just one more day."

"It's the middle of January, and we've had plenty of Christmas spirit." Knowing he wouldn't be able to force her hand away from the wall, he leaned forward instead, kissing her sweet lips. "You're going to be a terrific mother. Celebrating the holidays so...intensely" —he cleared his throat — "isn't necessary."

Her eyes narrowed. "You mean, stop acting like a psycho."

Half the time, he was damned if he did, damned if he didn't. Not much he said swayed her when she got tunnel vision about being the best mother. The makeup sex was great. At least he had that to look forward to.

Sauer liked to tread carefully and watch what he said. She was six and a half months pregnant. Anything he could do to keep her calm and stress-free was important to him. She switched to thinking she would be the worst mother on the planet to thinking she had to be the best mother that ever lived. He walked a very fine line every day. A fine line he'd continue to walk until he died because he loved his wife so damn much.

He kissed her lightly again. "That's not what I said."

Then a lightbulb went off. Probably a terrible idea, but it was better than anything else he thought of yet.

"You don't want to offend Valentine's Day, do you? Isn't it time we start decorating for Valentine's?"

Not that he wanted his house looking festive in reds, pinks, and hearts galore. But since she had gotten pregnant, she went overboard on decorations, no matter the holiday.

Like vicious laser beams, her eyes narrowed into tiny slits, weighing whether or not to skewer him from head to toe. Like he was messing with her or something. Oh no. He was dead serious.

Then, like a magical switch, a bright smile pierced her beautiful face. "I just bought the cutest thing ever yesterday." Her hand dropped the plug to the Christmas tree lights. "It's a countdown to love calendar. I thought I should wait until February 1, but you're absolutely right. We should take down the Christmas decorations and decorate for Valentine's."

Whew! Crisis averted. At least, the Christmas crisis. He'd probably have a hard time when Valentine's ended. Oh, boy.

Helping her stand, he pulled her closer, wrapping his arms gently around her so he didn't crush the baby.

"Why don't you make a quick lunch for us and I'll start taking down the tree and the other decorations. When I'm done with that, we'll hang up the few Valentine's decorations you have."

A wide smile touched his lips, even though he dreaded decorating all day on his day off. But hey, he was with his wife and nothing beat that. It wouldn't be too bad. Anything to keep her stress levels down.

"I actually have two full boxes." The beaming smile on her face made him chuckle and press his lips to hers.

"Perfect."

She patted his cheek like she knew he wasn't looking forward to decorating, then started walking toward the kitchen.

His phone vibrated in his pocket, ringing merrily, a peppy Christmas tune Dee insisted he use. He knew he'd have to change it to a love song now for Valentine's.

Pulling it out of his pocket, he froze as the number glared at him.

What...? It couldn't be.

His heart pounded as he stared dumbfounded.

"Sauer? Aren't you going to answer it?"

Looking at Dee, who stood in the hallway, his hand shook as he lifted it. "It's Newman."

Brows furrowing low, she looked ready to spit at his phone. She couldn't stand Newman. Not after everything he had done. Then her features softened.

"You've been calling him since he left. Day after day, and he never picks up. And now he's calling you. Answer it, silly."

"I don't know what to say."

"What were you going to say when you called him all those other times?"

He shrugged.

The ringing stopped.

Rolling her eyes, she stalked to him with determined

steps, then snatched the phone from his hand. "I love you. That's the only reason I'm doing this."

"Doing what?"

She tapped his screen a few times, then put the phone to her ear.

Oh, boy.

Not good.

He should've answered himself.

"Oh, hello, douche man. Finally decided to grace us with a phone call. How sweet of you." Her eyes narrowed like the devil himself stood before her. He was scared for Newman, even though he wasn't in the vicinity. "You say one word to my husband that upsets him, and I'll gut you from your sternum to your stupid dumb ass." Then her voice turned cheery. "Such a great talk. Bye."

She held out the phone toward him. "Here you go."

All he could do was nod, unable to even process the right thing to say.

"Hello?"

Damn. That should've come out more assertive and aggressive as Dee managed. But he wasn't Dee. He didn't do confrontation well. Or at all. Probably why he didn't answer the call in the first place.

"Hey, man. Umm..."

Well, that was a good sign. Newman was as unsure as him.

"Hey."

So dumb. Hey? He already said hello. Why was he repeating himself?

"Dee sounds...the same."

A chuckle slipped out. "Yep. Same beautiful, loving wife."

Dee smiled at his words, then nodded that she was leaving. He blew out a breath as she walked away. Not that he didn't want her near, but it would be easier to talk to his friend without her in the room.

"How are—"

"How is—"

They both laughed.

"Look, I'm...I apologize." Newman got the first word in this time. "For everything. Not answering your calls. Not calling you back." His voice lowered. "For everything that went down before I left."

"Yeah, me, too."

Not the most eloquent response, but he honestly didn't know what to say. He *was* sorry about everything as well. He just wanted his best friend back. By his side as his partner. Which would never happen, unfortunately.

"Don't apologize to me, man. I'm the...idiot." Newman swore, then blew out a breath. "I...I have a reason for calling. I'm still the same selfish bastard that left."

Well, damn. At least he was an honest selfish bastard. Here Sauer thought he was finally calling to repair their friendship. Apparently not.

He was being used. Once again.

Did he even want to know the reason he called? Why should he care what Newman wanted?

"Sauer? You there?"

Of course he cared.

Because he wasn't that kind of person. He didn't turn people away, especially if they needed his help.

"Of course I'm here. What's going on?"

NEWMAN TURNED AWAY from Amelia as he tried to figure out where to start. He hadn't been sure how receptive Sauer was going to be when he called. His friend had been calling him since he left, but he never answered. He didn't know what to say. What could he say? He acted like a jackass toward everyone, and saying I'm sorry didn't seem good enough.

Not to mention, Sauer hated the words I'm sorry. Dee was attacked by a lunatic that used those same exact words as if it would give him some sort of forgiveness for his actions.

Glancing at the rickety worn table, he was grateful it was empty. He couldn't destroy more plates and cups. He excelled at destroying things.

"Newman? Are you there?"

Three months away put a lot of distance between them, and not just in mileage, but in their friendship. The awkwardness through the phone was palpable.

"Yeah, I'm here. So...umm..." He hated how uncertain he sounded. But how did he explain he was calling for a woman? When he left, that's where all his problems stemmed from. Women!

Glancing over his shoulder, his gaze connected with Amelia, who stood near the couch appearing alert and ready for anything. Good. She shouldn't trust anyone, especially him.

"There's this girl..." He smirked at Amelia when she glowered at the word girl. "She's trying to find her brother and the police won't help her yet. He's run away before and they think it's the same thing going on. She thinks something bad happened to him. Some guy creeped her out last night, watching them. She grabbed a license plate number. I was wondering...I know it's a lot to ask...but..."

Wow. He couldn't even get the question out. Who was he

to call Sauer after how many months of ignoring him and ask him for help? How damn selfish was he?

Sauer should hang up on his ass. Tell him to go to hell, call him a douche, like Dee would say with pure venom, and hang up.

"You want me to run the plates. I can do that."

Except Sauer would never hang up on him no matter what he said. He couldn't finish his question, yet Sauer was willing to help, knowing exactly what he wanted.

He looked back at the old, rickety table, at the marks littered across it. His grandfather had done everything at this table—ate his food, did his paperwork, cleaned his fish, sharpened his knives. If he had something to do, he sat down at this trusty table and did it.

Every time Newman visited, he always relied on his grandfather to do the same thing over and over. Without fail. He couldn't say the same about himself. He wasn't reliable for anything.

"Why?"

The simple question popped out before he could stop himself. Like a knee-jerk reaction that he couldn't control.

"Why what?" Sauer asked, the concern prominent in his tone.

"Why are you helping me? Why don't you yell at me? Why don't you tell me what a damn bastard I am? Why don't you ever say what you really want? I'm an asshole, Sauer. Just say it."

Silence answered.

Well, did he expect any different? Sauer didn't do confrontation. It was something he loved about him. He could say something, knowing Sauer wouldn't snap back. If that didn't say he was a worthless friend, he didn't know what else would.

He took advantage of Sauer's friendship way too much. Took it for granted that he'd always be there for him, no matter how cruel he was.

"You *are* an asshole."

Finally.

Sauer finally spoke some truth to his face, or sort of. Over the phone was close enough.

Unlike last time when he goaded Sauer to get on his case, egging him on to make him confess his sins, he didn't lash out. He didn't tell him to go to hell.

He stayed silent. He waited for Sauer to continue. To lay into him and say everything he should've said a long time ago.

He'd take it all like a man. He wouldn't interrupt or say anything cruel in return. Because he deserved to hear every single word.

"But we're all assholes at some point." Sauer sighed heavily. "You're doing it again. I didn't notice it before. But I've had three months to think about everything, and I see it clearly now."

Newman's brows puckered low, frowning. "See what?"

What the hell was he talking about?

"You want me to get mad. You're looking for a fight. Instead of facing the issue, you..." Sauer blew out a breath. "You self-sabotage yourself in a way. Trying to piss me off. Keeping secrets. The thing with Chrissy...maybe."

Nope. He wasn't going to talk about Chrissy. And he wasn't—

Was he?

When things got serious or he didn't want to address an issue, he acted out. Like now. Instead of accepting Sauer's help without complaint, he wanted Sauer to get mad at him. He didn't want to help Amelia.

Because he would fail her. Like he failed everything else in life.

"Give me the license plate number and I'll call you back as soon as I have any information. You can say whatever you want, Newman. You can act like an asshole. When Dee gets pissy like this, it's usually PMS or someone pissed her off and she doesn't want to talk about it. I don't let that bother me, so I'm not going to let this bother me either. You're my friend."

A chuckle floated out like a whisper on a windy day. "Are you saying I am PMSing?"

Sauer returned a small chuckle. "Well...yeah. You are."

"Thanks, man."

He rattled off the license plate number, and then Sauer said good-bye. Newman slipped his phone into his pocket once he disconnected. Twisting toward Amelia slowly, he saw she was in the same spot with the same alert look.

"My friend is going to run the plates. We should know something soon."

When he said the word friend, it didn't taste like a nasty dose of cough syrup. The really terrible kind where you had to plug your nose to get it down in one swallow.

Because Sauer *was* his friend. He couldn't forget that. If Sauer hadn't walked away from him yet, then how could he not see that he was his friend.

"Who is this friend?"

Sauer said he liked to start fights when he didn't like where a situation was heading. Very true now that he thought about it. He didn't want to answer her question. Because it meant he had to talk about his past, and that wasn't something he liked to think about.

But, to move on, have a semi-decent life, he had to face his problems. He had to answer questions he didn't like.

"He's my old partner. He's a great detective."

A gentle smile touched her lips. "I bet you were, too."

Newman averted his gaze. Maybe he wasn't *that* ready to talk about his past.

"So, what do we do while we wait for him to call back?" Amelia asked, thankfully understanding he didn't want to delve deeper into his past.

Meeting her brilliant hazel eyes once again, a devilish smirk touched his lips. "I could think of something entertaining."

4

THE LOOK of disgust on Amelia's face at his suggestive words was enough to make him sick to his stomach.

Why did he do this to himself? Why did he make people feel uncomfortable? Why did he make an already tense situation more awkward?

Even if he did want to have sex with her—oh, and he did, he wasn't going to lie to himself—he usually didn't go this long without sex. But right now wasn't the time for that. Especially when her brother was missing. He was a bastard, but he wasn't that cruel of one.

Looking away, he coughed before saying, "I didn't mean anything by it." Then he walked to a small desk near the fireplace and grabbed a large notepad and a pencil. "I meant this."

Of course he didn't. But she didn't need to know that. Deep down, he'd rather take her to his bedroom and release the anguish filling up every cell in his body instead of what he was about to do.

Working a case...

Jumping back into his old shoes...

He didn't think he could do it. Not without failing once again.

That's all he was in life. A big failure.

Amelia eyed him funny, then looked at the notepad and pencil in his hand. "I don't understand what's so entertaining." Then she narrowed her gaze.

Smart woman. She knew he was lying.

"When I work a case..." He swallowed, then took a small calming breath. "I always start at the beginning. Usually the crime scene, but we don't have one of those yet."

Her eyes widened in panic.

God, what an idiot. Holding up his hands in an apologetic manner, he tried to offer a soothing smile. "I didn't mean to say..." He shook his head, remorseful. "I didn't mean anything by it. I'm only trying to explain how I do—did—my job."

Raising her hand, the trembles noticeable, she pointed at his notepad. "So, how does paper help us?"

A tiny grin appeared. A real, authentic grin that he hoped would ease the terror still written in the golden depths of her eyes. "I always use a notepad. It helps me remember stuff, and it helps me to see everything in a different light."

He gestured at the couch. "Let's have a seat and I'll ask you some questions about your brother. You can take your jacket off. I do have the heat on and a fire going. You have to be sweating to death."

Seriously. She had to be hot with her large winter coat on. But hey, if she didn't feel comfortable enough around him to shed her coat, he wasn't going to argue with her. She could sweat to death for all he cared.

Except she nodded, unzipped her coat and slid it off, setting it on the end of the couch, and then took a seat.

His heart started pounding. He averted his gaze as he took a seat at the other end of the couch as far away from her as he could.

She had on a light-blue sweater, form-fitting, that displayed all her gorgeous curves. Curves he wanted to trace with the palm of his hand ever so slowly. Savor the beauty before him.

But he wasn't going to do that. Because that wouldn't be appropriate. He swore off sex. It wasn't good for him. It was a defense mechanism. A way for him to drown his problems.

Not fix them.

"So..."

Tilting her head, sweet laughter left her lips. "So?"

"Your brother. Tell me about him."

Another adorable laugh floated his way. "Right. My brother. Umm...what else do you want to know? Our lives are messed up, but I'm trying my best."

"Why did your mother leave you custody?"

He couldn't claim he had a terrible mother, but she always wanted the best for Roger, his older brother. Him, on the other hand, he always stayed in the background, forgotten, the mistake. He had to fight for their attention, both his mom and dad, especially when his brother was the perfect child. No matter how hard he tried, he could never manage the feat. He always fell short of perfection.

Perhaps he asked the question with bitterness coating his tone because Amelia narrowed her eyes in a way he was starting to find oddly cute. He never thought a woman narrowing her eyes, piercing him with a nasty glare would ever be something he'd consider cute or adorable. But on Amelia, he couldn't resist loving it.

He enjoyed getting a rise out of her.

And she still reminded him of a pink warrior fairy. It might not be a thing, but he was making it a thing.

"The truth?"

"Of course. I always want the truth."

Her golden hazel eyes glittered with sudden venom. "I expect the same courtesy. I want the truth from you, no matter what. No matter the circumstances."

She wasn't talking about the fact if they happened to sleep together and he wanted to move on to another woman, he should just tell her instead of cheating on her.

Oh, no. Why would she think that? She didn't want to have sex with him. He was the only one with the crazy, erratic thoughts about sex.

She definitely wasn't thinking along those lines.

She wanted him to tell her the hard, brutal truth if, or when, they found her brother. All the gory details. And when it came to his line of work, the details were usually very messy and disturbing.

It was time to act like a gentleman. Time to act like a decent human being that cared about others.

"I promise you, Amelia, I will never lie to you. Ever."

Fiddling with the sleeve of her coat resting near her leg, she nodded, looking down at the old, worn couch. "Good. I don't like lying. I need to hear the truth."

"It's not always pretty." She wanted the truth, he'd start right now.

"Oh, I know. It's downright malevolent sometimes." Her eyes met his, pain dripping from them. "My mother left me custody to turn herself in. She's sitting in jail waiting for her trial in New York."

Okay. That was completely unexpected, but he was glad to know. His hand tightened around the pencil, making his wound ache. He wasn't sure he needed to write that piece of information down.

"You're not from Minnesota?"

She shook her head. "We moved around a lot. I've lived in Texas, Florida, and Maryland. I moved out when we moved to New York. My mother moved here after…"

He wasn't sure he wanted to hear the answer. But he had a job to do. Find her brother.

"After what?"

Her bottom lip wobbled. She was trying to hold back a dam of tears.

He couldn't believe she was about to cry. It was the first sign of weakness. Not a bad kind of weakness either, but a crack in her armor. Those other times she took a step back or flinched when he touched her, he didn't consider those actions a weakness. That was a reaction. A split reaction she probably hadn't meant to reveal.

This was something else entirely.

It was something serious.

"It's okay, Amelia. Take your time."

She let out a tiny breath, inhaled deeply, then smiled. "You're not as bad as some people say."

He grinned, chuckling. "Thank you? I don't know what to say to that. Because I *am* as bad as people say."

"No, you try to live up to that hype, but deep down, you're a good man. You just don't believe it yet."

"Amelia, I'm not—"

"Don't bother arguing with me. I'm not always a good judge of character. I've made some stupid mistakes. But I definitely know when I see a good man. Because I had my father as an example." Her expression turned downright horrifying, filled with hatred. "He was not a good man."

"He's dead, then?"

"My mother moved here after she killed him. She got Adam far away from everything. Then she called me to come here and take care of Adam so she could..." Her voice broke, as a tear slid down her cheek. "So she could face the consequences. So she could turn herself in. For killing a man who deserved it."

And there was his answer.

Someone had hurt her before.

Her father.

And her mother killed him.

No wonder her brother had issues.

Her eyes developed that steely gaze he adored a little too much. "I know that look. I've seen it before."

"What look?"

"That my brother has issues. And why wouldn't he? My father was abusive and my mother is a murderer." She leaned forward. "He didn't run away. I'm telling you, he didn't."

He leaned forward, too. Her hazel eyes sparkled with intensity. He knew it was a very serious discussion they were having, but he wanted to kiss her. Drown out her worries and her fears with a hungry, searing kiss.

But he was a changed man. He didn't use sex to deflect the issues anymore.

Why did he keep turning to sex in his head? He had to stop it.

"I believe you."

MEL HELD HIS GAZE, not sure if she believed him. She told him he was a good man. But was he? She had terrible judgment when it came to men, thanks to her deadbeat, asshole father.

Well, she dated her neighbor Matthew for four months, until the day her mother called begging her to come. They parted amicably. They still talked every few weeks. He was one of the few people who never ran away or ignored her after learning about her past. And she usually revealed pretty quickly when meeting anyone. Why should she have to hide from her past?

Other men she dated, she couldn't say the same thing. They usually dropped her like a sack of potatoes. They couldn't handle how outspoken she was.

Newman's expression softened. "I believe you, Amelia. I do."

Did the anger displayed on her face intensify as they stared at each other for him to repeat himself? He didn't seem like the type of guy who repeated himself.

Besides Mary and a few other ladies who loved to gossip, everyone had good things to say about Newman.

And when he said her name—Amelia—she believed everything he said. It came out so soft and endearing. Like a sweet whisper of affection.

Okay. She believed him. But she couldn't trust him. He was a known cheater and liar. She was here to use him to find her brother and that was it.

And maybe have sex once because, when he looked at her with such passion, she didn't want to resist. Like her mother always said, never pass up an opportunity.

"Well, that's my life, my brother's life, in a nutshell." She glanced at his notepad, unable to bear the intensity in his eyes. He looked like he wanted to ravish her right there on the couch. "You didn't write anything down."

He looked at the notepad and shrugged. "My partner—"

His lips thinned into a tight line. Then he smoothed out his features into indifference. "Maybe he rubbed off on me. He never writes anything down. He has such a great memory." He met her gaze. "I don't think I need to write down anything you just said."

Good. She didn't either. She didn't even like to think about what happened sometimes. Most of her past was an open book. Except...her mother killed a man. Every time she thought about her mother spending the rest of her life behind bars for defending herself and Adam against a man who deserved death, it made her so...so...angry. So filled with rage and despair she couldn't stop the tears.

But the tears, well, they never solved anything. She had to work hard to keep them in every time she thought of her mother.

Somehow, some way, she'd get her mother free.

Her father was a monster. He would've never stopped beating them, cutting them down, making their lives miserable if her mother hadn't stepped up and defended herself.

She wasn't sorry he was dead. She would never mourn his death. Her father had been dead to her far longer than before he died.

She hated thinking her mother was going to rot in prison for doing the right thing. It wasn't fair.

"Let's start with the last time you saw him. What was he wearing?"

Mel noticed he had his pencil poised, ready for action once again. She let out a breath and then thought back to yesterday.

"He had on blue jeans with a white T-shirt. Maybe some kind of band on it. I don't remember exactly. He had on his red winter coat. The pocket is torn. He never wears a hat or scarf or mittens, so he wasn't wearing anything like that. I tell him all the time if he's going to ride his bike in this cold weather, he should at least wear a hat."

Newman paused in his writing, sharing a look with her. She turned away before they could have some sort of moment. A moment of understanding, of shared pain. She didn't know what the look might've been, but she didn't want to click with this guy in any way. She just wanted her brother back.

And how could they share pain? Or understanding? Did his brother ever go missing?

She knew he had an older brother from all the gossip around town. Although, his brother hadn't been to the cabin in years, even before Pappa Roy passed away. If anyone was the golden boy of the town between the two, it would definitely be Newman, not his brother. She deduced that pretty quickly.

"Does Adam ride his bike to the store often? You said you two were at the store before that. Why did he need to go again?"

Exhaling a slow breath, she didn't look away from his wary gaze. If she expected honesty, she would display the same trait. "Because I asked him to clean his room. Just because we had a heart-to-heart about not running away again doesn't mean he's this perfect child all of a sudden."

Newman flinched. The pencil dug into the notepad before his features relaxed as if she imagined his reaction. Odd. Why did he flinch?

She decided to overlook it. "He ignored me, rummaging around in the kitchen to find a snack. He claimed I forgot chips. I didn't. I chose not to buy them. He grabbed his backpack and hollered he was going to buy some chips. He really didn't ask me. He simply left. Even if he would've asked and I said no, he still would've left."

"So he rides his bike to the store often? Does he bike the same route each time?"

A tentative smile graced her lips at his questions. Because when she told the chief of police the same thing, he jumped to the conclusion her brother ran away again.

But not Newman.

He believed her.

He was asking questions like he believed her brother was in trouble. Oh, and she knew he was in serious trouble because her stomach had been twisting in knots since last night when he never came home.

"I think so. I never followed him. It's a straight shot from our house. There is a big hill that he has to bike. It's kind of a winding road, too."

"There's a light snow on the ground. Nothing that I would think would impede his biking, not if he does it all the time, which it sounds like he does. But..."

Her heart started hammering in her chest. She didn't appreciate how he uttered the word *but* then stopped speaking because it wouldn't be something she would like to hear.

"But?"

A muscle ticked in his jaw. "But maybe he had an accident. Did you check the route from your house to the store?"

Her entire body started to shake. "It was dark out last night when I first started to get worried. Then this morning I paced the house from one end to the other before going to the chief of police, who told me to get lost. So...no, I didn't....I didn't...look for him...on the side of the road."

Oh, God. Her brother could be lying in a ditch, hurt, cold and dying. She was a terrible sister. Horrible.

"You said a few folks had things to say about me. When

exactly did you speak to them? How did you know where to find me?"

His questions jolted her out of her sudden panic. She eyed him quizzically, repeating his questions in her head.

"Oh, this town loves to gossip. They gave that information willingly without me even asking. People love to talk about everyone all the time. I don't even want to know what they say about me and my brother behind my back." She huffed out a trembling breath, realizing she wasn't thinking straight. If she wanted to find her brother safe and sound, she needed to stop, take a deep breath, and think before answering a question. "Okay, so after the visit with the chief, I stopped at the store to see if he bought his chips. That's where I spoke to Rebecca Sue, who said he never came. Then she mentioned you, and I asked where I could find you. She gave me your address. That's all the searching I did before coming here."

Newman stood up. "Then let's start looking."

She slowly stood up as well. Her knees buckled from the thought of what they might find on the side of the road.

He reacted with an ease that surprised her. His arms swept around her waist, guiding her back down to the couch gently. She couldn't stop shaking as his arms wrapped around her comforted her. His touch was soothing, light and tender.

"We'll find him. I promise."

"Are you supposed to make such promises? What happens if we don't? Or maybe we will. Maybe he's been lying in a ditch all night and I was an idiot, not thinking to go look there."

His arms tightened around her. "You're not an idiot. And I'll find him. I will not fail you, Amelia. I promise. I won't stop until I find him."

She turned her face slightly, meeting his powerful gaze that spoke the truth. An hour ago, if that, he wanted to kick her out of his house. He refused to help.

Now, he was promising he'd never stop until he found Adam.

She was right when she told him he was a good man.

He only had to start believing it himself.

5

NEWMAN GRIPPED the steering wheel hard as they slowly drove down the hill. Not because he was afraid of going too fast and hitting the ditch, but because he didn't want to miss Adam in case...

He stole a glance toward Amelia, who sat rigid in the passenger seat, her eyes darting back and forth outside.

...in case they found Adam lying hurt, injured—dead—in the ditch.

If he had fallen off his bike or got hit by a car, lying outside all night in the freezing cold didn't bode well for his chances.

Newman didn't know what was worse. A freak accident where it left him for dead in the freezing cold or abducted by a sicko. Either scenario sucked. Both scenarios wouldn't make Amelia happy.

For some odd reason, he wanted to make her happy. He wanted to make her proud, to have faith in him. Something nobody had for him anymore. Not even his parents when they found out why he quit his job, the things he did to Chrissy. The look of disappointment wasn't something he'd ever forget. In a way, he was glad his grandfather wasn't alive anymore. His look of disappointment would've gutted him straight to the core. Trying to gain his parents' approval was a lost cause. He stopped trying years ago when he was a senior in high school and he knew he wasn't going to make the honor roll. But his grandfather...Newman always tried to make him proud. He always tried to slow down and be patient about things like he always told him. And he always failed.

"I'm not seeing anything."

Yeah, neither was he. He still couldn't decide if that was a good thing or not. The panic in Amelia's tone didn't go unnoticed either, but he didn't know how to respond. How to make a little glimmer of hope cheer her up.

Was there hope? If they didn't find Adam lying dead in a ditch, he was most likely in the hands of someone dangerous. Good people didn't abduct kids. Bottom line.

"We'll find him."

That's all he had to offer her right now. Whether he was dead or alive was another story.

Amelia looked his way. They shared a small look of understanding, unspoken words that, although the truth hurt, they'd find him.

By the time they reached the store, taking the same path Adam would've taken, Newman refused to get frustrated. Because they didn't see a single thing.

No new snow had fallen overnight, the ground relatively clear, besides the already packed snow coating the sides of the road. It was a well-traveled road, so deciphering Adam's bike tracks from other markings from a car, truck, or even a snowmobile was impossible.

They didn't find Adam, and they didn't find his bike.

"Come on. Let's go talk to Rebecca Sue and some of the

other people inside." His hand started to reach for the door handle.

"I already did."

A soft, hopefully soothing smile touched his lips. "It never hurts to try again. Trust me."

Then he stepped out of the vehicle without waiting for a response.

He didn't want to hear a rebuttal that she didn't trust him. Why should've he earned her trust anyway? He hadn't done anything to show he was worthy of it. If anything, he had done everything in his power to show her how much of an asshole he was.

They spoke to Rebecca Sue, who kept offering shy, teasing smiles and silly giggles the entire time. Usually, he flirted back because he couldn't help himself. It came as natural as breathing, just another extension of himself.

But with Amelia by his side, watching him, judging him, he didn't joke back or deliver a suggestive smile. He kept it professional like he had a badge strapped to his belt, as if he were still a detective working a case.

Rebecca Sue didn't have anything helpful to offer. Neither did any of the other co-workers or the few visiting customers in the store. He made sure to stop and talk to each person he saw.

When they got back in the vehicle, he started the car to turn the heat on but didn't shift it into gear. He took off his gloves and grabbed the hand sanitizer he always kept in his car.

Even though he took his gloves off in the store, he didn't touch anything, but he still felt the need to lightly dab a small amount in the palm of his hand. He was careful not to get any on the bandage wrapped around his wounded hand.

"I'm sorry we're not finding anything yet, but don't give up hope. I said I'd find him and I will."

He wasn't sure why he said it, whether it was to reassure her or to reassure himself he still had the power to be a good cop. Maybe all the good in him died when his life started unraveling how many months ago.

Who cheated on a good woman? Who lied to his partner? Who acted like a jerk to his friends?

He did.

Wiping off the germs with this dumb sanitizer wouldn't get rid of the bad inside of him. No matter how much he applied. He sure wished it would.

"Well, I didn't expect much results. I've already looked here."

He met her gaze and nodded.

She suddenly looked down at her lap, fiddling with the edge of her coat. "It's..." Her head whipped in his direction. "Tell me the truth. What do you think is the worst-case scenario?"

Worst-case scenario?

Shit. He didn't even want to think it, let alone say it out loud. This was her brother they were talking about. She didn't need to hear the horrible things that might be occurring to him right this very second.

Worst-case scenario...

The first thing that popped in his head was the abduction of ten boys between the ages of twelve to sixteen from seven years ago. They were tortured, starved, deprived of everything, then killed brutally, cut from limb to limb still alive. Once the killer was all done, he disposed of the bodies by leaving pieces all over the woods. Some pieces he buried. Some pieces he left out in the open as a small tease. At least, that's what the officials theorized. They never caught the guy.

At the moment, that was the worst-case scenario filtering through his brain. It went on for two years, ten boys went missing from the surrounding towns, until one day, it stopped.

And there was no way in hell he would utter one word of that. Never.

"Newman?"

She could repeat his name over and over, but he wasn't going to answer the question. Not even with something less brutal than the imagery he just concocted in his mind.

"Detect—"

He caught her wrist before her hand could touch his shoulder. His eyes narrowed as a vile expression emerged. He wanted her trust, yet the crazy part inside him didn't want her to trust him. He was bad news, and it was better all around if she didn't trust him.

"Don't touch me. I don't like it. And don't call me anything other than Newman."

He still couldn't say such a simple word as detective. If he couldn't say it, he didn't want to hear other people say it.

Defiance etched into her golden-hazel eyes. His pink warrior fairy flashed with a vengeance. What would she say if he called her that?

"I can't even use your first name?"

"You don't know my first name."

Her brows rose as her lips twisted in mockery. "I thought I heard Rebecca Sue call you Robbie." The boldness in her eyes intensified. "She even tried to touch your hand."

Which was why he had the sudden need to get rid of the possible germs lingering when he got in the car.

He wouldn't call himself OCD or anything, but he had a

thing about germs. He usually carried a travel size of hand sanitizer anywhere he went. Whenever he shook hands with someone or left a crime scene, regardless if he touched anything, he always had to clean his hands immediately.

Amelia looked at the sanitizer sitting near his leg. "I didn't see you clean your hands with sanitizer in the cabin."

No, he didn't clean his hands in the cabin, did he? That was his living space. It didn't occur to him to do it then. But as soon as Rebecca Sue tried to touch his hand, he had been itching to get out of there and put on sanitizer.

Her eyes darted to his hand still wrapped around her wrist. He wasn't moving a muscle, although he was tempted to rub his thumb softly across her silky skin. Make her feel alive and wanted in a way she probably never felt before.

Or was it himself he wanted to make feel alive? To make him feel human, normal, and worthy of her affection.

"You're going to need to clean your hands again. Is that what you do, Newman? Act like a jerk, do something assholery, then slap some sanitizer on it and it clears away your sins?"

He dropped her hand as if she were a fire pit of hot coals burning his skin. She didn't know what she was talking about.

How in the hell did this conversation unravel to the intensity it had? They were talking about—

Of course.

She wanted to know worst-case scenarios and he refused to answer. She decided to lash out at him instead.

Coldness hit his hand.

"What the—"

He jerked away as Amelia tried to pour more sanitizer over his hand. Grabbing the bottle, he threw it on the floor, sucking in a sharp breath. So many nasty words teetered on the edge of his tongue. But he would regret it the minute they left his mouth.

Sure, she was acting like a child right now. But she had a reason. Her worry for her brother.

He didn't say anything as he tried to rub in the sanitizer as best as he could on his hands. Although, she had poured quite a bit out.

"Do you feel clean now? After touching my hand. Doing something you don't want to do."

Exhaling slowly, he looked at her, blown away by the pain in her eyes. She looked so broken, like a doll badly torn and ripped, hanging on by one thread.

"My name is Robert. Some people call me Robbie. I hate it. I like Newman. I don't like other people touching me, because yeah, I have a thing about germs sometimes. But I don't like it when you touch me—" He sucked in a sharp breath. "Because I want to do more than simple touching. I want to kiss you so hard, you won't be able to catch your breath for a week."

He said he would always be truthful with her. Well, there was some truth. Straight to her face and painting just how much of an asshole he truly was. Her brother was missing, most likely abducted by a maniac, and all he could think about constantly was sex.

"You want the truth? Worst-case scenario?" he shouted, the rage filling his veins because he promised the truth to her no matter what. For some reason, he couldn't lie to her. He couldn't break his promise. "There are sick people in this world. And hearing the worst possible thing your brother could be enduring is not going to help you. It's only going to further cause you to worry, so much worry, where you could make yourself sick. I'm not a goddamn savior, Amelia. I can't save you and save your brother. So I need you sane and in control. I won't be giving you any worst-case scenarios."

He turned his gaze away, staring out the window at the bleak, dreary day. The sun wasn't shining, blocked by gray, murky clouds. It's as if the weather knew it would be a tragic day.

He shuddered as a small dose of sanitizer slid underneath his bandage, seeping into his wound. He couldn't hold back a sharp breath, but he held in the roar of pain that wanted to unleash.

Maybe he should add more to his wound. He deserved to feel the pain.

He should apologize. Amelia didn't deserve his rage. Deep down, he wasn't angry at her, but himself.

"You can kiss me."

He turned toward her sharply, his brows puckered low. What? Why would she even want to kiss him? Didn't she know what kind of man he was? He'd only use her, then toss her to the side when he got sick of her. Because that's what he did.

A shy, tentative smile graced her red, kissable lips. "When we find my brother. You can kiss me."

"You don't mean that."

"Why not? I'll even have sex with you."

She couldn't possibly mean that. She had to be messing with his head.

"Don't say things like that. We promised we wouldn't lie to each other."

Her eyes narrowed. "What is it with men that they think it's okay they can have simple no-strings-attached sex, but oh no, if it's a woman, it's not okay. Well, screw you. If I want sex for the hell of it or a simple kiss, it's mine to take." Then she shrugged, averting her gaze. "I can pay you with a kiss.

So there, if it makes you feel better for me to have a reason to kiss you."

Without thinking, he raised his hand and brushed her cheek softly before letting his hand fall to his lap. She looked at him. "I don't want anything from you for helping. I want to help." He gave a lame laugh. "Even if it doesn't seem like it."

She bit her lip coyly with the desire flaming in her eyes. Was it always there and he simply didn't see it because he was so blinded by his own desire?

"I'll still take the kiss when this is over. Or sex. Whatever. You can pick."

"I'm bad news, Amelia. If you know what's good for you, you'll forget I ever said that. You'll forget me."

He refused to believe her. To think she'd actually want him in that way. How could she think he was worthy enough for her sweet warrior fairy goodness?

"I have a feeling you're not going to be easy to forget, Newman." Looking out the window, she squared her shoulders. "Where to next?"

Okay. The odd, confusing fight—or was it a conversation —was over. That was clear.

"I guess we talk to the chief of police."

She rolled her eyes, which made him chuckle. "Good luck with that. I'll stay in the car."

"That's fine."

And it was. He'd get a better read on the chief of police on his own. Not to mention, he'd be able to make a phone call without Amelia hearing.

Because the more he thought about the worst-case scenario, the more his gut was speaking loud and clear. Maybe he did have a small idea where her brother could be.

And it wasn't any place good.

6

HE DIDN'T SAY a word as he pulled into the police department's parking lot and got out of the vehicle. Amelia didn't say anything either.

Her grim expression, the slight fear in her eyes, and her silence was loud and clear. She didn't mind waiting in the car.

What had the chief of police said to her?

When he asked to speak to Chief Dodson, waited a few minutes for him to appear and followed him to his office, he understood why she didn't join him. The guy was a douche. Dee approved level kind of douche.

The insolence in his tone, even in a simple hello. The judgmental glare in his eyes. The arrogance in the way he walked.

The guy thought he was better than him, that he knew it all.

Well, he was about to get a rude awakening. Amelia was all alone and had no one to fight for her.

She did now.

She had him.

And if there was one thing he hated to see, it was people in need and not given the time of day.

"What's this about?"

Newman took a seat with his own arrogant smile. Two could play that game, and oh, boy, he could play it well. Just ask his friends and co-workers. Well, former friends and co-workers.

"I'm helping Amelia find her brother Adam." He propped his leg over his knee, indicating he was getting comfortable. He wouldn't be leaving until he had some answers. "How's your search going?"

A cocky laugh echoed out of the chief's tainted lips. "I'm not bothering with that family again. Do you know how many times that troublemaker has run away? Do you know how many times I've seen that juvenile delinquent in my building? I'm going to let him do his thing and he can come home on his own good time."

Troublemaker?

Juvenile delinquent?

His building?

Oh, it wasn't hard to see how much Chief Dodson did not like Adam.

But damn it. Chief Dodson didn't need to like the kid. He needed to do his job, which was to find him and return him home.

"Did you forget how to do your job, Chief? I can remind you how it works."

Chief Dodson flexed his fingers together, cracking his knuckles. "Remind me, uh? From a man that was fired from his job."

"I quit."

"You surrendered instead of enduring an investigation that would've ultimately fired you. Semantics."

Newman refused to let this asshole get under his skin, even if he was right in his assessment. He did quit before they could fire him. It would've happened. Everyone knew, including him.

Back in the day when his grandfather was alive, this asshole had only been a police officer. Chief Dodson's father had been the chief of police then. Sitting in the power of authority ran in the family, obviously. Now he sat in the chair of authority like he knew it all. But he didn't know anything. His grandfather hadn't even liked the guy, nor his father. That said enough.

"And if something terrible happened to the kid, how are you going to explain that?"

Chief Dodson leaned forward, his hands clasped tightly on his desk. "Nothing terrible happened. He's a loser, being taken care of by another loser, and you're falling for it. She must be good in bed."

Newman clenched his teeth, a muscle ticking in his jaw. Yet he forced his body to remain relaxed and not leap up and grab him by the shirt and knock him on his ass with one swift punch.

He painted his own past. He couldn't get upset when others took the information and expanded, creating new scenarios that could be plausible. He did *want* to get in Amelia's pants. She was a beautiful woman and she was available.

But he also had self-respect. He had a conscience for what was right and what wasn't. On occasion, he chose to ignore what was right. He would start learning from his mistakes. Quick and easy sex wasn't the right answer to his problems anymore. It never had been.

Damn it, Amelia wanted to sleep with him, which was shocking as hell to find out and terrible news to know.

How was he going to resist her now?

Chief Dodson's smirk grew as Newman said nothing to his derogatory remark. He acted like he won the battle between them. Not even close. He'd be the victorious one between the two when he found Adam and brought him home safe and sound. Hopefully.

Newman stood up. Chief Dodson didn't flinch or say anything.

Newman couldn't hold in a chuckle, which made Chief Dodson narrow his eyes in a vicious gaze. "You've been a great help. Thank you, Chief."

"I told you the truth. You're welcome."

Newman shook his head, an evil sneer twisting his lips. "No, you showed me how much of an idiot you are. How you don't care about the citizens of this town. And when I find Adam—and I better find him safe and sound—I'm going to make sure you lose your job for your mistakes." He stepped closer to the desk, pressed his hands down, and leaned forward. "Because I'm an expert at mistakes and losing a job I loved. So I know what it looks like when someone's repeating the same thing I did. Enjoy your comfy chair while it lasts. Because you won't be sitting there much longer."

He turned around and walked out of the office. It was petty and childish, but it felt good to be walking away with the last word.

His phone started ringing as he stepped outside.

"Hey, Sauer. I hope you have good news for me." Something he desperately needed. He was running out of good leads to find Adam.

"Umm...not really."

He sighed. "Lay it on me."

"The plates came back stolen, about a week ago. Not far from where you live. A town over."

He could work with that. A semi-lead that could guide him in another direction to a full lead.

"Thank you, Sauer. Can I have the address?"

"Of course." He rattled off the owner who called in the report, then paused. "Are you okay? Do you...you know..."

Newman shivered. Not from the cold seeping into his bones as he stood outside, but from the deep yearning to have his partner by his side helping on this case. Which was what it sounded like Sauer was trying to ask.

It was better if Sauer stayed away. He was bad news, and he wouldn't do anything but stain his life.

Sauer coughed and cleared his throat. "Do you need help? I can come help."

He should've hung up, ended the call before Sauer found the nerve to finish his question.

"Newman? Are you there?"

"Dee wouldn't like it."

"You're my friend. If you need help, I'm there."

"She hates me."

Silence.

Well, he didn't need a response. He knew Dee hated him. And yet, it was an excuse to keep Sauer away. An easy excuse. One that Sauer would take.

"She does hate you. But she loves me, and if I want to help my friend, she supports that."

Hearing Sauer say that made him instantly jealous. He wanted that kind of love. He wanted to find that kind of woman. One that supported you through anything. Through any difficult trial in life.

He didn't think that kind of woman existed. Not for him, anyway.

His gaze caught Amelia's as she sat in the warm car watching him intently.

No, she wasn't the right woman for him. Even if she was beautiful and sexy and sassy and not afraid to get in his face about anything.

His warrior fairy.

Wait. No. Not his anything. She was simply a woman he was helping.

"You're ignoring me again. Newman?"

"I got this, Sauer. But thank you." He inhaled deeply, then let it out. "I'll call if I change my mind."

"Will you?"

He deserved that. The uncertainty. The worry he was lying.

"We never talked, did we? Like, we talked about stuff, but not like Zeke and Ben do about every single dirty thing in their life."

"No, we didn't," Sauer said quietly.

"I was always jealous of you, Sauer. Of your quiet confidence. Of your relationship with Dee, because at that point in your life, I had officially ruined mine. Why? I don't know. Because commitment scared the crap out of me. Because I wasn't sure Chrissy was the one, even though I loved her."

Oh, man. He didn't want to think about Chrissy. He never did because it always made him think of himself and his actions. But he couldn't keep ignoring it. He had to eventually face his issues and now seemed like a good time. But only to make Sauer understand one thing.

He could trust him.

"I cheated on a good woman. I won't say we were a perfect couple because we weren't. Instead of owning my mistake, I lied to you about it. Because I was ashamed of myself. Because, here you were, perfect, starting a new, fresh relationship, and I was jealous." He blew out a harsh breath. "I've never been perfect, even though I tried my damndest to be the perfect son, the perfect cop, the perfect boyfriend. I always fall short. Always. No matter how hard I try. So, sometimes I give up and give in."

"Nobody is perfect, Newman, not even me. I'm far from confident. You do remember how I struggled to talk to women, even Dee in the beginning."

"No, man, you're confident. You just don't see it. And you're far more perfect than I'll ever be."

"You're my best friend. I don't care what anyone says, I don't want a perfect best friend. I want someone who's always going to be there for me. We all make mistakes. I forgive you for yours. Can you forgive me for mine?"

Forgive him? Sauer hadn't done a damn thing to him.

"You should hate me, man. There's nothing to forgive. You didn't do anything to me."

"I didn't see my friend was in pain, struggling. I should've. I know struggle well."

A small smile touched his lips. Sauer was the best friend a guy could ask for. He wanted to accept his help and ask him to come.

His smile died.

He would never ask him to come.

"Okay, enough going back and forth. I forgive you, Sauer. Although, I don't think you needed to apologize."

Sauer chuckled. "Is this how heart-to-hearts are supposed to go? I think we nailed it."

Newman joined in laughing. "It wasn't bad for newbies."

The laughter was still in Sauer's tone, yet a hint of seriousness lingered. "You better call me if you need me. I'll be there."

"I will."

"Good." This time it sounded like Sauer believed him.

Maybe they honestly had a decent heart-to-heart.

He hung up with Sauer and then slid into the car, reaching for the sanitizer.

"That bad, uh?"

Glancing at Amelia, chuckling as he rubbed his hands clean, he nodded. "The chief of police is a jackass of great proportions. I might need the whole entire bottle to clean his stench off."

"Now you know why I had to come to you."

Newman grinned. "I'm glad you did. We'll find him."

Amelia returned a sweet smile. A smile filled with admiration and trust. And damn it, he wanted her trust, even though he shouldn't. He wanted to prove to at least one person they could put their full trust in him and he wouldn't let them down.

He started the car.

"Where are we going?" she asked as she buckled her belt.

"We have a new lead. It's not much, but it's something."

And in any case, that's all he needed to keep the trail hot.

MEL WASN'T sure who Newman had been talking to—or what about—but he seemed more relaxed as they drove. Not as tense holding the steering wheel. They even engaged in light conversation and laughed together a few times.

Or maybe he was trying to make her feel more relaxed and keep her mind off the fact her brother could be dead.

Nope.

She wasn't going there.

Her brother was alive and...well, maybe not *well*. He could be hurt in some capacity, but he wasn't dead.

As soon as he pulled into the driveway in an upscale neighborhood, her anxiety skyrocketed. He said he wanted to interview the owner of the stolen truck she had seen. The truck didn't come from this residence. It was a dirty white truck with dents, scratches, and rust spots lingering everywhere.

The house before her was something she'd describe as magnificent. Rich and full of money. The yard and shrubbery looked well manicured, as well as could be in the winter. Of course, the expensive SUV sitting in the driveway also said the homeowner had money. Lots of money. She found it hard to believe they owned a rusted old pickup truck.

Newman put the car in park but didn't turn off the ignition. "Why don't you stay in the car?"

She liked that idea. All too much.

But this was her brother missing and she wanted to be involved in everything. Next time, she'd even go with him to speak with Chief Dodson. No one scared her, and she wouldn't let the chief of police think he scared her either.

She started to open her mouth to argue when he lifted his hand in protest.

"I know what you're going to say. And I completely understand. I would want to be involved in everything."

The knowledge he did understand reflected in his ocean-blue eyes. "Then I'll come with you."

"It's going to be hard enough to explain how I got their information, considering I'm not a cop. Neither are you. I think it's better if I go by myself."

"You were a cop. Can't you just..."

Brows puckering, he looked at her odd. "Just what?"

"Just say you are. And I'm your partner and—"

"I'm done lying, Amelia." His entire face went hard as granite. "I won't lie for you. Lying has never gotten me anywhere, except to a special kind of hell that I don't like. I lost my job"—he gritted his teeth— "as a *cop* because I lied. Don't ever ask me to lie again."

Before she could respond, he whipped open his door and stepped out. A rush of cold air hit her in the face. The door slammed right away, although, the chill from outside still lingered in her bones.

Not necessarily from the weather, but from her actions. For thinking because he did shady things in the past, he'd still do it. Chief Dodson slamming the door in her face, refusing to help her, wasn't the only reason she sought out Newman.

He walked a tight line before; she figured he might do it again.

She wanted her brother back, and honestly, she wasn't afraid to do things that might skirt the line. If that included lying to find some answers, then she was prepared to lie.

But, she hated to admit, it wasn't fair to ask Newman to do the same. He was right. He lost his job because he lied. About what? She didn't know. But it wasn't right of her to ask him to go down that path again.

It's just...her brother. What was he enduring right this very second? Was he being tortured? Was he cold and alone? Was he locked up, injured?

If Newman wasn't prepared to lie, and he wasn't a cop, what would he do if—or when—faced with a difficult choice? What would he do if the only way to get a lead was he had to lie?

What if...

No. That was a crazy thought.

But it was better than nothing, and he wouldn't have to lie.

If he was a PI, he could get information without skirting the truth. How did one become a PI? Could you simply say you were one? Sounded simple enough to her.

Grabbing her phone, she started searching for answers. Because Newman would not take her word for it.

Jumping, startled when the door opened, she waited for Newman to look at her. He slid into his seat, shut the door, and rested his hands on the steering wheel.

But he refused to look at her.

That could mean one of two things.

No useful information was gained from questioning the owner of the truck.

Or he learned some bad news and he didn't know how to tell her.

"So?"

She couldn't take the silence. If it was bad news, she wanted to know now rather than later.

"I didn't find anything useful. He owns a construction company and he used that truck for hauling supplies sometimes. He came home about a week ago after work, and the next morning it was missing from his driveway. He didn't see anything odd or strange around the neighborhood, nor did he hear anything strange. We're at a dead end right now."

Well, that was disappointing, especially by his tone of voice, so destitute and broken. Why would he sound so disheartened by the news? It's not as if he ever met her brother.

"We'll keep looking. Maybe we should drive by the route he took to the store again. Maybe we can walk it this time and keep an eye out for something we might've missed driving. On the drive back I can tell you—"

"I'll bring you home, Amelia. I can search that route myself."

He still refused to make eye contact, staring out the window like he was waiting for something to happen. Something to jump out and surprise them.

"My car is at your house. And I *will* help search."

"I think it's better—"

"I've had enough of people telling me in my life what's best for me. I won't let you tell me, too. He's my brother, not yours." Gripping her phone hard, she resisted the temptation to scream like a banshee. The man was insufferable, frustrating, and she wanted to shake some reason into him. "Look at me!"

He took his time, but he finally swiveled his gaze to her. No expression, nothing for her to decipher what he was thinking echoed in his features.

"I'm sorry for asking you to lie. I'm prepared to do anything to find my brother..." She turned her eyes to her lap. "But I shouldn't ask the same of you."

"I said I'd find him and I will."

She looked up. The determination glittering in his eyes made her hopeful they'd find Adam soon.

But the lack of any leads to point them in another direction dashed those hopes quickly.

"Where you go, I go. That's non-negotiable." She made sure her determination was just as prominent as she met his intense glare.

"Fine. For now." He looked away, put the car in gear, and started to back out of the driveway.

"Umm...for always. I said it was non-negotiable."

A tiny smirk emerged, although he still didn't look at her. "We'll see."

"No, that—" She stopped speaking, figuring he was

looking for a fight. No matter what he said, she wasn't going to argue about it. Until they found her brother, she was glued to his hip.

The conversation needed to change before the tension swirling between them magnified to dangerous levels.

"So, I did some research while you were interviewing that guy. I didn't get all the way through it, but I found a way for you to say you're a cop but not lie about it."

A brow arched, yet he kept his eyes on the road. "Sounds like you're creating a way for me to lie, but not make it sound like a lie. Let's not go there again, Amelia."

"Okay, not so much saying you're a cop, but sort of like one. A PI."

"A what?"

She rolled her eyes, laughing. "Don't play dumb. You know, a private investigator. It didn't look too hard to apply to become one. You have the experience since you were a cop. You look like you have money for the filing fees and such. Oh, and you'll need a Surety Bond. You'll also need five references. That's kind of a lot, but we can brainstorm together who you can ask and how fast we can get that. You came back before I could finish reading. I'm not sure how long the process takes, but maybe we can—"

"Stop."

Her mouth froze in a circle as the venom in his tone sliced her to the core. Somehow, she managed to upset him once again. That's all she'd been doing since she knocked on his door. He had some serious anger management to work through.

Not that it was her problem. But if it was the only way to find her brother faster, she'd make it her problem.

Except she wasn't sure how to help lower his anger.

"You miss being a cop. You can still be one. Kind of. A PI isn't much different."

"Amelia..."

He still sounded angry. Yet, his tone had changed a bit. As if he knew he was in a losing battle with her. She could be very, very tenacious when she wanted to be.

"Yes?"

His hands tightened on the wheel. "Stop talking before I pull over and make you walk back."

Or maybe she was the one in the losing battle.

He didn't ask her to help him, so why was she bothering?

No more words were spoken as he drove back to his place.

7

NEWMAN ALMOST SLAMMED the door but stopped when he heard the shuffling of feet behind him. The damn woman was following him inside, even though he gave her a curt good-bye-see-you-tomorrow farewell outside.

Earlier, they grabbed a quick bite to eat, since she skipped lunch, then drove to her house and started the cold, blistering walk to the store. They stuck to one side, roaming over every inch of the ditch and road looking for any signs of her brother. Nothing of importance stuck out. Once they hit the store, they grabbed a coffee and started the walk back on the other side of the ditch.

Nothing.

Nodda.

Zilch.

They didn't even see any distinctive bike treads from Adam indicating he made it to the store. Newman figured he was nabbed the second he started biking.

It wasn't something they talked about. In fact, not much was spoken since she tried to tell him the process of becoming a PI. He didn't want to hear it.

As soon as she said he'd need references, he knew it wasn't a possibility. No one would vouch for him. Not a soul. Why would they?

Maybe Sauer would because he was just that kind of guy, willing to help out his friends. But he'd never ask him. Newman had already used and abused that relationship. It wouldn't be right to ask him for anything, especially with the way he treated him.

So, yeah. It was better not to talk about it, or even think about it.

When they reached her house, he drove her back to his cabin. She had insisted he drive in the first place, whining and complaining until he didn't want to hear it anymore and caved in.

He was done with her for the evening. He couldn't be around her anymore. They didn't have anything else to do tonight, nowhere else to look for her brother.

Failing once again.

So he shot out of his car, muttered a good-bye, and tried to escape into his domain.

And she wasn't letting him.

He heard the door close quietly as he stalked to the kitchen. A nice strong drink of liquor would be perfect right now. Calm his nerves, the rage simmering inside.

Who did she think she was? Following him. Ignoring his wishes—or demands. He didn't exactly tell her to leave politely.

He wanted to be left alone. He liked being alone. It was definitely better if he was left alone.

"What's for supper?"

His hand gripped the fridge handle hard. He could go for the liquor in his cupboard, get drunk, and get really nasty with her.

"We could order pizza."

Or he could try to keep his cool until he got her out of his house. He whipped open the fridge and grabbed a bottle of water.

Taking a long swallow, he turned toward her. "I told you to go home."

A devious smirk twisted her lips as she took a seat on the couch. She took her jacket off as well. "And I told you you're stuck with me. Like glue. Joined at the hip. I'm like a flea that doesn't die."

"I told you I wanted to screw you ten ways to Sunday, so you better get the hell out of my house before I actually do."

Her smirk inched up a notch. "You didn't quite describe it that way, but..." She shrugged, as if nothing bothered her. "We can totally pass the time having sex if it'll put a smile on your face. Do you ever smile?"

Damn...

This woman could get under his skin with finesse. Without even trying.

Here he was, trying to scare her away and she wasn't taking the bait.

He turned away from her penetrating stare, squeezing the bottle tight. Some of the water shot up, coating his hand and the floor around him.

Not even the threat of sex was chasing her away. Crazy laughter almost bubbled up his throat.

She kept saying she would sleep with him.

He kept saying he'd screw her without blinking.

Maybe he should test her. Stalk over there, tease her, entice her, and make her beg him to give her the pleasure they both obviously were dying to have.

"Newman—"

"Stop talking." His hand squeezed the bottle again, more water spurting out.

He didn't want to hear what she had to say. Most likely, he'd hate it. Because, so far, he had hated everything she said. Most of it the truth.

Like applying to become a PI. It had crossed his mind before, although, he didn't go as far as her researching information. It only scattered around his thoughts, making him believe he could have a semblance of his old life. He never actually looked it up because he wasn't worthy of it.

He didn't help people.

He screwed up their lives.

Just like he would screw up hers if she stayed.

Screwed.

Yeah, he could screw her brains at the same time he screwed her life. A double whammy.

A soft hand touched his shoulder.

He flinched. The water bottle fell to the floor. He jerked away from her hand. A hand he wasn't sure what it was offering. Comfort? He didn't want that from her. Understanding? She didn't understand a damn thing about him.

"You have a serious anger problem."

Damn her. Right about everything.

He hated know-it-alls.

Finally meeting her gaze, he didn't try to hide the fury blazing through his veins. "You need to leave, Amelia."

"Or what?" She took a step forward. He took a step back. "Are you going to hit me? Are you going to rape me? Are you going to hurt me? Kill me? Bury my body in the woods out back?"

She kept advancing. He kept retreating for every step she took. He had nowhere to go when he hit the counter. She stopped right in front of him, trapping him.

He'd never been trapped by a woman before. He did the chasing, flirting and teasing with ease, dating like it was a game until he reconnected with Chrissy, his old high school sweetheart.

Which he didn't want to think about right now. Conjuring thoughts of Chrissy never took him to a happy place.

She hesitated, then touched his chest, her hand over his heart. Her eyes flashed with compassion. And why? Because she could feel his heart was racing a mile a minute? Because she thought she understood him?

Nobody understood him. Nobody ever would.

"Answer me, Newman. Just answer one of those damn questions."

He inhaled deeply. Her hand followed the movements.

"No."

"To which question?"

His eyes were locked with hers. The intensity, the strength in her eyes made him think he could heal from the pain he inflicted upon himself.

He couldn't blame anyone but himself for everything that happened in his life. He did it all. He was the culprit.

Her honest, warm gaze nearly told him he could recover from it.

"All of them."

Then he grabbed her hand and pulled it away from his chest. Except when he tried to let go, she twisted her fingers, grasping his hand instead. She refused to let go.

"I don't know where all this anger stems from."

"I'm not standing here having a goddamn heart-to-heart about—"

"And I'm not asking for you to tell me." A tender smile touched her lips as he tried to twist his hand out of hers.

"But I'll help you in any way I can. I want to find my brother. Keeping you coolheaded and in control is the only way we can do that."

Unless he grabbed her hand with his free hand, he wasn't going to be able to escape her embrace.

Not that he was trying hard to get free.

"You're tense. If sex will loosen you up and calm you down, then okay. Let's do that."

Yeah, he was definitely not trying hard enough to get away from her. Maybe he was looking for any excuse to touch her.

Because damn.

He wanted to toss her over his shoulder and never leave his bedroom for a week.

"It'd be like selling your body, Amelia. Is that the kind of woman you are?"

He wouldn't lie and say he never slept with a hooker before, because hey, he wasn't perfect. He had done things he wasn't proud of. When he started sinking, instead of jumping off the boat and swimming for help, he took a seat and prepared to go down with the ship.

"I'm whatever kind of woman you need me to be right now."

Instead of grabbing their locked hands to tear them apart, he reached up and cupped her cheek.

"Never be anyone but who you are. Not for me. Not for your brother. Not for anyone. You're better than that. You're not like me."

"You keep saying you're this terrible person, but I haven't seen it yet. Yeah, you cheated and you lied. So have tons of other people. That doesn't mean they're terrible. And okay, you have a bit of a temper." She leaned into his hand holding her cheek. "But I know what a temper is and what a toddler tantrum is. You're acting like a big old baby right now, Newman. Trust me when I say, I wouldn't be this close to you if I thought for even a second you'd hurt me."

Who was this woman?

Messing with his head.

Making him believe things he shouldn't believe.

Leaning closer, he couldn't resist anymore. Not when she said every word like she honestly believed it. Like she truly believed he was a good person. His lips touched hers gently. Soft and tender, like a sweet caress, as if he were savoring the most delicious chocolate in the world.

And oh, man. He suddenly had a sweet tooth. For her.

The kiss barely lasted a few seconds, but it was enough time for him to know if he kept kissing her, he'd never stop. He'd do something he'd regret. And when it came to Amelia, he never wanted to regret anything.

For the first time, he was going to start thinking about someone other than himself.

He cleared his throat. "I should apologize for that."

She cocked a brow.

A devilish grin emerged. "But I'm not going to." Then his smile disappeared. "And it won't happen ever again."

He gripped her hand and tugged her to follow him.

"So, where are you dragging me? We're having sex, but no kissing. Where's the fun in that?"

A chuckle slipped out. This woman kept surprising him. Instead of slapping him hard across the face for taking advantage of her, she was making jokes.

He heard a short inhale of breath from her when he turned right instead of left to the bedroom. Stopping in front of the punching bag, he let go of her hand, and then whipped his shirt off.

Probably torturing himself by letting her eyes roam all

over him, but what could he say? He liked the torture, how her eyes devoured him like she was eating the tastiest snack she ever had.

Rotating his shoulders, stretching out the kinks in his body, he smiled. "You want to help me release some tension? This is how I release my tension these days. Not with sex."

"Even if I'm willing?"

He ached to reach out and touch her once again. But he didn't. He resisted. Touching her was a little more torture than he could handle at the moment. He might actually cave in and take the pleasure they both craved.

"There's evil in the world, Amelia. In every corner of life. I want to know if you can protect yourself while also releasing some of my tension. It's a win-win."

Flexing her hands, a smile spread across her face. "You're not one of the evil things roaming this world. And if you do think so, I guess I'll have to beat it out of you until you believe you're a good man."

He almost wished her luck.

But it'd be useless.

Nothing—no one—would ever get the evil out of him.

WIPING HER BROW, she took a step back, breathing heavily. "I need a break."

Newman, the bastard—the totally sexy bastard with no shirt on—smirked at her, then continued to pound the bag.

Compared to him, she was out of shape. Yeah, she took self-defense classes and learned the best techniques to help herself if she were ever in a position where she needed to get away. And yeah, she liked to work out at home, doing a few exercises to stay in shape. Exercises she thought were brutal.

But no.

Working the punching bag, learning how to properly throw a punch, now *that* was pushing her past her limits.

And damn.

She loved it.

She understood now why Newman liked to release his tension this way. The power she felt in each jab. The strength she knew she had confirmed with each motion. It was intoxicating.

Except when Newman opened his mouth and said she was doing it wrong. Which he did quite a bit.

Her form was off. Her balance wasn't right. Her punch too slow.

The man had nothing encouraging to say.

Wiping her brow once more of sweat, she inhaled deeply, enjoying the show in front of her. She might not appreciate the things he said, but in all honesty, she was grateful he took the time to correct her form and make her a better fighter. But he could have more tack, more grace, more kindness in the way he delivered his messages. Of course, that wasn't his style. She totally knew that from the beginning.

She wanted to be as fluid as him, as graceful in her movements. She was mesmerized watching him swing punch after punch, his muscles flexing in his back and arms, enhancing the beauty in his features.

She never thought a man was beautiful before, more so usually hot or yummy man candy or downright sexy.

But watching Newman attack the punching bag with such agility, it was so breathtakingly beautiful.

He paused a moment, rotating his shoulders, but didn't

look at her. "You should go home. Take a shower, relax. We'll start searching again tomorrow bright and early."

Geez. He just didn't get a clue. She wasn't leaving. Not now. Not tomorrow. Not until she found her brother.

And they would. Newman said they would and she believed him. She had to; otherwise, she'd go out of her mind with worry.

When she didn't respond, he looked at her. Honestly, a response wasn't going to make a difference. She knew they were about to argue either way.

"You don't give up, do you?"

"Giving up means I don't care, that I'm a loser, that I'm not good enough to follow through to the end. I don't ever give up."

"Someone say that to you before?"

She forced herself to stay calm, like his question didn't affect her. Because what he thought of her actually mattered. "Maybe. What do you care?"

He shrugged and looked away. "I don't."

"But I think you do."

Damn infuriating man. Why couldn't he admit it? He cared.

Of course, why did she bait him in the first place?

An irritated chuckle floated out as he glanced back in her direction. "You always think you know me so well. You don't, Amelia. You never will."

"Well, if you didn't care at least a little bit, you would've tossed me out of your house a long time ago."

His eyes narrowed, his fists tightening. "I'm tempted to throw you out right now. I said we're done for the evening. Go home."

She planted her feet more firmly to the ground. "I said I wasn't leaving. You're not getting rid of me."

"Who said those things to you? They obviously don't know you very well. You don't give up."

A bout of laughter echoed between them. She couldn't hold it in. Because he had no idea how right he was.

"Random people here and there. But mostly my father said those things. He cut me down every day of his life. From the way I did my hair, to the way I dressed, to the way I talked. If I so much as looked in his direction, he had something nasty to say. Sometimes, just to piss him off, I would laugh for no reason. I don't know why I did. He always hit me right after until I stopped laughing."

Newman's eyes shifted around the room, hitting the floor, the walls, the punching bag, unable to hold her stare.

Yeah, most people weren't comfortable when she talked about her father.

It never stopped her, though. Every time she confessed about her past life, a tiny slice of her damaged soul drifted away. It was cathartic in a way she couldn't describe, and she tried so many times to explain her reasoning. Most times, her friends simply stopped calling or visiting. They didn't like how open she was about everything in her life. People couldn't handle the truth. The only thing she found hard to talk about was her mother and what she had done. Because she wasn't sorry that her mother killed her father. Did that make her a terrible person? She didn't want to think so or to find out what others thought.

"I hope your mother has a damn good lawyer."

"Excuse me?"

He met her gaze once again. "Your mother. I hope she has a good lawyer. I'd hate to see her spend life behind bars when it sounds like she was already living a life behind bars."

Mel actually stumbled back as his words hit her like a punch straight to the gut.

No one ever said that before. No one ever understood the kind of cruel man her father had been, even when she told them horrifying stories.

Yet Newman did. He didn't think her mother deserved to be locked up like a monster for killing another monster.

"Are you okay?" The compassionate look in his eyes said he wanted to step closer.

"I'm fine. You surprised me. I'm not sad or angry that my mother killed him. If anything, I'm happy. He deserved it. And she doesn't deserve to be locked up. You're the first person to agree. At least, vocally."

"I just call it as I see it." He cracked a smile. "How did we get on such a depressing topic?"

She matched his smile. "You told me to get the hell out of your house."

"Right. That worked well." He chuckled as he brushed a hand through his hair. "So, what? You're my new roomie until we find your brother. Is that what you're telling me?"

"You obviously don't listen." She shook her head as a crafty smile twisted her lips. Then her expression dropped into a frown. "There has to be something we can do right now. I mean, what are we doing tomorrow? Searching some more? Where? What's your plan?"

"I have no plan. When I work a case, I follow the leads and go from there."

"We don't have any leads, Newman." She couldn't keep the dejection out of her voice.

"I know. But I've lost leads many times. You just keep at it."

"So you have a one hundred percent closing rate on your cases? You've solved every single one?"

He winced, his fists tightening once again. "No, I can't say that. But it doesn't mean I ever give up. People can call me some nasty things, but I was a damn good detective."

She clapped as one would praise a toddler for putting their toys away nicely. "Yay. You can say the word."

Rolling his eyes, an exasperated breath escaped. "You're impossible. I'm trying to tell you that you can't give up hope yet."

"Did you not understand the beginning of this conversation? I don't give up on anything. I will not give up on my brother. And until we find him, you're stuck with me. So yeah, roomie, pull out some blankets and a pillow because I'm sleeping here tonight."

She wouldn't even mind if it was in his room. With him. Right next to her. She hadn't been kidding when she said she'd sleep with him. Punching a bag was fun and everything, but she was all for releasing the tension in the form of hot, raunchy sex.

When he displayed his tender, understanding side, which wasn't very often, it made him that much more attractive. It made him into a man she respected.

"You can have my bedroom. There are two rooms here, but the other one is full of storage. I'll sleep on the couch."

"I don't—"

"Non-negotiable. I can act like a gentleman on occasion. Take the bed and try not to argue with me for once." An adorable grin touched his lips.

"Fine. I'm going to take a shower. Then I can make us something to eat. I need to borrow some clothes until I can grab a bag tomorrow."

"There's some sweats and shirts in my room. Grab whatever." He flexed his shoulders like he was preparing to start jabbing at the bag again. "I'm not hungry, but feel free to eat anything you like."

"You should—"

"Stop." His expression hardened. "Don't think because I'm giving in and letting you stay means you're the boss of me. Because you're not. You need to stop thinking you know me and can control me. You can't. The sooner you figure that out, the better."

A smirk emerged. "You need to stop saying *stop* all the time. It's starting to get old. You need to know that I will and can boss you around. Because it's been working so far. I'll always get my way because I don't give up. You yourself just admitted to giving in to me. There's the difference between us. You gave up. I didn't. The sooner you figure that out, the better."

With that, she twisted around and walked out of the room to clean up.

And boy, she loved getting the last word in.

His shocked expression was too damn adorable.

8

STARING AT THE CEILING, his eye caught a cobweb. He'd take care of that first thing in the morning. He couldn't have spiders crawling in his cabin. There could only be one nasty thing living in the cabin, and spiders weren't it.

He was.

Two long days of torture.

Two long days of snapping and yelling at Amelia and she still wouldn't leave.

It didn't matter what he said, what he did, usually beating her body to the bone with the punching bag, she refused to give up and leave. He didn't want to take his frustrations out on her, but no one else was around. So she took the brunt of his anger, his irritation, his disappointment that he was once again failing.

Two long days of dead ends and no leads to help him locate her brother.

He canvassed her neighborhood, the surrounding neighborhood—basically, the entire town. Not a scrap of evidence. No sighting of Adam. No clues to point him in the right direction.

Yesterday, when forty-eight hours rolled around, he accompanied Amelia to the precinct to file a missing person's report. Something that should've happened right away, and he didn't hesitate to inform Chief Dodson of that several times. What a prick. While the chief finally did his job, he still thought the boy ran away of his own accord.

Newman knew it wasn't true.

Although he despised it, he researched the cases of the missing boys from seven years ago. He dug deep, attempting to find every piece of information he could based on news articles. He knew without even asking Chief Dodson wouldn't supply him with the official records.

Nothing useful panned out. The boys were abducted without any eyewitnesses, usually playing outside or riding their bikes around town, just like Adam. Over the course of two years, ten boys went missing. Sometimes, a month went by before another boy went missing, and other times, two to three months would pass. The killer had no set pattern in his method. Based on the few body parts recovered, the coroner was able to determine they were tortured, indicative of the marks on the body, and they were starved.

Because they were cut up, the coroner couldn't determine a cause of death.

Whoever this killer was, they were beyond sick. Beyond psychotic. Beyond reasoning. Newman couldn't even find the right word. Since they only found a few body parts scattered around the woods—an arm here, a leg there, a few fingers lying around—they could never determine what the killer had done with the other parts. Buried them? Kept them? They weren't positive about that part of the puzzle.

Then, like the sun immediately appearing after a torrential downpour, the disappearances stopped. Finding body pieces in the woods stopped. The evil and terror just stopped. For five long years.

Thinking about those murdered boys made him think about his grandfather. Although his grandfather didn't have a background in law enforcement, he loved to talk cases with him. Whether it was a crime committed up north where his grandfather lived or a case he was trying to solve with Sauer. They talked about anything and everything. It never helped him solve any particular case, but it had been nice to talk to him about things. No matter what it was.

Then his grandfather suffered a massive heart attack and died.

One day here, the next day gone.

Newman left and never came back. It didn't matter his grandfather left him the cabin. The memories were too painful. He missed him too much.

Moments like this, he wished his grandfather was here. Maybe he'd have some insight on the missing boys from seven years ago.

Because it appeared to be happening again...maybe. He couldn't be absolutely sure Adam was taken by the same killer. Why wait five years? Why start taking boys again? Was it the same lunatic?

Newman didn't know, but he was determined to find out. He wouldn't rest until he found Adam because failure was not an option. Never again.

Unfortunately, since she was like a nauseating fly that wouldn't leave him alone, Amelia was right by his side as he researched. A few times she clutched her stomach as if she were going to throw up, something he wanted to do right along with her.

But she didn't, and he didn't offer any words of encouragement. What could he say that would be encouraging? It had been officially four days since her brother disappeared. Three days since he'd been helping.

Long days and nights with her living in his house, invading his space...his mind.

He couldn't help but watch her out of the corner of his eye, not wanting her to catch him staring. She was beautiful. In every aspect. Her gorgeous lithe body, her pink fairy hair, her luscious red lips. Oh, and her strength, determination, and willpower to stay strong was so damn beautiful he wanted to drop to his knees in agony. He had never met a more gorgeous woman in his life.

Because of that, he needed her to leave. To do his job in peace. She was a distraction. So many times he wanted to shove her against the wall, kiss her breathless, and show her how much he craved her.

He was starting to think it wasn't because she was a woman and available, but because she was...Amelia.

Strong. Sexy. Bossy.

So damn bossy.

She never stopped ordering him around. Eat this. Take a break. Let's do some punching. Sometimes, he would stop what he was doing and listen. Well, kind of. She didn't leave him alone until he caved or he lost his temper that had her arching her brow in a way that said she was about to skewer him to the bone. It was her way or no way. Infuriating woman.

Beautiful, infuriating woman.

Groaning, he closed his eyes and tried to think of how he'd get those cobwebs off the ceiling. He needed to occupy his mind with something else because he was aching to leave the uncomfortable couch and slide into bed with her.

He'd have to grab a chair and use a broom to get the cobwebs. The ceiling was pretty high. It was a good thing his hand was healing well and not bothering him as much. It shouldn't be too hard to clean.

First thing on his agenda tomorrow: clean the cobwebs.

Second thing on his agenda: resist the temptation of sleeping with Amelia.

Third thing on his agenda: find her brother.

Just another day in his crazy, messed-up life.

MEL PUT two bowls on the table as she tried not to laugh at Newman. "What are you doing?"

Standing on a chair with a broom high in the air, he waved it with mockery. "What does it look like I'm doing? I'm getting these cobwebs."

She didn't even bother to ask why as she turned toward the cupboard where he kept his cereal. The first morning she made a big breakfast with eggs and toast and bacon. And the obstinate man didn't touch a bite. The second morning she tried just eggs. He still ignored it.

To give him credit, he didn't usually ignore lunch and supper, so maybe he wasn't a breakfast person.

She'd find out this morning. She was skipping the eggs altogether and going with cereal. It was stocked in his cupboards, so it had to mean he ate it on occasion.

Pouring both bowls halfway, she grabbed the milk from the fridge and poured it over the cereal.

"Breakfast time."

"Not hungry."

Her lips pressed into a tiny line as she watched him circle the broom around the ceiling. He had been in the same spot for the past few minutes. The cobwebs were gone. The man was certifiable right now.

"Get down from there and eat your cereal. Now."

"You're not the boss of me."

Well, maybe she wasn't. But every day should start with a good breakfast. It made a person think better. If they were going to find her brother, which they needed to do soon, he needed all of his wits. He had to eat breakfast.

Stalking over to him, she pushed at the chair, which made him lose his balance. She tried not to laugh as he stumbled—not quite falling, but he didn't get down gracefully. Of course, she failed miserably. Her laughter came out strong and clear.

"You just pushed me and almost made me break my neck. How is that funny?"

"Because I caught you off guard and I love doing that." Her eyes narrowed. "Now come eat."

Moving the chair, he stepped into her face. "You're not the boss of me. Stop thinking you are."

"I made breakfast the past two mornings and you didn't touch a thing. You're eating today."

"I never asked you to make me breakfast."

"Well, I did. It's only polite to eat some, even if you don't want any."

He inched closer. Close enough to touch her lips. "I'm not a polite guy."

Two long days of circling each other, not including the first day she knocked on his cabin. Two torturous days trying to find her brother. Two agonizing days holed up in a cabin with a man she wanted to sleep with, a man who wanted to sleep with her, yet held back.

He said she wasn't the boss of him.

Oh, how wrong he was.

She closed the distance, pressing her lips to his. Before he could pull away and break the triumph coursing through her for catching him off guard once again, she stepped away first.

"When you stand that close to me, I'm liable to do anything."

His eyes glittered with mischief. "I'm all for more kissing."

She threw him a wicked smile. "Or how about a quick, swift kick to the nuts. You just never know what I might do."

"Amelia..."

"Give in, Newman. Stop fighting me. I will always win. Go eat breakfast. I made you cereal this morning. It was in your cupboard. It must mean you eat breakfast sometimes."

"You didn't *make* cereal. You poured it into a bowl."

"Semantics," she said as she waved a flippant hand in the air. "Chop, chop. We have a busy day ahead of us."

Ignoring the sadness that poured off him in waves, she walked back to the table to eat her breakfast.

Oh, yeah. They had a busy day today. Pacing the cabin trying to think of where they could look for her brother. Didn't get any busier than that.

They had run into a dead-end wall. They talked to all her neighbors, questioned people around town. Nothing panned out. They even researched some abductions from a few years ago that gave her the chills every time she thought about it.

Which she tried hard not to do.

Because if her brother was in the hands of that sadistic—

Two loud knocks on the door interrupted her thoughts. And she was oh so grateful for it. She already ruminated too long last night about what her brother was enduring.

"Who is that?"

Newman shrugged and eyed her funny. "It's probably somebody you know. Nobody visits me."

She almost laughed but stopped herself. It wasn't funny. He wasn't joking. Nobody visited him. It made her sad for him. Because she knew the feeling. Nobody visited her either, or her brother, who was an outcast at school. He liked to keep to himself. That didn't stop kids from being mean, bullying him because he happened to be an easy target. Before she moved to the wilderness, nobody visited her much in the city. She was a loner. She preferred it that way. The few times she tried to be social and make friends, it always fell apart. People didn't like the real her. They couldn't handle her honesty. She could be a little too brash sometimes.

Stepping away from the table, she waited impatiently for Newman to open the door. The second he swung it open and a strange man walked in, she didn't know what to think. Did they find her brother? Was he dead?

Then the man smiled and Newman hugged him. It was an awkward hug, not very long, but a hug that said they knew each other well.

"What are you doing here, Sauer?" Newman asked.

"We're here to help."

"We?"

She was curious, too. And help with what? Finding her brother?

A smile wanted to burst free at the adorable confusion on Newman's face. Flabbergasted was not a common look she saw on him. She quite liked it.

She walked farther out of the kitchen and closer to the couch as two other men walked in along with a very pregnant woman. More awkward hugs went around, besides the woman. She didn't do anything but stand there and glare at

Newman with her arms crossed. She was definitely sending the I-hate-you vibes.

Oh, no.

Nope.

Nobody was going to upset Newman. Not these men. Not this woman. No one.

She needed him clear-headed and stress-free to find her brother. She had faith he would. He promised. Even if it was crazy and illogical to trust a man who cheated and lied in his past, she had to cling to something. To some kind of hope that her brother would be found safe. She was going to cling to Newman. He was her savior, and nobody would be messing with that.

"Who are your friends?"

Newman flinched, then glanced at her, as did all three men and the woman.

"Umm...this is Sauer," Newman said, pointing to the man standing closest to him.

"Oh, your partner," she said with a smile. This was good. Having someone familiar and someone he used to work with was a very good thing.

"Former partner. I'm not a detective anymore." The glower on his face said it wasn't as good as she thought.

She started clapping excitedly, ignoring the confusing looks from everyone but Newman. "Yay. You said the word. I'm so proud of you." Looking at the others, she broadened her smile. "We've been working hard on saying the word detective. Baby steps. He rarely says it."

"I like you. Who are you?" the man with short black hair and piercing blue eyes said with a sexy smile. Not as sexy and alluring as Newman's when he chose to offer a smile, but pretty darn close. And she adored his eyes. So vividly blue.

"Well, who are you?" she countered. She wasn't sure whether she wanted to like these newcomers yet. Especially with the angry vibes still pulsating off the woman.

Newman cleared his throat. "Before this conversation takes a serious derailment, and with Amelia, it's possible, let me make introductions."

She smiled at his assessment. She wasn't going to apologize for her behavior. People either liked her or hated her. There was no in-between.

"This is Zeke," Newman said, pointing first to the man with the gorgeous blue eyes, who smiled wickedly at her. Then he pointed to the man standing next to Zeke, who had a sweet, gentle smile on his face. "This is Ben."

Then his hand swung toward the woman with the obvious disgust on her face. "And this is Dee, Sauer's wife."

Dee didn't offer any sort of smile, not even a smirk.

Then Newman pointed at her. "This is Amelia. She's Adam's sister."

Sauer stepped closer to the couch and held out his hand. "It's nice to meet you. We came to help find Adam."

She eyed his hand, then stepped closer as well and shook it. "Thank you. Newman didn't tell me you were coming."

There was a gentleness in Sauer's eyes and compassion she wasn't used to seeing from complete strangers. "He didn't know."

"Because he probably would've told you not to come, so you just decided to come."

"Yep. Exactly."

"He can be so obstinate. I appreciate your help."

"I'm standing right here, you know. And who says I would've told you not to come," Newman grumbled.

Sauer took a step back and laughed. "Really? Last night when we talked...it sounded like some help would be good."

"We've hit a dead end. No good solid lead. We could use the help." She honestly meant it. She was going to reserve judgment whether she liked these people yet, but any help to find her brother...well, beggars couldn't be choosers.

"You sound like a detective," Zeke said with a chuckle.

"Well, I've been learning from the best. Haven't I, Newman?"

His fists clenched, but he didn't respond.

Too soon. Maybe she shouldn't have said that in the first place. She still didn't know why he quit, or how he lied to his partner. Apparently, it couldn't have been too bad. His partner was here right now willing to help.

"Eat your breakfast and then we can get started." She held his gaze, refusing to look away.

"I already said I wasn't hungry."

"Just a teeny tiny bite."

"How about not." His glare said to knock it off, especially in front of company.

"How about—"

"Stop." He smirked as he interrupted her with the one word that irked her. "I bet Ben or Zeke would love some breakfast. I'm going to go over everything I have with my partner, and that's final."

"I am hungry. We left super early. The breakfast I had wore off," Ben said with an eager smile.

Tilting her head, she held Newman's gaze as they had a tug-of-war with emotions. Arguing with their eyes.

Finally, after what felt like hours but was merely seconds, she smiled. "Well, considering you said Sauer's your partner, which is what I originally said, which makes me right, I'll let you skip breakfast."

"Former. I meant *former* partner. So you're not right. And you don't boss me around. So it's not about letting me. I'm choosing not to eat. So there." Newman nodded as if that settled the argument.

"You're so cute when you're wrong." She looked around the room at his friends. "Isn't he adorable when he's wrong?" Then she waved at Ben. "Want some cereal? It might be soggy by now, but I don't mind soggy cereal."

"I'm starving. I don't mind either." Ben beelined it for the table. Zeke chuckled.

"Where's the bathroom? I have to pee."

Mel met Dee's gaze. "Down the hallway. First door you see."

A smile slowly grew on Dee's face as she walked around the couch and looped arms with her. "Walk with me, Amelia. I have a feeling we're going to get along fabulously."

Mel wasn't so sure about that—not if she had a problem with Newman—but she'd indulge the woman for now. She was pregnant. It didn't seem right to be mean to a pregnant woman.

By the devilish gleam in Dee's eyes as they walked out of the room, Mel wasn't sure what to think. Did this woman think they'd be friends? Why the evil look?

What was about to happen?

All she wanted to do was find her brother.

Hopefully, she did. She now had not just one, but four detectives on the case.

9

NEWMAN WANTED to ignore the three sets of eyes on him as soon as the women walked out of the room. Except it was extremely difficult, especially when Sauer cleared his throat, then chuckled.

"Do you have something to say, Sauer?"

"Amelia's...refreshing." Sauer chuckled some more.

Newman finally looked at him, a small laugh escaping. "Refreshing is an interesting way to describe her. You can now see why I'm helping her. She didn't give me much of a choice."

"That's putting it mildly," Zeke said, his soft laughter circling around them.

"I like her," Ben said as he chomped away at the cereal.

He felt sort of bad not eating the breakfast she always made, knowing she was only trying to be nice. But he didn't want her in his domain. He wasn't going to pretend he wanted her here. And he wasn't a breakfast person. He liked a cup of coffee in the mornings and that was about it. Sometimes, he would sneak a donut from the break room...

Well, he used to when he actually had a job.

"Sauer gave us an update as we drove. Anything new pan out since last night?" Zeke asked, eagerness on his face and in his tone of voice.

Newman appreciated they came to help, especially Zeke and Ben, who he hadn't spoken to since he left three months ago. He didn't even speak to them when they finally let him out of the interrogation room. When he had been considered a suspect in four murders.

He didn't understand why these two were with Sauer. Neither of them had tried to reach out since he quit and left town. Neither had any encouraging words to say. They hadn't believed he was innocent, not like Sauer had that fateful night he was taken in for questioning.

Why did they come with?

A supportive hand touched his shoulder. "Newman?"

Glancing at Sauer, he tried to smile, managing to produce a small grin. "Nothing new." He sighed. "Other than I don't think her brother is anywhere good."

Sauer's hand fell away. "Well, I know you canvassed this town from top to bottom. With more of us here to help, we can tackle the surrounding towns. Someone else had to have seen the truck. Since Amelia didn't get a good enough look at the guy for a decent description, maybe someone else did."

"I appreciate you guys coming. I know Amelia does, too." Newman looked at Zeke and Ben, broadening his smile. "Thank you for coming." Then his smile vanished. "I know you didn't want to."

Zeke's friendly demeanor fell. "I never do anything I don't want to, Newman. I can't say I understand what you did, but it doesn't mean I won't help when Sauer asks, especially when a thirteen-year-old little boy needs our help."

"Well, I apologize for the things I did." Newman

shrugged. "I know it's not much, but that's all I got. Hopefully, we can be cordial enough to work together and find Adam."

"I don't hold any hard feelings towards you, Newman." Zeke held out his hand. "Unless you start acting like an asshole again. Then I'll have to do something about it."

Newman wasn't sure what Zeke meant, but he didn't plan to find out. If Zeke thought he liked acting the way he had in the past, the way he still acted on occasion, then he was wrong. He just didn't know how to turn off the assholish part of himself sometimes.

"Co-workers again?" Newman said, shaking his hand, although not with as much strength as he should've. His damn nerves were taking over.

Zeke tightened the grip, a grin appearing. "Friends again."

Suddenly, Ben was by their side, pulling them all in for a group hug. "Aww, I love these moments."

Zeke playfully shoved him off, cracking up laughing. "Ignore him. It's a lack of sleep since Rina had Corrine last month. He's gone bonkers."

Newman clapped Ben on the back, smiling wide. "Congrats, man. I'm so happy for you."

"Thanks. She is the best thing that ever happened to me. And Rina, of course. She's only three weeks old. She's tiny and beautiful and..." Ben blew out a breath. "I miss them both and I've only been gone about four hours."

"He's been back to work for only a week and you should see how many times he calls Rina to check on Corrine," Zeke said with a snicker.

"Hey, man. Let's not forget how psycho crazy you were when Zoe had Zabrina," Ben shot back.

"Yeah, but I don't think I was as bad as you. You've been..."

Sauer shuffled away as they continued giving each other shit about who was crazier. Newman followed him.

"Nice to know nothing changes with them."

"Still the jokesters at work. Now it's just about baby stuff and who's going to get pregnant next," Sauer said, the happiness shining in his eyes.

"How's Dee's pregnancy going?" Newman tried to keep the distaste for her out of his tone. He didn't think he excelled very well when Sauer's brows rose. "I know she doesn't like me, but I do care about you guys."

"I know. You know Dee, she's not as forgiving. She's doing good. The baby is good. She, uh, she stresses out a little too much sometimes, but they're both healthy."

"Let me know if you ever need anything. I know I've been in my own little world for the past few months, but..." He looked down, his nerves ramped up, hating to say anything but knowing he had to. He raised his gaze back up. "But I'm done hiding. I'm done acting like a jackass. If you need me, I'm there. I'd like to know when she has the baby. I wasn't there for Ben, but I don't want to miss out on yours."

"Thanks, man. That means a lot." Sauer smiled, then looked at Zeke and Ben who were still squabbling with each other. "Are you two done yet? We should talk logistics."

"I'm trying to tell him the best kind of diapers to buy and he won't listen. Corrine will thank you when she's older," Zeke said with a smirk.

"Yeah, because she's going to remember the kind of diapers she wore." Ben rolled his eyes as he laughed.

Sauer leaned closer and whispered, "Three hours of this. I can't take much more."

Newman laughed.

Oh, boy. It felt good to laugh. Like old times. Walking into work for a brand new day, getting ready to solve cases, seeing Zeke and Ben at their desk, arguing in the jovial way they loved to argue.

He missed this.

And damn it. He'd never have it ever again.

Because he screwed up.

His laughter died, as did the short burst of happiness he experienced.

This wasn't the time to reminisce or get all emotional. He told Sauer he was ready to move on and start living again. But it wouldn't be with them. It would be in his new life—all by himself.

Without Amelia aggravating and upending his world.

The sooner they found her brother, the faster he could get her out of his life.

"Well, you and I can search together while Zeke and Ben go out on their own. We meet back here for lunch to give each other an update, unless we find something sooner than that." Newman figured that was the best plan. Just like they used to.

"What about me?"

Newman turned toward the sound of Amelia's voice. She stood next to Dee, who still had an angry look on her face when they made eye contact.

He swallowed, prepared for the ensuing argument that was about to happen.

"You can stay here with Dee."

"Okay." Amelia nodded, yet her expression was oddly blank.

"Okay?"

"Yep. Okay." Then she turned to Dee, whispered something, and they walked away to the kitchen.

"That was way too easy. I should be worried, shouldn't I?" Newman muttered.

A soft chuckle fell from Sauer's lips. "Oh, yeah. You should be very worried. Especially if my wife has a hand in it."

Damn.

Maybe he should have Amelia tag along.

Which meant Dee would, too.

Which was probably the ladies' objective all along.

He just got played.

MEL WIGGLED IN HER SPOT, trying to find a comfortable position. She couldn't complain about being cooped up in the backseat of Newman's car because she wasn't six and a half months pregnant like Dee, who sat next to her. Dee rarely shifted in her spot either, making her wonder if she was even uncomfortable. How couldn't she be? She didn't understand it.

Well, to be fair, she didn't understand a lot that happened this morning.

The second Dee got her alone in the bathroom, she peed first, which was so odd standing in a bathroom while another woman peed and she didn't even know her. It hadn't seemed to faze Dee, though. Then Dee washed her hands. When she was done, her brow rose and the interrogation started. How was Newman treating her? Was he being mean? Taking advantage of her? Respecting her? Acting like a gentleman? She made a few remarks of bodily harm against him if he was being mean. Physically or emotionally.

It actually made her smile.

This woman didn't know her. She didn't know she could take care of herself.

And as quickly as her smile appeared, it died.

Because she didn't know Newman either.

He would never hurt her. Or anyone else.

Okay, emotionally, sure. He could be an asshole at times. But to be affected by something you had to let it in. You had to let the other person hurt you.

Since her father, she had learned how to switch off that sensitive part of herself. Not much could hurt her anymore.

Besides, Newman didn't act like an asshole on purpose; he simply didn't know how to express himself. At least, that's how she saw it. Every time she looked into his baby-blue eyes, she saw nothing but pain. When there was pain, there was deviance and acting out.

Explaining that would've been pointless with Dee, so she didn't say anything other than, "You mind your business and I'll mind mine."

That garnered an arched brow that looked so steep and sharp, one glare could've sliced her in two.

Oh, but this woman didn't know she had sharp claws, too.

Then Dee switched tactics. "They're going to want us to stay here. Trust me, my husband doesn't like me in the thick of things. He didn't even want me to come with. Although, probably so I wouldn't murder Newman."

By the devious twinkling in her eyes, Mel didn't think she was joking. Dee hated Newman. Part of her wanted to know why right that second. The other part of her wanted to escape the small bathroom and get far away from her.

She opted for the second one.

"Newman knows better than to make me stay back. It won't happen."

When she tried to open the bathroom door, Dee had stopped her. "There's four against two out there. The best offense is to agree."

"Agree to stay behind?"

Dee had nodded. "Sometimes, no argument is an argument in itself. I always win those."

Mel had followed her plan, ate her bowl of cereal, and ignored Newman's odd, nervous stares. When it had been time to leave, she donned her jacket and smiled at him.

"It's pointless to argue with you, isn't it? What do you two have planned if I say no?"

She only smiled wider, laughing inside that Dee's crazy plan of agreeing was working. They didn't have some master plan. Dee said to agree and it would work. That's it.

Her smile must've frightened him because he shook his head with aggravation and then gestured for her to walk out first.

Now she sat in the backseat of his car, while he and Sauer talked to the police in the first town they planned to search. They said they wanted permission and to ask them questions. Particularly if they had seen anything strange or odd lately. She didn't care about getting permission, and she doubted they had any useful information, but whatever. She figured they were the ones with the knowledge, not her.

They said it would be better if she and Dee stayed in the car.

She had agreed without question. After the treatment by Chief Dodson, she preferred never to deal with another cop again, unless it was Newman. Not that he even considered himself a cop. So yeah, she never wanted to deal with any cop ever again. Period.

"I hit a nerve in the bathroom. I didn't mean to."

Mel gradually twisted her head from staring outside to Dee, who was waiting for her to look at her.

Although it sounded like Dee was apologizing, the sharp gleam in her eyes said she wasn't. "Whatever do you mean?"

Dee laughed. "It's like dealing with myself. I'm not sure I like it."

"Well, I don't let people run all over me."

"Why do you trust him?" Dee arched a brow.

"Why don't you?" Mel mimicked her.

"He obviously didn't tell you anything if you're asking that."

She dropped the façade, trying to one-up her in sass. "You *obviously* don't look behind the mask. You see an asshole when you look at Newman. I see a man in pain. I know pain well. It didn't take me long to see it either. I don't need him to tell me anything. I know something happened. I know it wasn't good. I know he had a hand in whatever it was. But it doesn't matter. I trust him. Out of everyone here, I trust *him*."

Dee looked taken aback. The first real sign things could affect her. Her haughty attitude vanished, replaced with astonishment. Then she shifted in her seat for the first time since they entered the car and looked straight ahead.

"He's a douche. He cheated on his girlfriend. He lied to his coworkers." Dee sucked in a huge breath. "He lied to my husband."

Ah, there it was. The real reason she didn't like him. Because he lied to her husband. Hurt him.

"And you're this almighty saint? You don't do anything wrong?"

Dee whipped her gaze at her. "Of course not. But—" She stopped speaking.

"Yes?" Mel smiled. She loved how Dee's face morphed

from arrogance to distress as if she realized something she didn't like.

Dee pierced her lips. "I don't like him and I never will."

Amelia shrugged, refusing to drop her smile because it seemed to make Dee uncomfortable. "Well, I do like him. And anyone who upsets him upsets me. Which won't be good."

"Is that right?"

Mel leaned closer. "That's right."

The doors suddenly swung open and Newman and Sauer entered the car.

Dee shifted in her seat again. Mel straightened and grinned sweetly as Newman glanced at her.

"Well?" she asked, hoping to hear good news.

Dee didn't say a word, which she didn't expect her to. Neither would she. Their little argument, or whatever you wanted to call it, would remain between them. She wouldn't say she hated the woman. But if she upset Newman, they certainly wouldn't be friends.

As much as she wanted to say it was because he promised he'd find her brother and she was clinging to that hope, she didn't think that was the only reason she didn't want anyone messing with him.

He was in pain. Buried so deeply, so heavily in pain, one more rough shot and he might never recover. She couldn't live with that. Because she had been to that point of torture before. She barely survived.

She wouldn't let that happen to Newman. He didn't have anyone on his side.

He did now.

Whether he knew it or not.

A reassuring grin punctured his handsome face. "We have permission to ask questions unofficially. It's always better to have the local police's blessing. They had no useful information, though. I didn't expect any. Now we start searching and finding a lead."

She didn't doubt him. Not when he spoke with such conviction.

"AREN'T YOU WORRIED?" Newman asked as he and Sauer made their way to the next store.

They started going house to house near the road that led into town, coming up empty with any good leads. The ladies took one side, as they took the other. Now they were going around town hoping for something better to pan out. Maybe the same guy from the store Amelia saw stopped in this town, too. Not that they had a picture of him. Only a brief description of his clothing from Amelia and the description of the stolen truck.

A white male wearing a black hoodie. He never stepped out of the truck when she saw him, and he had kept the hoodie on at all times, covering his features well.

"Of course. This kid is only thirteen. Each day that passes..." Sauer shook his head. "It's not good."

Newman rubbed his hands together trying to keep them warm, even wrapped up in gloves as they walked from store to store.

"I know that. I wasn't talking about that."

Sauer looked at him, puzzled. "Then what are you talking about?"

"Amelia and Dee. Couldn't you feel the tension when we got back in the car at the police station? I thought they became friends in the bathroom, but now I'm not so sure."

"Yeah, I felt it. Dee's...it's probably nothing."

"She hates me. I get that. But she doesn't have a reason to dislike Amelia."

Sauer stopped in front of the door to the hardware store. "I don't think it's about dislike. She's worried about her."

Newman wanted to punch something. The brick wall next to him would work. "I'm not going to hurt her. Is that what Dee thinks? I'm not a monster."

"I know you're not, but Dee's not a very forgiving person. She's also very pregnant and her hormones have been out of whack. I mean, I have to tiptoe around her sometimes. One minute she goes from thinking she's the worst mother in the world, to thinking she has to be the best. It's damn stressful, man. I just want her to be happy. I knew bringing her with wasn't the best idea, but she didn't give me a choice."

Well, what was he supposed to say to that? He wanted to understand. He wanted to be forgiving, even if Dee wasn't willing. But why should he? Why should he have to put up with her attitude?

And Amelia...

She was a mystery. Why the tension between them? The last thing Amelia needed was more tension when she was worried about finding her brother.

"I'm always going to be that guy. The one who lied and cheated and screwed up. If she can't handle that, if she can't leave it alone while we're trying to look for this kid, maybe it's better if you guys leave."

"I'm not leaving." Sauer's intense expression said they wouldn't be arguing about it. "I'll talk to her. But I'm not leaving. You're right. This is about Adam. Not about the shit in the past. Adam needs us."

Newman nodded. "Well, I'm glad we agree. Look, Dee shouldn't worry. Amelia knows the kind of guy I am. I haven't exactly been shy about it. She can hold her own."

A chuckle floated around the icy cold air. "I don't doubt it. Those two are so much alike. Maybe that's why there's tension. They're both used to getting their way and neither one is conceding."

"I hope we find Adam soon," Newman said with a laugh, "because it will not be pretty if they keep fighting for the upper hand."

"So not pretty." Sauer laughed with him as they stepped inside the hardware store.

They walked to the counter where an older gentleman sat on a stool writing in a notebook. When he saw them approach, he smiled jovially. As soon as they introduced themselves and explained what they needed, the same spiel they said to everyone, his smile didn't waver.

"You know, that truck sounds familiar." The gentleman snapped his fingers. "The guy was wearing a black shirt, could've been a hoodie, except he didn't have the hoodie up when I saw him. He had a nasty scar on his face. Ran from his eyebrow to the corner of his mouth on the left side of his face. I only know this because he almost hit me at a four-way stop. He did one of those roll-and-go stops. He didn't fully stop. It was my turn. I flicked him off. It made me feel better."

Newman suppressed a chuckle, especially when the gentleman still had a friendly smile on his face as he told them everything. He could just imagine him flipping the bird at the guy with a bright smile shining as he did.

"When was this?" Newman asked, feeling giddy for the first time in three days. It wasn't a huge lead, but it was better than nothing.

"Yesterday." The gentleman furrowed his brows, a serious expression lining his features as he thought hard. Then a bright smile appeared. "Yep, yesterday. I had to run to Burt's Hardware Store for a plumbing part that I didn't have in stock. Burt usually has anything I don't and vice versa. We share all the time."

"Did the other guy react in any way?" Sauer asked.

"Barely seemed to faze him. He looked focused like he didn't even see me."

"What four-way stop was this?" Newman asked.

"Oh, Closyter Road and Dewing Street. Not far from the store you were talking about."

Not far from Amelia's house. It was the same four-way stop at the bottom of the hill on the same path from her house to the store that Adam would've taken. The same man that gave Amelia the creeps was seen on that road only yesterday. What was he doing? Buying more supplies? Did that mean Adam was still alive?

Or was he searching for another victim?

"You've been very helpful, sir. If you think of anything else, please call me." Sauer handed the gentleman his card.

"Will do. I hope you find that boy. Just terrible. I'll keep my eyes peeled for anything else."

They thanked him and left.

"Well, our first lead of the day. And he has a scar on his face. We should do a rough sketch. Do you know anyone in the area that can draw well?" Sauer asked as they kept walking down the sidewalk to the next store.

"Not really. We can go to Chief Dodson with this news and he can find a sketch artist. Honestly, the chief and his department should be doing all this heavy work, not us."

Sauer rolled his eyes. "With everything you told me, he doesn't believe Adam is in serious trouble. We should go back to the police department here and see if they have a sketch artist."

"Good idea. Chief Dodson's an asshole."

So was he, but he was trying to find the good inside himself.

He couldn't wait to see Amelia, who was walking the other side of the street with Dee, and tell her the good news. They finally had a small lead.

10

Mel shoved her gloved hands into fists, hoping to keep them warm as she sat on the porch in a rocking chair. If she *really* wanted to keep them warm she'd be inside the cabin instead of sitting outside in the brutal cold. It had to be close to single digits.

But she needed air.

After spending all day with Dee cooped up in the back-seat of the car and walking from store to store asking questions about her brother and the guy in the truck, she needed more than air. She needed another whole state between her and that woman.

They didn't speak much, but they didn't need to. They both could get their point across with a single nasty glare.

Dee wanted her to give up on Newman and declare him a douche for his past sins.

Mel wanted her to let it go and see him for the man he was now.

A man worthy of redemption.

A man working tirelessly to find her brother.

Her brother who was probably enduring the most brutal, horrific—

"Hey—"

She screamed, jumping, the chair rocking with intensity.

Sauer winced, then took a seat in the other chair next to her. "I didn't mean to startle you."

Offering a laugh, she started to rock the chair slowly, fisting her hands even more. Not that she could tighten them much more. If she did it any harder, her nails would start to dig through her gloves straight through to her skin.

"No worries. I didn't hear you come out. I guess I was lost in thought."

"If it was about Dee, I want to say—"

"It wasn't," she replied, cutting him off before an apology slipped out. If she wanted an apology, which she didn't, it would have to be from Dee herself. But Dee had nothing to be sorry for. She had every right to her opinion about Newman. She only wanted Dee to stop, think, and process before she said things.

"We sensed some tension today. I—"

"Don't try to apologize for your wife."

Sauer opened his mouth to counteract, then shut it again and smiled. "She means well."

Mel chuckled. "She has a funny way of showing it."

"She does." Then Sauer looked out into the woods surrounding them and inhaled as if the weight of the world sat on his shoulders. "It's peaceful here. I like it. I'm sorry about your brother. We'll do our best to find him."

Mel followed his gaze, looking at the woods, the dark night, wondering if they *would* find him. It had been almost four full days since she last saw him. The first twenty-four hours were the most crucial. At least, she assumed they were. Every day that passed, the likelihood they'd find him dwindled away. Of course, she didn't do anything the first night he didn't come home. She should've called the police that first night.

"I appreciate your help. All of you. It's better than what I got from the police around here."

"Yeah, Newman mentioned the chief of police. That he's not too friendly. Hopefully, with the help of Chief Banner in Kelting finding a sketch artist, we'll know who this guy is soon. They can run the sketch through a database and, if we're lucky, they'll find a match. Technology is amazing these days."

Mel produced a half grin, even though she didn't feel like it. She knew Sauer was only trying to be helpful, trying to make her see a silver lining when in reality her brother was already dead.

Murdered.

Like those other ten boys from seven years ago. Chopped up and buried and scattered around the woods.

Probably these very woods surrounding them.

"Do you honestly believe that, Detective Sauer? Because I can handle the truth." She didn't look at him as she asked the question. She didn't want to see the lie in his eyes. Because that's what people did when a serious situation sat before them. They lied. They stretched the truth. They made it appear better than what it was.

"Some cases never get solved. It's a sad reality in life. Some cases eat at a person, never quitting, never giving up, until they solve it and then some. Newman's very deter-mined. We'll..."

When he stopped speaking, she turned in his direction. "We'll, what?"

He huffed as if he didn't want to finish his sentence, then he met her gaze, even though his eyes told her he didn't want to. "I want to believe we'll find Adam. I'm...not sure if he'll be alive, though."

Her lips trembled as soon as he voiced what she feared. Well, she asked for the truth. Surprisingly, he gave it to her.

"That was harsh. I shouldn't have said that. I—"

"It's the truth. Not many abductions turn out with a happy ending. Do they?"

"I should've said it better. I..." His eyes turned to the porch, his foot tapping with a rhythm that said he was agitated.

"You can never say the truth pretty, detective. I appreciate you saying it straight. I'm not even sure Newman would say that to my face, and he promised he would never lie to me."

Sauer glanced up and met her gaze once again. "He's a good guy. I know my wife doesn't think so, and I know he's made mistakes, but we all have. Nobody is perfect."

She smiled. "You don't need to convince me. I know he's a good man. I would've never begged him to help me if I didn't think so. I can usually look at someone and tell what kind of person they are. It's a blessing and a curse sometimes."

"So, you're a psychic?" Sauer asked with a chuckle.

She knew he was joking around, asking a silly question to lighten the dreary mood and the conversation they had about her brother being dead. And it helped—somewhat. It made her laugh.

"Sure, you can call me that. Or very perceptive. When your father beats you all your life, it's easy to see evil. You learn very quickly who's nice and who's not." She shivered, and not from the brutal cold seeping into her bones. "Probably why the guy at the store creeped me out so much. I should've listened to my instincts."

"And what?" Sauer said with a sharpness in his tone. "What would you have done? From what I hear, your brother did what he wanted anyway. He was going to go biking no matter what you said. Blaming yourself won't help."

Mel's smile inched up a notch. Not because he spoke to her so harshly, but because he didn't react or say something awkward about her confession about her father. Most people either flinched, looked away, or immediately poured the pity in their eyes.

"I like you, Detective Sauer. I'm glad Newman has you in his life. Make sure it stays that way."

Sauer chuckled, removing the intense glare from his earlier reprimand. "I like you, Amelia. I should've never stayed away as long as I did. But I thought I was doing the right thing giving him space like he asked." More laughter floated out. "You remind me of Dee."

She arched a brow, not sure she wanted to share similarities with that woman. But she didn't say so, not wanting to offend him when he was being so nice.

"Will you be staying in Newman's life as well? I don't know how long he plans to stay here, but he could use a friend while he's here."

She rolled her eyes, looking out into the woods once again. "He's the most infuriating man I've ever dealt with." Then she met his gaze and smiled wide. "I adore getting on his nerves. He's going to have a hard time getting rid of me."

They laughed together.

"I can't promise you we'll find Adam soon, but I can promise I'll do everything in my power to find him as quickly as we can."

Just like that, the conversation went sour. But she appreciated his direct honesty. False hope wouldn't do anything but hurt her as the days went on.

He shook his head as a strangled laugh escaped. "That came out wrong again. I didn't mean—"

"It came out right. As the truth."

A tiny grin appeared on his face.

"You always tell people the truth, don't you, even if it's not something you want to do."

He nodded.

"Don't ever change. I hate hearing it, but I need to." Her lips trembled once again, the tears wanting to break free without notice. "I hate thinking what he's enduring, but I do. I hate torturing myself, but I can't help it. He's my little brother, and no matter what I tell myself, what you tell me, what anyone tells me, I failed him."

Before she knew it, warm arms were circling around her and tears were falling down.

Even though she appreciated Sauer's comfort, it wasn't his arms she wanted holding her.

It was that damn infuriating man who crawled under her skin, rankled her nerves, got her heated with a few words or no words at all.

She wanted Newman holding her, reassuring her everything would be okay.

Hell, maybe false hope would be better than the truth.

The truth sucked.

Her brother was probably dead. And now she couldn't get it out of her head.

———

NEWMAN NEVER FELT hot rage before. Sure, he'd been upset, angry, vibrating mad when his friends and colleagues thought he was capable of murder. Losing his job sent him into a madness he didn't think he'd ever fall trap to in his life. Even losing Chrissy, although he screwed it up with his own actions, pissed him off.

But this.

He'd never felt such rage towards another guy because of a woman. And with his best friend and partner no less.

Why in the hell did Sauer have his arms around Amelia? And why in the hell did he care? She wasn't anything to him but a woman he was helping. She aggravated him, pissed him off, bossed him around. She wasn't anything special.

Then Sauer leaned away and he saw the tears marring her face.

His pink warrior fairy was crying.

That punctured a hole in his rage, deflating it, replacing it with a deep, searing agony that almost brought him to his knees.

He'd seen her on the verge of tears before, but she never shed any. Seeing it now, it wasn't right. It didn't fit the picture he had of her.

"Newman." Sauer immediately stood up, glancing from Amelia to him, then back and forth once more.

There wasn't a bright light illuminating the porch, only a small yellow bulb giving just enough light to feel safe surrounded by the darkness, so he couldn't see the red likely tinting Sauer's face, but he figured it was there. Sauer appeared nervous, like he had done something wrong.

Of course, Sauer would be wrong again. *He* did something wrong. He wasn't there to comfort Amelia. And he should've been. The only arms that should be encircling her were his.

Damn it. He didn't have a right to demand that. To want it.

He did, anyway.

Why? What made Amelia different from other women? Geez. What made her different from Chrissy, the woman he thought he'd marry?

Probably not a good time to think about her, so he didn't.

He shoved his hands in his pockets for safe measure. He didn't want to do something stupid, like hit Sauer for touching Amelia, even if he was comforting her for some reason.

"Everything okay?" He meant for that to sound like he didn't care either way. Unfortunately, the anger wasn't completely masked in his tone.

"Yeah, we were just talking..." Sauer's words trailed off as if he wasn't sure he should share what they had been talking about.

Him, most likely. How bad of a guy he was. How she should stay far away. How she shouldn't trust him. All reasonable things to tell her.

"About what?" he snapped. Damn it, he hadn't meant to ask that. He shook his head, averting his gaze, and turned to go back inside. "It doesn't matter. Forget I asked."

It didn't matter. Sauer had every right to warn her away. He was bad news. Amelia could do and say anything she wanted. He had no control over her. Hell, even if they were an item, not that he wanted to date her, he wouldn't be able to control her. Of course, he didn't *want* to control her even if they dated. Which they never would.

What was he thinking? Dating her?

But he sure in the hell wouldn't want her wrapping her sweet, delicate arms around another guy, even if that guy was his friend that he knew loved his wife. Sauer would never do anything to ruin his marriage.

Unlike him.

A cheating bastard.

What right did he have to get jealous?

He was such a hypocrite. Another nasty trait he could tack on to the list of traits he already possessed, ones he didn't even want to have.

A strong hand on his shoulder stopped him from stalking inside the cabin. He knew right away it was Sauer's hand and not Amelia's. He didn't turn around or throw a punch like he ached to do. He didn't do anything but stop. He wasn't even sure how he would've reacted if Amelia had been the one to stop him from proceeding any farther.

"She needs you, Newman. I barely know what to do when my wife cries. I'm clueless with a woman I don't even know. And you two seem..." Sauer's hand stiffened, not necessarily in a bad way, more so like he was comforting him. "You two seem to have a connection. She was asking about her brother, and I said things I shouldn't have."

He turned slightly, enough to look him in the eyes. Sauer's hand fell away from his shoulder. He made sure to keep his voice low, as low as Sauer had. "What things?"

Sauer huffed. "You know I hate giving false hope. It's never felt so terrible before to speak the truth. You and I both know the likelihood of Adam still alive...is not promising."

He closed his eyes, then popped them open, shocked Sauer would say something so brutal to her. "Please tell me you didn't say her brother was dead."

When Sauer winced but didn't respond, he had to fist his hands so hard, he could feel his nails digging into his palms through his gloves.

"I have never wanted to hit you more than I do right now. Even more so than when I saw you hugging her."

Despite the seriousness in his tone that he wanted to sock him a good one, Sauer grinned.

The man had the audacity to grin at him. Did he think he was joking? Because he wasn't. He still might throw a punch.

"Care to explain why you're grinning at me like a damn monkey?"

"Do monkeys really grin?"

"Sauer..." he all but growled low and menacing.

Sauer's grin immediately disappeared, yet there was still laughter in his eyes. "You like her. It makes me happy to know you're moving on. And I like Amelia."

He did *not* like Amelia.

He was attracted to her. He wanted to sleep with her. But he did not like her—as in potential girlfriend material. Absolutely not.

Why did his thoughts keep going in that direction? It needed to stop.

"It's nothing like that, Sauer."

Sauer clapped him on the shoulder, producing another small grin. "You keep telling yourself that lie if it makes you feel better." His grin vanished. "I should've worded what I said to her differently. I didn't mean to upset her."

Then Sauer stepped around him and walked back inside the cabin.

Newman looked at Amelia, who sat huddled in the rocking chair gazing out into the darkness.

As a small child, he had been scared of the woods at night. His grandfather always told him nothing could hurt him unless he let it. Nightmares. The boogeyman. The darkness. If he let those things take over his mind, it would hurt him. But if he let it all go, nothing could hurt him.

Surprisingly, his grandfather's logic helped him keep the monsters at bay as a child.

Why didn't it work as an adult?

Because he couldn't seem to let the past go.

But now wasn't the time to be focusing on his issues. Amelia needed him, even if he wasn't sure how to proceed at the moment.

He took a few steps toward Amelia. Her features were rigid. Not from the cold, trying to keep the frozen temperatures at bay. More so from his reaction and him and Sauer whispering fiercely with each other.

Although she wasn't crying any longer, tear stains still marked her cheeks.

She didn't look at him as he stopped right by the empty rocking chair next to her.

Before he could think about his actions, he scooped her up out of her chair and then sat down with her wrapped in his arms. She felt so good in his arms that he never wanted to let go.

She stared at him wide-eyed, one arm wrapped around his neck that she had immediately secured when he picked her up.

Neither said a word as he slowly started to rock.

The shock in her expression didn't die down, but after a few seconds, she gave in and rested her head against his chest.

It felt comfortable and…right to be sitting with her like this. The rage that consumed him when he first walked outside vanished, disappeared in the blink of an eye. Something close to contentment filled his soul.

His arms tightened around her.

She started to tremble.

Damn. Maybe he should take her inside because the

cold was finally getting to her. Take her straight to his bedroom so she could have some privacy. Or they could have some privacy together. He didn't want to leave her alone. Not like this.

The shaking in his arms increased.

Shit. It wasn't from the cold. She was crying again.

"He's dead, isn't he? Those other boys seven years ago..." she whispered between sobs.

Damn Sauer.

He wanted to beat the living shit out of his best friend.

And for what?

Speaking the damn truth.

"You can't think like that. You have to keep the hope inside. You can't give up. It's not in you to give up. You don't believe your brother is dead. You can't."

"Now you think you know me."

Newman kissed the top of her head because he couldn't resist and squeezed her tighter as a small chuckle slipped out. "It's only fair since you think you know me."

The shaking in his arms gradually stopped.

"I'll find him, Amelia."

"How? Nothing has gone our way and nothing seems like it ever will."

He wished he had an answer.

"I have no idea. But I refuse to give up." He rubbed her arm and back, trying to keep her warm. She had to be freezing sitting outside as long as she had. The coldness was burrowing into his bones rather quickly. "Let's get you inside. You're freezing. Take a shower and get some sleep. Those guys will be leaving soon. They got a hotel in town, and we'll be back at it in the morning looking for Adam. We'll find him."

She pressed her hand against his chest, right over his

heart that hadn't stopped beating erratically since the moment he picked her up. "Stop bossing me around. I'm the boss around here."

He had no answer to that.

Because he feared she might actually be right.

11

FINGER COMBING her hair to get the tangles free, she headed out of Newman's bedroom and to the kitchen. She should go to the bathroom first and see how terrible her hair really looked, maybe brush her teeth, hell, take a shower, but she was eager to see Newman.

The reason why, well, she didn't stop to contemplate. It wouldn't do well to sit and wonder and dissect her feelings for the man. He was complicated and arrogant and downright nasty sometimes.

Then there were times he was sweet, caring, and thinking only of others and how he could make it right.

Like last night when he held her in his arms, comforted her, swearing to find her brother. She believed him when he spoke with such passion and conviction.

She paused in her place when she found the living room and kitchen empty. Retracing her steps, she opened the bathroom door without knocking. Rude, yes, but she wanted to see him.

Empty.

Okay. Odd. Where was he?

The only other room was the spare room filled with a bunch of junk. At least, according to him. She had never bothered to look in there. Time to rectify that.

She opened the door and looked around. Although it was filled from top to bottom with boxes, bins, and cluttered piles of various things everywhere, it was empty for the one thing she was looking for—Newman.

It wasn't that late in the morning. The sun had woken her up, shining into the room, fanning her face. But she hadn't slept in. Not to mention Newman said they were going to start searching bright and early.

Where did he go?

He couldn't have left without her. Unless he didn't think she could handle helping in the search after her breakdown last night.

She should've never cried, and in front of him, forget it. That was a bad idea. Now he knew how weak she was, and if there was one thing her father ever taught her, it was not to show weakness. Every time she displayed an ounce of weakness, he pounced on her like a predator honing in on their prey.

She vowed never to be weak again.

Except, last night she broke down like a little baby. No more. She had to stay strong and in control for Adam. He needed her. She was all he had left and vice versa. She would like to say they had their mother still, but the likelihood she'd beat the charges was slim to none.

Deciding she wouldn't be put off, she grabbed a change of clothes and headed for the shower. If he thought he could leave her behind, he was wrong. Nobody left her out, especially when it concerned her brother.

She should've known better than to trust him.

And last night... He had shown her a side of him she had never seen before. He had been so tender and gentle holding her in his arms, rocking her, soothing her rattled nerves.

By the time they ventured inside the cabin, her tears had abated and she felt more optimistic. Her positivity wavered when she made eye contact with Detective Sauer and his words slashed through her once again. But she decided to let Newman's reassurance overshadow Sauer's dejected words.

Then they all left, saying a quick good night like they knew she didn't want the company anymore. She wouldn't have been rude, demanding them to leave, but she would've excused herself and went to the bedroom. But that didn't happen, and she and Newman were left to themselves.

She almost went to bed, except Newman stopped her with a brilliant smile, one she had never seen before, and asked if she wanted some hot chocolate.

With the adorable smile on his face and the hope in his eyes, she couldn't say no. He made one of the best cups of hot chocolate she ever had. Her mother never had the chance to make such a simple thing most people enjoyed every winter. Hot chocolate was considered a treat in her house, and her father didn't allow treats of any kind. Ever. She couldn't compare his hot chocolate to anything else, but so what? She still thought it was the best hot chocolate out there.

They drank the delicious hot drink on the couch, a fire roaring in the fireplace, and talked. They didn't delve into anything serious or too personal. They spoke about random, silly stuff, like sports and great places to take a vacation. That topic kept her interest because she had never been on a real vacation. Besides moving around a lot, her family never went anywhere. And when they moved, they never stopped along the way for anything fun. Even though she didn't confess her lack of traveling, she sensed Newman understood by her enthusiasm as he spoke about the few places he had visited.

By the time midnight rolled around, she couldn't believe how fast the time flew by. She had debated for about one second to invite him into the bedroom—his bedroom—but chickened out. He already knew she was willing to sleep with him and he had yet to take her up on the offer. In fact, he seemed repulsed by the idea. Well, maybe not repulsed, but he didn't seem enthused to sleep with her.

She had walked toward his bedroom with one fleeting look his way in case he decided to speak up, but he didn't even watch her walk out.

It had been a wonderful night. The first night where she felt close to him as if they could be friends once they found her brother.

And he finally decided to show her his true colors. The same thing she heard over and over from Mary and the other gossipers in town. He was nothing but a liar.

She slammed the bathroom door.

How dare he leave without her. How dare he think he knew what was best for her. She already imagined that was what he would say when she saw him. Well, he could think again. Only she knew what was best for her. Nobody bossed her around.

Taking a shower in record time, she barely combed her hair before throwing it into a wet, messy bun. She knew she'd regret not drying it before stepping outside, but it couldn't be helped. She had to catch up to them...wherever they might be.

She tossed her dirty clothes onto his bedroom floor, then stomped toward the kitchen. A quick bowl of cereal, or even better, a granola bar from the pantry, and she would be out the door.

A piece of paper lying on the counter stopped her in her tracks.

Her anger slowly depleted.

Went for a run. Be back soon. We're meeting the gang for breakfast in town.

Well, shit.

He left her a note.

He didn't leave her. He didn't lie.

She stared at the note as the distress of what she thought of him swept through her and nearly brought her to her knees. And more tears. She wanted to cry from her misplaced anger, for not trusting in him. Sure, he might've lied in the past, but he had been nothing but good to her. Swearing to find her brother when he didn't have to help her at all.

Steeling her spine, she swore she'd never think badly of him again until he had a chance to explain himself. She misjudged his actions without even thinking because of his past deeds.

Well, never again.

She didn't want people to judge her for her past, so why would she for his?

Picking up the note, she almost crumbled it up and threw it away. Instead, she folded it gently and put it in her pocket. It's not like it was a love note or anything. She couldn't even picture Newman writing a love note, let alone expressing any sort of affection, but she couldn't help herself.

For some reason, she wanted to keep it.

Because, honestly, he didn't have to leave a note. He didn't have to explain himself if he wanted to go for a run.

He didn't have to help her.

He certainly didn't have to comfort her in a moment of weakness.

He didn't think he was a good guy. Except, all she kept seeing was the goodness in him.

She couldn't wait for him to return to plant a sweet kiss on his lips.

Just for fun.

And because she was dying for another kiss.

HE LEFT the cabin without a jacket, but he wore a long-sleeve shirt over another T-shirt. The chill swept through him as he ran through the woods, his legs eating up the distance. He welcomed the cool breeze, the cold air that brushed across his face as he sprinted through the snow as if his life depended upon it.

In a way it did.

Last night, when they walked back into the cabin, he should've let Amelia walk out of the room when everyone left. But what did he do like a colossal idiot? He asked her if she wanted hot chocolate. He tortured himself all night with temptation sitting right next to him.

He had her in his arms. Sure, she had been crying, and he wasn't a complete jackass where he would've taken advantage of the situation while she was in a vulnerable state. But he had her in his arms.

It made him want more. So much more.

Which in turn made him crave more of her company.

Talking and laughing with her as he reminisced about his favorite vacations. He couldn't recall the last time he had so much fun sitting with a woman and enjoying her company—and not in a bed.

Even with Chrissy. The last few months before he cheated on her had been good, but not great. They had a solid relationship. They lived together. They ate together. They slept together. They had, in all appearances, a good relationship.

He couldn't deny they didn't. He had it all with her.

Maybe that was the problem. It was too perfect. Not enough...he wasn't even sure what it had been missing. When he thought about it, which in the last three months he tried not to think about her, it hadn't been missing much. Perfection right down to the clothes situated in the closet. More so Chrissy's doing than his. She was a neat freak, while he could handle a little mess.

Maybe that was it. He couldn't handle living up to perfection. That's all he ever did. Try to be as perfect as he could be and he always failed.

He failed with his parents.

With his brother.

With his job.

And especially with Chrissy.

He couldn't remember a time he ever laughed with Chrissy as hard as he had with Amelia.

He started to run harder and faster, forcing himself to stop thinking about everything. He came outside to clear his head. To forget how sexy and alluring Amelia looked last night, her eyes lit up with excitement, her laughter ringing in his ears, filling his soul with happiness he'd been missing for the longest time.

This damn run wasn't helping.

He couldn't get her out of his mind.

But at least this jaunt in the chilly morning would put some distance between them. Distance they seriously needed.

He barely hung onto his control the entire night, since the moment she walked out of the room. His thread on sanity had been so thin, he couldn't even look at her when she left the room. One look into her dazzling hazel eyes and he would've swept her into his embrace and did things to her he'd been dying to do since she uttered she wanted to sleep with him.

So, yeah. He needed this run. Just to get his equilibrium back. He couldn't sleep with her no matter how much he wanted. Because he swore off sex. It didn't matter how beautiful she was, how strong and brave she was while they searched for her brother.

He was a bastard. But he wasn't that much of a bastard to sleep with her right now when her brother was missing.

The pressure in his chest from running so hard for such a long time started to expand and burst free. Almost falling to the ground, as if he'd run head first into a brick wall, he managed to find his balance before collapsing in a heap. Bent over, resting his hands on his knees, he tried to catch his breath and wondered why the hell he ran so hard.

It didn't help one iota.

He still wanted Amelia as fiercely as the moment he stepped out of the cabin.

What a cad.

Thinking about sleeping with her when he should be thinking about where to look for her brother next.

Standing up in slow increments, his breathing gradually came down from the high. He glanced at his surroundings.

White, frosty snow as far as his eyes could see. Trees standing here and there, scattered in no particular pattern. Some tall and proud, trying to reach up high into the sky. Some short and stout, hugging the ground.

It was so quiet. So peaceful. And so damn refreshing.

He hadn't had a moment of peace since Amelia knocked on his door.

Even his mind quieted down as he let his breathing catch up to him.

He glanced at his watch, noting only about fifteen minutes had passed since he left the cabin. Not too bad for a novice and while running on snow. He didn't usually run. Attacking the punching bag was more his style, but with Amelia in the cabin, it hadn't been doable.

He needed a break, a little breather from her.

Blowing out a deep breath, he knew this jog in the woods wasn't enough of a breather. Nothing would be enough until she was out of his cabin and out of his life.

He had to find her brother.

Once he found Adam, Amelia would go away.

A sharp ache hit his chest as that thought penetrated his mind.

Ignoring the pain, most likely from running too long, he rotated his shoulders and shook his arms. He had a long run ahead of him back to the cabin. He wasn't positive, but he assumed he ran about a mile. If he didn't run back, he'd waste too much time.

A branch breaking split the silence.

Twisting his head to the left, his eyes scanned the horizon once again. Nothing popped out at him except snow, trees, and bushes dotting the area. Not even an animal, maybe a deer, appeared.

Another branch snapped.

He angled his head another twenty degrees to the left, his gaze sharp and focused. Was it a squirrel? Some tiny animal he couldn't see.

Heading in the direction he heard the sound, he took his time, going slow and trying to be quiet.

About fifty yards away, a figure stepped into view from behind a tall pine tree. Newman froze and watched as the person hobbled slowly through the snow, their head down, not paying attention. They couldn't have been paying attention because the person should've heard him traipsing through the snow. He was being quiet, but he could only be so quiet when walking in the snow. The low crunching sound was impossible to hide.

The person had on jeans and a white T-shirt. That was it. No coat, no sweatshirt, nothing. The person—or more like, tall man with his short brown hair and broad shoulders—had his hands in his pockets, his shoulders hunched. Yet his movements were measured, his concentration focused on getting one foot in front of the other.

What the hell was this person doing walking out in the middle of nowhere without even a jacket on?

"Hey!"

The man turned his head in his direction, then dashed away in the opposite direction.

Well, it wasn't the first time a suspect ran away from him. He could count on one hand how many times a suspect got away when fleeing. Two times. The first guy got away because it had been dark out. He had hopped a fence and Newman hadn't been as agile as him to hop it with finesse. The other person got away because he slipped on the sidewalk. In his defense, it had been covered in black ice, and he even sprained his wrist in the process. Both times he had no control over the situation.

Although the ground was covered in snow and the fact he just ran about a mile already didn't mean anything. He took off after the guy.

It didn't take too long to catch up to him. The guy was limping, unable to run very fast. But he was trying his damndest to get away, zigzagging through the trees and bushes. Newman didn't hesitate; he jumped on top of the guy, slamming him to the ground.

"Get off me!"

"All I said was hey. You didn't have to run. People who run have something to hide."

Newman didn't like the fact this guy was walking around in his woods, or at least the woods surrounding his cabin. He thought he was in trouble, which was why he hollered hey instead of something crazy like, "Freeze, police!"

Which would've been dumb. He wasn't with the police department anymore.

The guy struggled underneath him, putting all his strength into it for a scrawny man.

Newman was stronger, though. Even though he didn't trust the guy, he knew something wasn't right with him walking around without a coat in these low temperatures. He swung one of the guy's arms behind his back, then grabbed his shoulder and made him stand up.

With a firm grip on his arm, holding onto his shoulder, Newman finally got a good look at his face.

At the first glimpse, he immediately released him, taking a step back.

"Adam?"

The man—now plain as day a kid, although tall for his age—looked at him puzzled, the fear blazing in his eyes.

Standing so far away earlier, he didn't get a decent look at him. But now that he was standing right next to him, it was easy to see he was a kid. Newman wouldn't have guessed thirteen years old—he looked more about fifteen or sixteen—yet he could see the youth in his face. Clean jaw, no hint of stubble or that he had started growing facial hair. Thin frame, but tall. Which was why from a distance he looked like a man, not a kid.

Newman held up his hands in an innocent gesture, keeping a neutral, friendly expression. And it was imperative Adam saw he wasn't out to hurt him, especially after he just tackled him to the ground. How in the hell was he supposed to know he was Amelia's brother?

"My name's Newman, and I'm a friend of your sister, Amelia. We've been looking for you." Newman offered a smile, hoping to ease the fear a little bit in Adam's gaze. "I'm sorry for knocking you down. I don't come across many people out here and you ran from me."

Adam took a step back, limping as he did. "I don't know you. I don't trust you. You could just be saying you know Mel. She's never mentioned you. Nobody calls her Amelia."

Newman nodded. "I just met her. She sought me out when you didn't come home. She asked me to help look for you."

Adam's eyes narrowed in distrust. "Why? You a cop? I've never seen you before."

And the kid would know based on Amelia's accounts. He was a frequent flyer through the station.

"No, I don't work there. But they weren't fast enough for her liking, so she asked for my help. My cabin's about a mile away. She's there. I'll take you to her."

"And if I refuse to go with you?"

Well, shit. Newman didn't want to answer that. He'd have to make Adam come with him. The kid was scared. He understood that. Adam didn't trust him, and he damn well shouldn't after what he'd been through—whatever it was, it couldn't have been good. Newman recalled Amelia said he left the house wearing a red jacket, which he wasn't wearing now. Why? What happened?

Adam hadn't been paying attention to his surroundings, which probably meant he didn't know where he was going so why bother looking. Newman could not, under any circumstance, let him walk away. If he had to use force, he would. For his own damn good.

"Why are you out here without a coat?"

Adam shifted, winced, then tried to play it off like he wasn't in pain. "Why are *you* not wearing a coat?"

Newman decided to ignore the flash of pain for now. One issue at a time. "I was running. I get hot with a coat on when I run. But now that I've stopped, the cold is seeping in. Aren't you getting cold?"

"I was running, too."

"You were walking when I saw you."

Adam shrugged. "I was taking a break."

Newman blew out a breath, trying to keep his cool. Losing his control because the kid didn't trust him wasn't going to do him any favors. But the longer they stood here hashing out whether he could trust him or not, the colder it would get. His hands were already starting to freeze like tiny icicles dangling from a roof. Adam didn't look any better. His lips were a light shade of blue, his body trembling. And if Newman wasn't mistaken, he wasn't keeping a lot of pressure on his right leg. And he was as pale as could be.

"You know, your sister is as stubborn as you. I can see where you get it from. I'm here to help you with whatever happened. I guess I was meant to go for a run. It was fate." Newman shrugged as a small chuckle escaped. "Or maybe we'll call it luck that I came across you. But if I let you walk away, you might not find your way back to anything. Do you even know where you are? Your sister will kill me if I let you walk away. And I would gladly hand her the weapon to do it."

Because damn it, he was not going to fail this kid, even if he had to wrestle him into submission and make him walk with him.

It was barely noticeable, but he saw it for a fraction of a second when Adam produced a tiny grin.

"I've been helping her look for you for four days." Newman pressed his lips together, forcing himself to keep it together. "She was thinking some pretty nasty stuff last night. She was thinking the worst. I am not out to hurt you. I will do everything in my power to keep you safe. You only have to trust me from here to my cabin and then you can do whatever you want because your sister is there."

Adam glanced around as if waiting for some boogeyman to pop out and snatch him. Then he met his gaze, biting his lip. "There were two guys. I only saw the one. I can't trust you. You'll have to kill me before I go back there."

Not what Newman wanted to hear, but it was a start. Because no matter what, he'd learn every wicked detail that happened to find the bastards who hurt him. Not just for Adam's sake. Not just for Amelia's sake. But for his sake, too. To prove to himself he wasn't a complete failure.

"Adam, if I wanted to hurt you, I would've when I tackled you to the ground. Everything I said is true. I'm here to help." Newman pointed in the direction of his cabin, the complete opposite direction from where Adam had been coming from. "My cabin is that way. About a mile. Your sister is there. She's been staying with me while we search for you."

Adam's expression hardened like he was preparing to fight to the death.

Well, shit. What did he do now? Keep talking his way to Adam's trust and freeze to death? Or make him walk with him?

12

NEWMAN REFUSED TO BACK DOWN. He didn't want to frighten Adam any more than he already was, but he couldn't let him walk away.

"I'm not—"

"Your sister said you were going back to the store for chips." Newman smiled, happy to see a flash of surprise on Adam's face. He didn't want to keep hearing he wasn't going to go with him because he didn't have a choice. So, he had to convince Adam he was telling the truth.

Why did it always come down to truth and lies? For once in his life, he wasn't lying, and the kid didn't want to believe him.

"She said you give her a hard time all the time and that she understands why. You've been through a lot with your mom and dad. She said you guys had a good chat about why you can't keep running away after the last run-in with Chief Dodson. Am I right so far?"

"Doesn't mean anything. You could've done your research. Spying on us and shit."

"Watch your language. I sure hope you don't speak like that to your sister."

A flash of fear touched Adam's eyes at his furious tone. Oh, Newman understood the kid had been through a lot, but so had Amelia. Not only had she stepped up to the plate to take care of her kid brother, but she also had to leave her old life when she moved to Minnesota. Adam should show a little respect. Amelia didn't do anything to him other than take care of him as best as she could.

"She doesn't correct me."

"Did your father correct you?" It was shitty of him to ask, but he was only trying to make a point.

When Adam flinched and looked at the ground, it was pretty easy to decipher what his answer would be.

"He would've never tolerated that kind of language."

"Well, out of respect, you shouldn't make Amelia have to play the bad guy, even though she doesn't. Why make things so hard on her? You know she's hurting just as bad."

Adam looked up, a very tiny grin puncturing his youthful face. "Okay, I believe you. You sound like her. Getting on my case." He hunched his shoulders and shoved his hands into his pockets. "It is cold out. How far did you say your cabin was?"

"About a mile." Newman pointed in the direction they'd have to walk. Then he removed his long shirt, thankful he had a T-shirt on underneath. "Here, put this on."

Eyeing the shirt dangling in his hand, Adam finally removed his hands from his pockets and put on the shirt.

"Thanks."

"Let's get moving. Amelia will start to worry if I don't get back soon, and by the looks of it, it's going to take us a while. How bad is your ankle?"

Adam shrugged as he started to walk next to him, limping as he did. "I'll live."

"Let me know if you need any help."

He didn't receive a response. Honestly, Newman didn't expect one. He had to give the kid props; he was putting on the bravest front he'd ever seen. All that he'd been through with his asshole father, he wasn't surprised. The kid knew how to survive.

"Want to talk about it?"

"No."

Adam's answer was short and clipped. He should leave it at that. But if he wanted to find the bastards who took him, he couldn't. Once Chief Dodson got his hands on Adam, he wouldn't be in the picture anymore. He needed some sort of information to work with.

"I know it won't be easy, but—"

"Dude, you're not the police. You said so yourself. What's it to you?"

A very good point Newman wouldn't dispute. Not the first time in the last three months he wished he was. God, to have his old job back. His old life.

"I used to work for the police department. Not here, but in St. Cloud. Once a cop, always a cop, I guess."

More or less. Newman didn't want to elaborate. The kid was only thirteen and it wouldn't be easy to explain to him why he needed to find these guys and make them pay.

"Why the hell would you move here?"

Adam said it with such disgust, Newman couldn't hold back his chuckle. Well, if he hadn't screwed up, he never would've. It was a small town, full of gossip, in the middle of nowhere, surrounded by nothing. It was not his ideal way of living.

But he liked the peace and quiet. He liked not having to explain himself and why he had done what he had.

Before he left St. Cloud, his parents wouldn't quit bugging him, nagging him, berating him for his behavior. When he left, they wouldn't stop calling. After a week of not answering their calls, they finally stopped. He didn't feel too remorseful because they didn't have anything pleasant or supportive to say, like, "We still love you. It doesn't matter what you did, we love you."

It would've been nice to hear something along those lines at least once.

How did he explain any of that to Adam?

"First, watch your language."

Adam huffed, muttering something under his breath.

"I didn't quite hear that. What did you say?"

Side-eyeing, Adam mumbled, "Yes, sir."

Newman laughed, knowing quite well that wasn't what he muttered. More like, go to hell. "I like you, kid. You're tough. That's good."

"So?"

Oh, yeah, he still wanted to know why he moved to this small-ass town. "Well, it's not a pretty story. I cheated on my girlfriend. I lied to my boss and lost my job. Lied to my friends. My life went to hell and I needed an escape. The cabin my grandfather left me provided that."

"Why can you swear and I can't?"

Good point. How did Amelia do this parenting stuff? He shouldn't be so honest with the kid. He was only thirteen.

"Because I'm an adult and you're not."

"Not setting a very good example for me."

Newman chuckled again. Another good point.

"Duly noted. I will watch my language as well." He tried to be unobtrusive as he watched Adam walk, his limp getting worse as they made their way to his cabin. It'd take forever at this pace.

"How did—"

"Why'd you lie to everyone?"

He should've expected that question after his confession. He only confessed because he thought he could connect with him somehow. Adam survived his abusive father. He survived an abduction and escaped. At least, he assumed so. If he wanted Adam to confess what happened, he figured the best way was to be honest first, even if he was only thirteen.

"Would you believe me if I said I didn't have a good reason?"

"It might not be good, but there's always a reason."

Wise kid. Newman liked him more and more as they walked and talked.

Did he want to get into his past with a thirteen-year-old? A thirteen-year-old who just went through a traumatic ordeal?

"I was scared. I knew I was in trouble and I was just scared to face the truth. So I did the only thing I could think of. I lied."

And damn, that was the honest to God truth. When he walked into the bedroom and saw Tonya's dead body, hell, when he got the call and he recognized the address, he had never been so scared in his life. Not only had he lied to Sauer about Chrissy cheating on him, when in fact he had been the cheater, he didn't know how to confess Tonya was the woman he slept with.

"That's a pretty...okay reason."

"Yeah, you think so?"

Adam shrugged. "It's not manly to admit you're scared. I can see why you wouldn't want to tell the truth."

"Did your dad tell you that? Because he's wrong. A man should always admit the truth, no matter how hard it is. And if some people find that unmanly, then so be it."

"No, he never said that. But he said plenty of stuff to get his point across." Adam produced a small grin. "You just called yourself unmanly."

He did. He was a poor excuse for a man. Lying, betraying his friendships, cheating on Chrissy. He was no gentleman.

"Well, it's not easy to admit, but I have to start somewhere if I want to redeem myself. And I do."

They walked in silence for a few minutes. Perhaps he shouldn't have been as honest with Adam as he thought. He made the kid uncomfortable, which was not what he was going for. He wanted to earn his trust so he could tell him what happened. The longer they walked, the more pronounced his limp became. Newman wanted to say something, offer his help again, but Adam was a defiant kid. He wasn't going to accept his help simply because he offered in a nice voice.

"Mel...she's cool. I don't mean to give her a hard time. I know..." Adam hunched his shoulders even more as if trying to hide from the words. "She has a lot going on. Trying to get Mom out of jail. I shouldn't be such a brat."

"Sometimes we can't stop it, no matter how much we don't want to act a certain way. She loves you. I hope you know that."

"Yeah, I know." Adam released a heavy breath. "So, like, can we keep this between us? I don't want to put more on her shoulders."

Newman wasn't sure what he was referring to or if he wanted to promise anything. It'd be lying to Amelia if she asked him, and he promised he'd never lie to her.

"Hey, we're a couple of guys chatting here. I'm sure your sister doesn't want to hear about guy stuff."

That answer would have to suffice. He didn't want to give him a clear yes or no answer.

Adam stopped walking, the expression on his face filled with agony. "I'm not talking about what we talked about. I... those men...you said you were a cop."

"In the past. I'm not anymore. But you can trust me when I say they will pay for hurting you. I will find them, Adam."

"And you won't tell my sister what happened? I don't want her to know."

He didn't want to say it, but he had to. "I can't lie to her, Adam. I promised I wouldn't, and I promised myself I wouldn't lie anymore either. But I will tell her if she asks what happened that it's your story to tell, not mine. She'll respect that."

Hopefully. Newman had no idea.

"Tell me what happened."

SHE COULDN'T STOP PACING from one side of the room to the other. And it was a small room. She was walking back and forth so much her agitated footsteps would start to imprint into the hardwood floor.

She was worried about Newman. Worried didn't even begin to describe how she felt. Her little brother was gone, kidnapped, lost, somewhere out there all by himself. Now Newman hadn't returned yet. Granted, it had only been about forty-five minutes since she found the note. But she was unsure of how long he had been gone before she saw it. He couldn't still be running. That was a long time for him to be running. Did people really run that long? She had no idea. She didn't run for pleasure. Thinking about it made her exhausted. While she liked to keep in shape, not opposed to getting sweaty from a good workout, running wasn't the way to go for her.

A knock sounded on the door.

She stopped pacing and raced to the door, then took a deep breath to calm herself down before opening it. Just because he wasn't back yet didn't mean something terrible happened to him. He was taking his time. The tension in the cabin was palpable. Maybe she should go for a run herself. Blow off some of the sexual frustration zapping her body every time she was near him.

Sauer and the rest of the gang, as Newman put it, were waiting with relaxed expressions when she opened the door. But she saw the concern in Sauer's eyes. Maybe she did have a right to worry if he was.

"Come on in." She took a step back and gestured them inside.

Newman didn't take his phone with him running. When it rang ten minutes ago, she answered it. So rude and not any of her business to be touching his phone, but she couldn't stop herself, especially when she saw Sauer's name flash across the screen. She answered, told him Newman went for a run and hadn't returned yet. He had to have heard the worry in her tone, but she wasn't sure. When he suggested skipping the diner and bringing some breakfast to them, she didn't hesitate to agree.

Dee beelined it to the couch and took a seat, gingerly sitting down, holding her back like she was in pain. Sauer followed and took a seat next to her. Zeke stood near the couch but didn't sit down. Mel closed the door and smiled when Ben handed her a bag.

"We picked up some donuts and croissants, and I wasn't sure what kind of coffee you'd like, so I ordered a few different kinds. A fancy latte and a regular coffee," Ben said with a smile as he held a drink tray filled with four coffee cups. He pointed to the front two when he said latte.

Offering a smile, she grabbed one of the fancy lattes. She was too wired to eat, though, and set the bag on the coffee table.

"Newman's not back yet?" Sauer asked.

To calm her nerves by the question she didn't want to answer, she took a sip of coffee. More like a gulp when she burned the tip of her tongue. But the delicious flavor swirled around her mouth and slid down her throat with ease. A little bit of vanilla and caramel. Delicious. Maybe she'd drink both cups if no one else wanted the other one.

"Nope. I guess he's still running."

"Never knew Newman to be a runner," Zeke said casually, although Mel swore she heard a bit of unease in his tone.

"In this cold weather, he's crazy," Dee muttered, rubbing her hand behind her back.

"You should've stayed at the hotel." Sauer kissed the side of her head, noticing her actions.

"I'm fine." Dee smiled, then winced when she shifted her position on the couch.

"Those beds were not the comfiest. I feel ya, Dee," Ben said with a chuckle.

Mel figured Ben was trying to make Dee feel better. Or more likely, Sauer, by the look of anxiety etched across his face every time his wife made an uncomfortable gesture.

"Maybe that's why Newman went for a run. To get the kinks out of his body. He's been sleeping on the couch," Mel said quietly, unwilling to give the other reason he went for a run. To escape the tension between them.

"And he didn't bring his phone with." Zeke said it more as a statement rather than a question since he knew he didn't bring his phone.

"Or his jacket," Ben said, nodding to the jacket hanging on the hook near the front door that he wore yesterday.

"Newman and I went running together a few times, even in the winter, just to relieve some stress. We didn't wear a jacket. The cold air can be relaxing and soothing." Sauer didn't look at anyone as he spoke, especially her, as if he knew the reason for Newman's stress.

So, was she supposed to be worried or not? She couldn't quite tell by the conversation.

Sauer finally looked at her. "I'm sure he'll be back any moment."

Mel took another sip of her coffee, this time making sure to sip, not gulp. The decadent flavor tasted good, but it did nothing to soothe her rattled nerves.

"Well, let's make a plan of attack for the day while we wait," Ben said enthusiastically, clapping his hands. "I say one team heads to Kelting and does some more canvassing, find another witness to this guy with the scar and the truck. Another team should ask around this town about the guy. And another team can check with Chief Banner about the sketch artist."

"Wouldn't it be more beneficial to wait for the sketch artist before you go asking around about the guy with the scar?" Dee asked, cocking a brow like Ben was an idiot.

Mel didn't think he was because his plan had merit. It kept them busy. So what if they bugged everyone again in this town about her brother and the man who grabbed him.

She had to do something. She couldn't sit on her butt waiting for some sketch artist.

But Dee also had a point. Would it help to ask people about the guy if they didn't have a picture to go along with their questions?

"It can't hurt." Sauer grabbed her hand and kissed the back of it. "Regardless what we decide, you're staying here today, or at the hotel."

"Oh, buster, we are not having this conversation. I came here to help and—"

Sauer cut her off with a kiss. Mel smiled, wanting to chuckle out loud. For some reason, she found it sweet and endearing how Sauer worried about his wife. She wasn't sure whether she liked Dee yet, but she was pregnant. Obviously, she wasn't feeling well with the way she kept moving around on the couch and touching her back. She understood why Sauer didn't want her tagging along knocking on doors, driving around town looking for clues. It wasn't strenuous work, but it wasn't easy either. It was a lot of walking from business to business, or from house to house. Getting in and out of the car constantly. Sauer was right. Dee needed to stay back and relax.

The kiss finally ended. Dee looked a little dazed, yet happy. Mel glanced at Zeke and Ben. They both had amused expressions like this was nothing abnormal. Ben winked at her and smiled. She returned a wink because it felt like he was including her in their little group and a joke they were all sharing.

Dee narrowed her eyes at Sauer, the happiness still twinkling in the depths of her eyes, but she was focused and ready to rumble. "Nice try distracting me, but it doesn't change anything."

"You're staying back and—"

"Why don't Dee and I head to Kelting and see about the sketch artist. Does that work, Dee?" Mel asked, feeling bad for cutting Sauer off, but she didn't want to hear them argue. It was her fault they were arguing to begin with. If she hadn't failed in being a good sister, watching her brother like she promised her mother, they wouldn't be here trying to help her.

Sauer inhaled but didn't respond as he met her gaze. Mel wasn't sure what he was trying to say, but she didn't care if she offended him. If he wanted to argue with her, fine. She was ready for a fight. But she didn't want to see him argue with his wife.

Dee nodded with a grin. "That idea works for me. Sauer, sweetheart? Does that work for you?"

The sweetness in her tone didn't fool Mel, or Sauer, apparently. It sounded more like a sarcastic question. Mel braced herself for more arguing. So unfortunate, because then she'd have to raise her voice and show these people— such wonderful people helping her out—the kind of brutal woman she could be. She refused to let them argue because of her.

Except Sauer laughed. A joyous, honest laugh, then kissed his wife. "I have no choice, so yeah, I guess that works for me."

Dee patted his cheek, her smile inching up a notch. "So glad you agree."

Ben coughed, then looked at his watch. "Well, that didn't take long to hatch a plan for the day."

Mel huffed, unable to hold it in any longer. "Something's wrong. He should've been back by now."

Zeke stepped closer, grabbing her gently by the shoulders. "Amelia, he's fine. I know right now it's easy to think the worst because your brother is missing, but Newman is fine."

Her heart started racing as nasty scenarios pelted her mind. But unlike last night when she imagined her brother being tortured and murdered, she saw Newman instead.

Her breathing became labored, then she whispered, "Why don't I believe that? I feel it in my bones. Something happened."

13

HE COULDN'T TAKE it anymore. From the biting cold to watching Adam limp even worse as he took one step after another, he couldn't take it. The silence was grating on his nerves as well. Even though he asked Adam to tell him what happened, he didn't respond. He decided not to press the issue. The kid was scared.

"I'd say we have about a half mile to go. You can't keep walking on that ankle, and I'm getting cold."

Newman stopped walking, which made Adam stop walking. He didn't miss the flash of relief in Adam's eyes.

Turning a bit, Newman threw a thumb behind his back. "Hop on. We're going to pick up the pace here."

"What?"

Newman caught Adam's puzzled expression and smiled. "A piggyback ride. Haven't you ever had a piggyback ride?"

"Dude, I'm thirteen. I'm too old for something like that and I'm too heavy for you."

Newman noticed he didn't answer his question. When he thought about it, it was a dumb question. With the kind of father he had, he probably never had a piggyback ride.

While he hated to agree Adam would be heavy to carry, he couldn't keep walking. Newman wasn't going to let him, even if he had to throw him over his shoulder in a fireman's hold.

He patted his shoulder, his smile still prominently displayed. No need for Adam to see his worry about whether this would be too much for him. "I got this, Adam. Trust me. Hop on."

Adam looked wary, glancing around the woods, then back at him. "You'll trip or something. I'm too heavy."

"I need you to trust me, Adam. Jump up on my back and hold on tight."

Adam hesitated, then wobbled closer and attempted to jump. Newman was ready for him, but it wasn't a very good jump and they both fell forward. Newman caught himself before tumbling to the ground and grabbed Adam, holding him steady.

"Big jump, kid. I'll catch you. That was more like slamming into me with your body rather than a jump," Newman said, trying to keep his tone teasing. He could feel the tension and nerves vibrating in the air.

He didn't know what Adam was so afraid of. If he thought Newman would fall and hurt him even more, he was gravely mistaken. If it was the last thing he ever did, he'd get Adam back to the cabin with no further pain.

"I've never done this before. I don't think—"

"Stop thinking and just do it. Let's go." Newman clapped his hands excitedly as if they were in a football huddle and about to complete the last play of the game to score the winning touchdown.

A determined expression touched Adam's face. Newman braced himself. Adam jumped. Newman caught him, hooking his hands under his legs.

"Hold on to me."

Adam's arms went around his neck, squeezing as if he were holding onto a raft drifting in the middle of the ocean.

Getting a good grip on his legs, Newman coughed a little before saying, "Not too tight, kid. I need to breathe."

A low chuckle sounded in his ear. "Sorry. Are you sure about this?"

Oh, yes, he was very sure. He'd be getting a good workout in now. Adam wasn't a lightweight. He was a scrawny kid, but he still weighed a lot. Newman didn't go around carrying things on his back.

And Adam trusted him. So yeah, he was definitely sure about this.

"I got you."

He started running with Adam clinging to him like his life depended on it.

Running with something on his back, something heavy, with the fact he was running on snow wasn't as easy as he thought it would be. But he couldn't fail Adam. He said he'd get him back to the cabin without falling and he wouldn't turn out to be a liar—again.

Except, a few times he stepped wrong or his foot caught on something covered beneath the snow. He never face-planted or tumbled to the ground, but he wobbled in his running. Adam always squeezed him tighter, restricting his air. To reassure him, he would lightly tighten his grip around his legs and mumble, "I got you."

It was his mantra as he ran.

I got you. I got you. I got you.

After a while, he found a rhythm. He still found pockets in the snow that would almost trip him up, but his pace stayed consistent.

Finally, after what felt like ages running, he saw his cabin in the distance.

Adam must've as well because his arms tightened around his throat.

"Adam," he grunted as he kept his pace up. If he slowed down now, he'd never make it. He'd collapse in a heap as soon as he stopped.

Understanding immediately, Adam loosened his grip. "There it is. Just like you said."

He didn't take it personally how it came out. That Adam doubted him telling the truth. The kid had been through a lot. Of course, he'd be wary about anyone and everything. As he should be.

As soon as he neared the porch, he slowed his pace but didn't completely stop until he was inches from the door. His breathing was labored. His chest felt like it was about to burst into a million tiny pieces. He had never run so hard in his life.

"Let me—"

Newman's hands gripped his legs. "Let me get you inside and on the couch. You need to stay off that ankle."

Newman hoped he could make it from the door to the couch. His breathing hadn't returned to normal yet, and his chest pounded and ached like a 2-ton vehicle sat on top of him crushing him to death.

Digging deep for another small ounce of strength, he grabbed the door handle and swung it open. He didn't stop to acknowledge any of the surprised expressions on his friends' faces, or even where Amelia was.

He didn't even see Sauer's vehicle out there. His mind had been completely on his mission. Get Adam inside the cabin.

Walking the few steps to the couch, he turned around,

then tried to crouch as much as he could, patting one of Adam's legs.

"Hop off, buddy. Take a seat."

A huge weight was lifted off his shoulders the second Adam slid off.

And not simply from Adam's heaviness, but the feeling that he had finally done something right without screwing it up.

Pushing the coffee table out of the way, he turned around, meeting everyone's gaze but Amelia's. Where was Amelia?

Adam looked at Dee, who happened to be sitting on the couch next to him. Then Adam glanced around the room to look at Sauer, who stood near Dee, then at Ben and Zeke, who had been standing by his punching bag but were now moving closer.

"I found Adam. We need to get him to the hospital. Where's Amelia?" None of that came out easily because he was still breathing like he was on his last legs of life, his words broken and mangled in jagged pieces.

He felt a hand on his shoulder, looking to his right to see Ben standing next to him.

"She's in the bathroom. Were you running...from something or..."

"Just to help get him back here. His ankle's swollen. And I didn't have a jacket." Newman chuckled, even though nothing was funny, but he was trying to keep the mood light for Adam.

The look in his eyes also portrayed to Ben, even though he hadn't been running from anything, it didn't mean there wasn't something dangerous out there. Adam had been wandering around the woods and he still needed an answer to why and how he escaped.

"I'll get you something to drink," Zeke said, walking past them, stopping near the couch. "What would you like, Adam?"

"They're my friends. You can trust them. They are actual cops." Newman smiled when Adam stared at Zeke like a deer in headlights, then looked at him.

Adam held his gaze for a few seconds before shrugging. "Water."

Zeke nodded and headed for the kitchen.

"I'll—"

His words were cut off by a sharp gasp from across the room.

"Adam!"

Newman couldn't hold a huge grin back as Amelia fled to Adam's side and pulled him into a tight hug. His legs wanted to cave in. His heart still beat rapidly, like he was hyped up on speed. His entire body raged with echoes of pain. But none of that mattered as Amelia and Adam clung together on the couch.

For once in his life, he didn't screw up.

MEL CLUTCHED HER BROTHER, never wanting to let go. The past few days, besides worrying to death, creating the worst scenarios in her head, she contemplated how she would tell her mother she failed in protecting her brother.

But now she didn't have to.

He was back. He was safe.

"I can't breathe, Mel. And there's a bunch of people around. Can you cool it?" Adam muttered.

She didn't care. She wanted to ignore everyone and everything and hold her brother tight.

"Mel," he groaned again.

This time she listened and backed away, although her hands still touched his shoulders. He looked pale, tired, and worn out. Dirt lingered on his face, his hair oily and messy from days of not showering. But he was safe. All of that could be easily fixed.

"We should—"

At the sound of Newman's voice, she stood up and ran to him, swinging her arms around him, cutting off whatever he was about to say. She pressed as close as she could, wrapping her arms around him like a snake coiling its prey. His heart raced, a crazy erratic pace. She swore it was beating steadily with hers because she couldn't stop the rapid race of her heart either.

He saved her brother. Just as he said he would. She would always be forever in his debt.

"Thank you." Tears wanted to escape. "Thank you so much, Newman."

Her words slipped out in a whisper. But they were enough to finally get Newman to embrace her back. His arms came around her and he squeezed her gently.

"I didn't do much, but you're welcome. We should get him to the hospital. His ankle needs attention, and I have no idea if he's hurt anywhere else."

That pulled her back to reality. Because she could've stayed wrapped contently in his arms all day long. She let go and stepped away, nodding.

Adam rolled his eyes as she met his gaze. "I'm fine, Mel. I need an ice pack and I'll be good to go."

There was the brother she knew. He might've been missing for a few days, but he hadn't changed. Still the same crabby, know-it-all buster that he was before.

"I didn't say anything."

"You never have to speak, but I know what you're think-ing. I don't need to go to the damn hospital," Adam mumbled.

A throat cleared behind her. She glanced at Newman, who smiled brightly at her, then she looked back at her brother. He shared a brief look with Newman before turning his gaze away, a light coat of red flushing his cheeks.

"We can go together, chump. It'll be fun," Dee finally said, breaking the weird tension filling the room.

Mel honestly wasn't sure what that exchange was between Newman and her brother.

Adam looked at Dee, confused. "What?"

"Yeah, what?" Sauer asked, placing a hand on Dee's shoulder. "Are you okay?"

"Of course." Dee smiled, then grimaced. "You know, besides the slight pain in my back that won't go away. And the slight pain in my belly. I don't know what contractions feel like. Maybe it's that. I don't know, but it...hurts."

"Oh, we're going. Let's go." Sauer stepped in front of Dee and helped her stand. "You shouldn't be having contractions yet, should you? How bad is the pain?"

"I'm sure it's all going to be fine. A trip to see the doctor can't hurt," Zeke said, joining Sauer and Dee. "Do you need help walking?"

"I'm fine," Dee said to Zeke, then looked at Adam. "Let's go, buster. To the doctor we go."

Adam nodded, his eyes wide as he watched Sauer walk carefully with Dee to the door. Zeke and Ben followed closely behind.

Newman touched her shoulder and smiled, then walked to the couch and turned around. "Hop on, kid. I've learned that if Dee says something, you listen. It's never good to ignore that woman."

Mel couldn't hold in her smile as she met Newman's gaze. He winked as Adam carefully crawled onto his back in a piggyback style.

She followed them out of the house, but not before grabbing Newman's jacket hanging from the wall and his car keys from the front pocket.

They made it to the hospital a short time later. Dee and Sauer went in one direction, as they followed a nurse in another direction.

Zeke and Ben didn't go in the room with them, but Mel was happy when Newman didn't hesitate.

She stood by the side of the bed as they waited for the doctor. The nurse took his vitals, everything appeared okay, although she said Adam was dehydrated and started him on an IV with fluids.

"Hey, so I'm going to call the police. Do you think you're up to talking to them?" Newman asked.

Adam fiddled with the blanket, not meeting either of their gazes.

"It's okay, Adam. You don't have to talk to them right away," she reassured her brother. She wasn't sure she wanted to know what happened to him.

Because if she didn't know, then it wouldn't make it real.

And the pain and heartache in his eyes was already real enough. What *did* happen to him? What had he endured?

Adam looked at Newman. "Will you stay in the room with me?"

Newman nodded. "Yep."

"Okay. Fine."

Newman smiled, then jerked his head toward the door. "I'm stepping out for a moment to call the police, but I'll be right back."

She returned his smile, hoping she played it off well

enough that she was as strong as he appeared. But she didn't feel that strong at all. She wanted to sit in a corner and ball her eyes out for the torture her brother endured.

When the door closed after Newman walked out, Adam spoke.

"I'm sorry, Mel."

She grabbed his hand, puzzled. "What for?"

Her brother looked at her with tears pooling in his eyes. "For everything. This is all my fault."

Hating the anguish in his voice, she wrapped him in her arms once again, not caring what he thought. They didn't do this kind of affection with each other. Hell, her brother barely told her how school went, let alone give her a hug or let her hug him in return.

She felt his tears soak her shirt. She didn't care. Pulling him tighter into her embrace, she tried to tell him without words that it was okay. Everything would be okay.

Especially because they had Newman in their corner.

For some strange reason, she didn't think whatever happened was officially over.

14

NEWMAN CROSSED his arms as he leaned against the wall near the window. He might've even thrown in a smug smirk because he couldn't help himself when Chief Dodson walked into the room.

He found Adam, although accidentally, but he still found him. Even though Adam hadn't told anyone yet what happened, he knew the kid hadn't run away like the chief thought. So yeah, he couldn't help but smirk at the guy.

"What are you doing here?"

Newman didn't react in any particular way other than to widen his smirk as Chief Dodson asked such a ridiculous question. He wasn't leaving Adam alone with the asshole and Chief Dodson knew it.

"Why wouldn't I be here?"

"You're not a cop or a member of the family. You can leave."

Newman finally straightened and walked closer to the bed. Chief Dodson stood on the other side. "I'm a friend of the family and I'm not leaving."

"I want him here," Adam spoke. His voice held a bit of apprehension.

Newman couldn't be sure if that was because he really didn't want him in the room, or if he was afraid to speak up to Chief Dodson. He figured it was the latter because he had asked him to stay.

"I have to ask you some questions and it's better if they aren't in the room," Chief Dodson replied. Not sympathetically either.

What did he think he was going to do if he got Adam alone? Try to make the kid lie that he actually ran away when he didn't?

"I'm not leaving either." Amelia stood next to him, her expression as fierce as a momma bear protecting her cubs. "My brother is only thirteen. I'm his legal guardian, and I will not be leaving this room. And as his legal guardian, I also wish for Newman to remain in the room as well. He might not be with the police department, but he'll know if you're stepping out of line."

"Excuse me—"

"You're not excused," Amelia stated with a slash of her tongue, cutting him off. "You've been nothing but rude and inconsiderate since we moved to this town. Okay, so my brother hasn't set the best example for the world's greatest kid, but when I needed you, you blew me off. So forgive me if I don't exactly trust you."

Chief Dodson swallowed, his eyes narrowing. Newman could tell he wanted to say something, but he didn't think Amelia would allow it. Chief Dodson obviously got the same impression since he looked away from her and turned toward Adam.

"Tell me what happened from the beginning."

Adam glanced around the room, meeting everyone's

eyes, finally landing on Newman. He gave him a slight nod to indicate it was okay to speak. He wasn't sure why Adam seemed to trust him so much—and so fast—but he'd take it. It'd been forever since someone trusted him wholeheartedly like this, and it felt good.

He was not about to fail this kid. Not ever.

"I left the house to bike to the store. As soon as I got on the road, this truck came up beside me and slowed down. I didn't think anything of it. The guy rolled down his window and started asking for directions. Out of nowhere this other dude came up behind me and shoved something over my mouth. I don't remember anything after that other than waking up in a small, dark room."

"Did you get a good look at the two men?" Chief Dodson asked as he pulled out a notepad and pen from the inside of his winter coat. "And how about a description of the vehicle?"

"Not really. The guy in the truck had a hood on, but I thought I saw a scar on his face. Maybe. I never saw the other guy's face that grabbed me. He was driving a white truck." Adam looked at Amelia. "That same truck that creeped you out at the store. I didn't think it was a big deal. I thought you were being...whatever."

Amelia smiled and laid a hand on his leg covered by a blanket. "It's okay."

"Tell me about this room," Chief Dodson said, writing in his notepad.

Adam shrugged. "Not much to tell. It was small and dark. There was never any light besides when the sun came through the tiny window. They never opened the door. There wasn't anything in there. Not even anything to lie on. It was cold, but not freezing."

"So they just let you go?" Chief Dodson raised a brow like he didn't believe a word Adam was saying.

Newman wanted to hit the guy like he attacked his punching bag every day. Hard and precise. Over and over. He thought Adam was lying. Couldn't he see how frightened the kid was? Couldn't he hear the terror in his voice? Couldn't he see the tiny trembles in his hands as he spoke?

He was a sorry excuse for a chief of police.

Adam shook his head. "There was a small window. Really small. I got it open and crawled out. I almost got stuck trying to crawl out. As soon as I got out I started running."

Which would explain all the scratches and marks Newman saw on his body when the doctor examined him. He hadn't meant to stay in the room, but Adam had insisted. When Adam looked at him with such fear and anguish in his eyes, Newman couldn't refuse him.

He also told the doctor he sprained his ankle running away from the tiny cabin.

It might take some searching, especially since Adam didn't remember the direction he ran from, but Newman would find that cabin. He wasn't trusting Chief Dodson to take care of it.

"Where is this place?"

Adam shrugged again. "I have no clue. I didn't stop to ask those assholes for directions."

Newman pressed his lips together to keep from laughing at the kid's attitude. Not the best thing to do, especially with such a prick like Chief Dodson, but Adam wasn't like other kids. Newman respected that, particularly with everything he'd been through.

Chief Dodson slammed his notepad shut, pursing his

lips in a disapproving manner. "The attitude isn't necessary."

Adam looked down, fiddling some more with his blanket.

Newman didn't blame him for averting his gaze. Chief Dodson didn't need to see how much the kid despised him. But Newman had no such problem expressing how much he hated the guy.

"That's enough for right now. Adam needs to rest, and I figure you have a lot of work to do to find that cabin."

Chief Dodson more or less grunted a response and shoved his notepad back inside his jacket pocket.

"I'll walk you out." Newman gestured toward the door. Chief Dodson surprisingly followed directions without arguing.

As soon as they stepped outside, he met Zeke and Ben's gaze, who stood right next to the door. Chief Dodson turned toward him with the evilest sneer he'd seen from him yet.

"The kid's lying. He ran away like he always does, got lost in the woods, and it took forever to find his way back home."

Wow.

Just wow.

Newman had no words. Utterly speechless.

He thought Chief Dodson might've had a tiny thought Adam was lying, but he didn't expect him to honestly *say* he was lying.

"He mentioned the guy in the truck had a scar. We also found a witness who can corroborate a guy with a scar in a white truck. He almost T-boned someone running a stop sign."

"Doesn't mean he kidnapped some troublemaker kid."

"Not sure what makes you believe the kid is lying, but

you're out of line," Zeke said, the muscles in his cheeks jumping, his jaw tight and rigid.

Chief Dodson looked at all three of them, his expression stern and without remorse. "I'm done here. I'm writing it up as a runaway. Case closed. He's a troublemaker. Has been since he moved here. I don't believe a word he's saying. You get in my way about this and you'll be sorry. All of you."

Then, without waiting for a response, he walked away.

Which was a damn lucky thing because Newman was one second away from knocking him on his ass.

A hand touched his shoulder. Glancing to his right, Ben gave him an encouraging smile. "We know Adam isn't lying. That guy can kiss our ass because we'll find out who hurt Adam."

Newman nodded, his throat clogged with too much emotion. What would he do without these guys here? He didn't know if he'd have the power to do anything by himself. But their moral support was enough to give him the strength.

"I have never wanted to beat someone so badly more than I do right now."

Zeke chuckled. "Dude, I'm right there with you. What an asshat. But Ben's right. We're not done with this case."

Newman smiled. "I appreciate it. You guys have no idea."

He didn't think they did. No idea how much it meant to him.

It was sad to admit, but if Adam hadn't gone missing and Amelia hadn't knocked on his door, he'd still be wallowing in his self-pity.

He owed Adam and Amelia everything.

He didn't save anyone today.

They saved him.

Now he would protect them and find out who hurt Adam if it was the last thing he ever did.

———

NEWMAN STRETCHED out in the lumpy hospital chair next to Adam's bed wishing the damn thing was more comfortable. The least the hospital could do was make comfier chairs to relax in while you visited a loved one. Not that Adam was a loved one, but he was a friend. And the kid still looked frightened. Adam hadn't asked him to stay, but he had seen it in his eyes when Zeke and Ben mentioned they were leaving for lunch. Adam hadn't wanted him to go with, so he declined before Adam said anything. The relief had been palpable, though.

Ben said he'd grab something for him on their way back. Newman only nodded. They had also given an update on Dee, who had been admitted for observation. With her back pain and the contractions, they wanted to make sure everything was okay. Sauer hadn't left her side once. Ben and Zeke had been back and forth between both rooms relaying information when necessary.

Adam also needed to spend the night. He had been extremely dehydrated. Not once had the suspects opened the room to feed him or offer him a drink of water. Nothing. He stayed in a tiny, dark room for four full days all alone.

God, Newman wanted to throw up thinking about what he had endured.

Pure torture, starving someone like that.

Which made him think back to those boys who went missing seven years ago. How much longer before the men would've started torturing him in other ways, cutting off his limbs? How would've Amelia reacted and survived to learn her brother was brutally murdered and pieces of his body tossed around the woods like trash?

He let out a silent breath.

Well, he'd never find out because Adam was safe. Nobody could hurt him now. He wouldn't let anyone. Especially Chief Dodson. The prick.

"I think you think you're being all quiet, but I can hear you huffing and puffing. You got something to say?" Adam mumbled quietly.

Newman met his gaze, surprised to find him awake. He thought he had been sleeping. Amelia had stepped out of the room to call her mother's lawyer and update him on her brother's status. Something she hadn't done yet, afraid to tell her mother what happened. But now that Adam was safe, she felt more comfortable sharing the disturbing news with her mother.

He didn't realize his agitation had been so noticeable. He tried to sit quietly so Adam could rest. He needed it. They had been pumping him with fluids, letting him drink some water and 7-Up, but he was still weak, recovering from everything. It was mind-boggling to even think that he escaped and managed to get away. He was one strong kid.

"I'm sorry for waking you. My mind is in overdrive right now. Go back to sleep."

Adam gave him a tired grin. He could see the exhaustion on his face. All the energy he had exerted escaping was finally catching up to him.

"Is it weird I can't sleep?"

"Not really. Your mind must be on overdrive, too." Newman sat up, offering the best reassuring smile he could. "You're safe, Adam. I promise."

He nodded. "Mel said we could trust you. I do." Adam looked down at his blanket, fiddling with it. "It was so dark in there. I've never considered myself a baby. My father made sure that would never happen. He beat in the importance of always acting like a man."

Newman almost held his breath waiting for Adam to finish. He didn't think the kid was always this forthright with people and sharing his feelings.

"I'm terrified for the night to come. For the darkness."

Pressing his lips together, he tried like hell to hold back the sudden tears threatening to consume him on Adam's behalf. He couldn't wait to find the men who dared to lay a hand on the kid.

"You're the strongest kid I know. The darkness can't hurt you. You didn't let it these past few days. You won't let it now either." Newman paused, trying to keep his composure. "I won't leave you alone. Not if you don't want me to."

Adam looked at him. The fear and pain echoed in his eyes. It swirled, hypnotizing him. He swore he felt everything Adam felt.

He didn't cry about things. There were times, after he lost his job and moved away, where he wanted to crawl into a corner and ball his eyes out for screwing up his life as he had. But he didn't. He held it in. He persevered. He kept going. Acting like a man, just like Adam said his father insisted on.

Right now, he wanted to cry. He wanted to shed tears for the agony and terror Adam went through. For such a young kid to have lived such a hard, brutal life and he was only thirteen years old. No kid should have to endure what he had to survive.

He couldn't stop the water pooling in his eyes. No tears ran down his cheeks, but his eyes filled to the brim.

"So it won't make me a baby if I ask you to stay?"

Newman sniffed, inhaling, hoping he could hold back

the dam of tears. "Nope. Not even a little. I'm afraid of things, too. We all are."

Adam tilted his head, contemplation wrinkled on his forehead. "What are you afraid of?"

He managed to gain control, his eyes not brimming with tears, although still sparkling wet. He could cry at any moment.

Then he spoke.

"Commitment. To anything. It terrifies me."

"Is that why you cheated on your girlfriend?"

Again, Newman was flabbergasted he was talking about this kind of stuff with a thirteen-year-old. It didn't seem appropriate. Yet, when he looked into Adam's trusting gaze, he also felt completely at ease, as if this kid would understand him. And that trust in his eyes, he didn't want to see it disappear.

"Yeah, I guess. Things were getting comfortable and the next step in any relationship is marriage. I loved her, but the thought of commitment scared me. It was a dumb reason, but I sabotaged my relationship. It was irresponsible and the worst thing I could've ever done. Don't ever act like me, Adam. I'm a very bad example of how a man should act."

A tiny smile appeared as Adam shifted on the bed. "I don't think so." He looked away, down at the blanket. "I can't talk to Mel about things. I feel comfortable with you."

Ditto, kid.

He even had a hard time talking to Sauer about stuff, and he was his best friend.

Adam's head popped up. "Do you like my sister?"

Newman froze.

Well, shit. How did he answer that? Yeah, he would say he liked her. She was strong and tough. Resilient, never backed down once when he wanted her to get the hell out of his life. Never backed off when Chief Dodson didn't believe her. How couldn't he like a woman like her?

And he definitely wanted to sleep with her. He had been attracted to her since the moment he laid eyes on her. She was a beautiful woman. He imagined most men were attracted to her.

But Adam wasn't asking in a friendly sense.

"Amelia is a special woman. I can't afford to like her more than a friend."

"Why? Because you'll end up cheating on her if things start to get serious."

Newman wanted to say no he wouldn't, but he couldn't. He had done it in the past. He always screwed everything up when things got serious. That's what he did. So who's to say he wouldn't do it again?

"She deserves better than me, Adam. I'm not sure why you're asking."

He glanced away, shrugging, then met his gaze. "She looks at you like I haven't seen her look at a guy before. And I've seen guys hit on my sister and how she reacts." Adam grinned. "I've seen how you look at her, too, when you think no one's looking."

"Your sister is beautiful. She's amazing. She's as strong as you are. I'm not surprised you're related."

The tiny grin on Adam expanded. "I'd be okay if you liked her. That's all I'm saying."

Newman nodded, chuckling. "Thank you for the blessing, but we're just friends." He leaned closer to the bed. "And we're friends, too. You can always count on me if you need me, Adam."

Always and forever.

Newman meant every word.

Did he want Amelia as he wanted his next breath? Oh, yes. He wanted her that badly.

But he couldn't have her. Not when he'd eventually screw things up and hurt her.

Even though he and Amelia would never be an item, Adam could still count on him.

Friends for life.

15

MEL SHUT the door quietly and let out a strained breath. The past two days had been hard. From watching her brother gain his strength back in a hospital bed, begging her to get him out of there because he hated the attention, to watching the fatigue in all the guys' features as they searched the woods for the cabin Adam escaped from, to the moment they were released from the hospital and she said they were going home.

Without Newman.

Adam had immediately glared daggers at her and he still refused to talk to her.

That brief moment where he hugged her and shared his feelings was gone. Back to the same old Adam who acted like he hated her.

She watched as he ignored her and stalked to his room. Even with a brace on his foot to help his sprained ankle, which was healing nicely, he managed to sulk to his bedroom with angsty teenager flair. He even slammed the door.

Oh, Mel knew Adam and Newman had grown close in

the past two days. She recognized it right away in the cabin when she walked in the room and saw her brother sitting on the couch. She knew even then they had formed some kind of bond.

She was grateful for that, considering her brother didn't connect with anyone, not even her. It was like pulling teeth with him asking how school went. He didn't make friends. He didn't ask to join any school clubs. He didn't attempt to put himself out there. Ever.

But they didn't live with Newman. They couldn't live with him. Which was something she tried to explain to Adam. But she said they could visit him.

Then Adam tried to say she liked Newman more than a friend and to do something about it.

Ha!

That's what she wanted to say to that.

She explained they were only friends, even though she'd be excited at the prospect to be more than friends. Newman, however, was not game for anything. Not even friends it seemed.

In the past two days, although he was in the hospital room the entire time, he barely spoke to her. She knew then that he was trying to distance himself.

Her hope for a little fun between the sheets had plummeted.

Hell, she'd take just talking to him over anything else. She enjoyed talking to him, spending time with him. He strangely understood her more than most people did.

But apparently, he didn't want anything from her.

Regardless, she owed him everything. He might've found her brother by accident, but was it? She knocked on his door begging for help and refused to leave. She told him she wanted to sleep with him and still refused to leave. The sexual tension between them grew and grew. If she hadn't acted the way she had, then he would've never gone for a run that morning. But because he did, he found her brother.

It was meant to be. She believed that.

She'd always be forever grateful.

And he was still their savior. Chief Dodson didn't believe her brother. Newman wouldn't accept his behavior.

He had gone straight to the town mayor, who had been great friends with his grandfather. A few words from Newman and Chief Dodson had immediately been in hot water. In addition to Zeke and Ben searching for the cabin, so was the entire police force.

And nothing. They still hadn't found the cabin where Adam escaped. Of course, Chief Dodson kept muttering they couldn't find it because it didn't exist. Because her brother hadn't been kidnapped.

Mel wasn't sure why Newman didn't help in the search, but she figured it had to do with Adam and the panic that always surfaced anytime Newman wanted to step out of the room.

Sauer couldn't help with anything because he had to drive back to St. Cloud with his wife, who had been given strict orders for bed rest. She was in the mild stages of preeclampsia and they didn't want the baby to come just yet.

Setting her purse on the table, she stood in the middle of the room trying to figure out what to do.

Should she check on Adam? Try to talk to him? Reassure him they'd see Newman sometimes?

When they left the hospital, Newman promised to visit them in the next few days, check on him and hang out. It was sweet of him to treat her brother like he mattered, as if he were someone special in his life. Maybe he was. Maybe her brother had become just as important to Newman as Newman had become important to Adam.

She couldn't ignore the ache in Newman's eyes as she drove away from the hospital. Maybe he didn't want them to leave either.

But what was she supposed to do? Ask him to spend the night? And for how long? Would Newman stay with them while her brother recovered? How long would it take for her brother to recover, to not be afraid?

Oh, she wasn't dumb. She knew her brother was terrified —and she might've overheard part of their conversation two days ago.

Her brother didn't like the dark. He didn't feel safe.

Slumping into a chair at the kitchen table, she stared into space. What did she do now? Where did she go from here? How could she help her brother and stay sane and in control?

Resting her head on her arm, she closed her eyes.

She felt so lost and alone.

With one phone call, she could beg Newman to come over for a little bit. But she was afraid that little bit would turn into a little bit more into a little bit more until he finally left because he couldn't take it anymore.

In the grand scheme of things, they weren't anything special to Newman. Just a woman and a kid who needed his help.

Well, he helped them. Done. Finished.

She couldn't, and wouldn't, rely on him.

She learned early in life she could only rely on herself.

Popping her head up from the table, she stared into the kitchen until her eyes zoned out.

Cookies.

She'd make her brother some cookies. That would cheer

him up. He loved her white chocolate chip macadamia nut cookies. It was the only time he ever let her in.

Donning an apron, a cute whimsical one she bought in New York, she knew this would cheer him up. She already felt better as she tied the apron around her waist. She couldn't resist buying it when she saw the saying etched across the front. "With a touch of fairy dust, cookies magically appear." There were five little colorful fairies waving wands over a plate of cookies. She might not be the world's best baker, but when she wore the apron it made her feel like she could create a masterpiece.

Since she loved these cookies, although didn't bake them often, she always made sure to have ingredients on hand if she ever had a craving. Getting to work mixing the batter, she prayed this would work to soften Adam up.

She needed a small reprieve. Staying strong and hopeful the past week hadn't been easy. Trying to be the best sister, trying not to upset her brother, trying to make sure he got through this ordeal with the least amount of stress as possible was tiring.

So this had to work.

Dropping small spoonfuls onto the pan, she couldn't wait for the first batch to be done. She could already taste the deliciousness. Popping it into the oven, she set the timer and stared at it as it ticked down. She had nothing better to do while the first batch baked.

She could do some work. Something she had let slide since Adam went missing. Something she honestly didn't think about once because she had been so worried about her brother. Her work would always be there. She wasn't too worried about losing her job, considering she was her own boss. Adam was more important right now.

Well, she could clean up her mess. That was one task

she could handle at the moment. She started to grab the dirty dishes lying everywhere, because hey, she wasn't the cleanest baker either, and turned on the hot water.

After adding some dish soap, she started to clean the dishes. Before long, she had most of the dishes drying in the dry rack and the timer finally dinged.

Once she had the first plate of fresh hot cookies ready to go, she took a deep breath and headed for Adam's room.

Knocking softly on the door, she waited for him to answer.

Nothing.

Silence.

Well, he could be sleeping.

Or simply ignoring her like he enjoyed doing.

Refusing to be deterred, she opened the door and tried to keep the smile on her face, even though her heart splintered at his annoyed look.

"I wanna be alone."

Yeah, she got the message loud and clear.

Lifting the plate of cookies, she tried to keep the pain of his attitude out of her tone of voice. "I made you cookies. Your favorite. Want one?"

His eyes definitely sparkled with craving, yet he frowned. "I'm not hungry."

"Just a tiny bite."

He glanced away, gazing out his window into the dreary afternoon day. Even the weather didn't want to be happy with the sun tucked away behind the clouds.

"I'm not hungry."

So the cookies didn't work. Her brother was still upset about Newman not coming home with them. Even though Newman didn't offer, it was obviously her fault in her brother's eyes.

Setting the plate on his desk, she nodded, as if it didn't matter. As if he didn't tear her heart out with his sour attitude. "Well, if you change your mind, here they are."

She walked out, closing his door as quietly as she opened it.

He might not want any cookies, but she was hungry.

The timer went off.

The next batch was done.

Good. She'd eat about a dozen, maybe even a pint of ice cream, and wallow in her self pity. She had nothing else to do for the day. Well, she had a deadline she needed to meet, but there was no way her mind would stay focused.

Ice cream and cookies it was.

———

NEWMAN HEADED out of the bathroom, grabbed a cup of coffee, not that he needed the extra caffeine, and joined Zeke and Ben at the table.

"We've covered a lot of the woods in the past two days. We should find something soon," Ben said casually with the hope lingering in his tone, then took a sip of coffee.

Newman figured Ben actually needed the fuel to keep him going. Both Ben and Zeke had helped search the past two days, getting up early in the morning and working late into the night. As soon as he left the hospital, he called them for an update. Zeke said they were headed in for a quick lunch break, then right back out into the cold, dreary day to find the cabin, and hopefully, the men who hurt Adam. Newman planned to go with them when they headed back out, so he suggested lunch at his place. All they had to do was finish their coffee and go.

"Me, too. For Adam's sake. Give him some peace of mind.

You should've seen his face when he left the hospital." Newman gripped his mug hard. "He's a tough kid, but I still see the fear in his eyes."

"He's a really tough kid. He'll be fine because he has a strong sister, too," Zeke said with a reassuring smile.

Newman didn't need that kind of reassurance. He knew Amelia was strong. The strongest woman he had ever met.

The most beautiful woman he had ever met. Not just in her features, which were gorgeous. Her sweet hazel eyes. Her vibrant smile. Her outrageous pink hair. Oh, he would never deny she was exquisitely beautiful. But it was her strength, her determination, her courage that made her the most beautiful woman he had ever met. He found it all sexy as hell.

Which was strange to realize. He never thought attributes like that in a woman would turn him on.

And he missed her. He missed them both. Adam had reached inside his heart so quickly, he knew he was going to worry about the kid all the time.

He even wanted to follow them home and make sure Adam was settled in without the fear lingering. But it wasn't his place. He didn't belong with them.

He didn't belong with Amelia. No matter how much he wanted to be with her.

After being confined in a small cabin with her, driving around enclosed in a small space, sharing a hospital room, he knew without a doubt he wanted her. Badly.

But he couldn't have her. He wasn't worthy enough for a good woman like her.

While she might want to have sex with him, he couldn't see her wanting a relationship. What woman would with the kind of past he had? A liar. A cheater.

No woman would ever trust him.

He wasn't even sure he trusted himself.

He was weak, and he knew it. Like he told Adam, commitment scared the shit out of him. He wasn't sure if he was strong enough to love a good woman and not run hard and fast in the opposite direction.

Love was frightening.

It could bring happiness and wonder to any relationship.

It could also bring destruction and sadness.

Love and commitment...

Yeah, those two things scared him more than anything else.

He could finally admit it to himself. And it only took a scared thirteen-year-old boy to make him see it.

"Newman?" Zeke waved his hand near his face. "You zoned out, man."

Blinking, he looked at Zeke, trying to figure out the last thing he said. He *had* zoned out. Because he couldn't stop worrying about how Adam and Amelia were doing. Adam, because although being home was a relief, the memories would haunt him for a long time. He wanted to be there for the kid. And Amelia, because helping her brother cope with everything wouldn't be easy. He wanted to help her in any way he could. Ease some of her worries and stress.

"Yeah, it's been a long week. Sorry. What did you say?" he asked Zeke, hoping a smile would appease both of them that he wasn't going out of his mind. Who knew what these two thought about him right now? Honestly, he wasn't sure he wanted to know what they thought about him. They all seemed to have let the past go, but that didn't mean they saw him as a friend any longer or an equal. He was a disgraced detective. He'd never be equal with these guys ever again.

"I was saying—"

Ben's phone buzzed and dinged in front of them, cutting off what Zeke was about to say. Ben picked up his phone, frowned, then a bright smile lit up his face.

"We finally have some success. It's a text from Officer Dawson. They found a cabin. Unoccupied, but it matches the description from Adam."

Newman stood up so fast, his chair nearly fell backwards. "Did he send a location?"

Ben shook his head. "He said to call for directions." He held out his phone. "I'll let you talk to him. You know these woods better than Zeke and I do."

Finally.

Finally, something going in the right direction with this case.

Except, where did the two men disappear? What were they up to?

And was Adam safe from them? Or would they try to grab him once again?

As he called the officer, he wondered if he made the right decision letting Amelia leave with Adam alone.

As soon as he checked out the cabin for himself, he'd head over to their house and check on them.

Not just for them.

But for himself, too.

He missed them so damn much. And it had only been two hours since he last saw them.

He didn't even want to decipher what that meant.

16

HE ENTERED the cabin with slow steps like it would hold back the terror running rampant through his veins. By the looks of the cabin from the outside, it wasn't too promising how the inside would look.

And nope. Newman wasn't impressed.

Garbage, at least what wasn't covered by snow, lingered outside on the porch and around the exterior of the cabin. Inside was no better. Fast food bags and cups littered the table and the ground. Empty pizza boxes as well. Beer cans scattered around the floor.

Adam had starved to death, aching for even a simple sip of water, while these men made sure their bellies stayed full.

Odd that they'd kidnap Adam in the first place. Although it held similarities of the missing boys from seven years ago, Newman doubted it was the same person. Especially since none of the reports he read indicated it was more than one perp. This didn't make sense.

Officer Dawson didn't offer a smile as he approached Newman. Zeke and Ben stood right behind him.

"I could get in a lot of trouble for letting you come here. Don't let me regret it."

Newman tried to reassure him with a friendly smile. He knew why Officer Dawson was hesitant about allowing them to enter the crime scene. Because of Chief Dodson. The man was determined to make this look like Adam ran away. Wonder what he thought about everything now?

"I appreciate it. I want these men caught."

Officer Dawson nodded. "Me, too. And your friends have been a big help the past few days. But don't touch anything."

"Of course. We know the drill," Newman replied. Officer Dawson eyed him funny, probably wondering whether Newman would follow directions. Sure, he lost his job, but not because he messed with evidence. He simply didn't tell his captain and his partner that he slept with the first murder victim.

Officer Dawson nodded, deciding he trusted Newman, then smiled at Ben and Zeke before heading outside.

"He's been great. Chief Dodson, on the other hand, is a real prick," Zeke muttered quietly since the cabin wasn't empty. A few crime scene officers were in the tiny cabin collecting evidence. Hopefully evidence they needed to find these bastards.

"Here, here. Can't argue with that," Ben said with a cheery tone and a broad smile. Then he tossed his head in the direction of the door. "I'm actually going to look around outside first."

"I'll come with you."

Newman didn't take it personally as they both headed outside. He wasn't even sure if he should take it personally that they wanted to look around together and not with him.

After taking a cursory glance around the living room and kitchen, close to the same setup as his cabin, he headed for the hallway. The first room had a bed and a dresser, but not much else. The room, like the front of the cabin, was a sty. Clothes were thrown around the floor, along with half the blankets from the bed. The slight stench lingering in the air told him the clothes hadn't been washed in quite a while.

Nothing significant was in the bathroom. A few toiletries and a garbage can overflowing with beer cans. Surprisingly, none were on the floor.

The last room on the right told him immediately it was the room Adam had been held in. Three deadbolt locks hung on the outside of the door. They wanted to make sure Adam couldn't get out.

Opening the door, he paused in the threshold. Nothing was in the room. Absolutely nothing like Adam described. Not even a blanket to sit on or keep warm. They had wanted him to suffer.

Why?

He was just a kid.

Taking a few steps inside, his fists clenched as he imagined every horrible second Adam endured in the tiny, dark room.

No wonder the dark frightened him now.

Newman couldn't see a single light bulb anywhere. Even if he wanted to attempt to flick a light switch, nothing would happen. They made sure he stayed hidden in the darkness.

There was a tiny window, about twelve by twelve inches, on the opposite side of the room. The window was shattered. Pieces of glass lay sprinkled all around the floor underneath the window.

Newman wasn't sure how it broke, because according to Adam, he pried open the window on his tippy toes and managed to escape without making a sound. Even though the window was high off the ground, Adam got the window open, hoisted himself up, and crawled out. Such strength and bravery. Adam never mentioned he broke the window. And based on the glass being inside the room, it stood to reason someone broke it from the outside. Why?

Walking closer, he saw dried blood on the windowsill and around the frame. Adam's blood, of course. He scratched and scraped himself pretty good trying to crawl out.

Looking at the window with his own eyes, he couldn't believe Adam even fit through it. He was kind of scrawny for his age, but he wasn't tiny.

Only pure survival got him out of this room. No food. No water. Barely a hole to escape from. Five nights trapped in this hellhole. It was a damn miracle Adam survived.

What a tough kid.

"Hey—"

Newman jerked back and started to laugh when Ben's head popped into view from outside.

A silly grin punctured Ben's face. "Sorry. Didn't mean to startle you. I guess this is where Adam crawled out from."

"Yeah. It definitely is. There's nothing in this room. Nothing."

Ben's expression fell into a frown. "We'll find the bastards. With all the junk around the cabin, we'll get some DNA. We'll identify them."

"If they're in the system," Newman replied, arching a brow.

"Oh, they're in the system. Douchecanoes like this are in the system."

Newman chuckled. "Douchecanoes?"

Ben cracked a smile. "One of Dee's new phrases. There's this new guy at work that keeps hitting on Rina," Ben's smile disappeared, "and she loves to call him that. To his face. I do love Dee for that."

More laughter filtered out. "Sounds like Dee. It's nice Rina has such a good friend like her."

Newman wished he could be as good of a friend. But he was nowhere near that level of kindness. He lied and even on occasion made fun of his friends. Something he had done to Sauer in the past. And why? Because he was jealous. No other good reason but that. *He* was a douchecanoe.

"It's very nice she does. Because otherwise I'd have to have a word with the guy, and well, I wouldn't be using actual words." The malice in Ben's eyes told Newman exactly what he'd do to the guy—beat the living shit out of him.

Everyone in his life was happy. Beautiful wives. Gorgeous kids. Ben and Zeke had both shown him pictures of their kids. Even Sauer had one on the way.

What did he have?

Shaking off the melancholy threatening to send him down the rabbit hole, he forced another laugh out. "You're a lucky man, Ben."

He hadn't meant to say it, but it slipped out. It was true. What was the point in lying? In pretending that he didn't notice?

Ben grinned. "I am lucky." His grin softened, concern flickering in his eyes. "You can be just as happy as us, Newman. Shit happened. It's in the past. But you can defi-nitely be as happy and lucky."

Did Ben honestly believe that?

Because he sure in the hell didn't.

He shrugged. "Maybe someday."

"Or soon." Ben winked, then nodded behind him.

"Come check this out." Then Ben disappeared from his view.

Soon? What did that mean?

Deciding to erase the conversation from his memory, he headed outside and met Zeke and Ben behind the cabin.

"It's hard to determine with all the footprints around the area how many people were here, but we're actually thinking three." Zeke pointed toward a crop of trees about twenty feet away. "There are snowmobile tracks. Three sets."

This mystery kept getting better and better.

"So three people were involved in kidnapping Adam." Newman shoved his hands inside his pockets, wishing he wouldn't have forgotten his gloves. "None of this makes sense. Two guys grab him and bring him here, starve him, make him sit in the dark, and left him to die. Who is this third guy? What was their endgame?"

"All good questions. None that Adam can answer. He only saw the one guy with the scar. He told you he heard some voices, but nothing distinct. As soon as we get DNA results back, and the sketch artist to complete a composite of the dude with the scar, then we'll have some answers." Ben sounded more hopeful than Newman felt.

Because that would all take time. A long time. In between all that waiting, Adam would be suffering. Afraid of the dark. Wondering if the men might come back.

Was Adam wondering about that?

Well, he was. His gut churned with unease this wasn't over. Whatever was going on.

Newman wanted answers now.

Zeke clapped him on the back and smiled. "We'll get those answers, Newman. In the meantime, you can only do one thing. Be there for Adam. The kid connected with you."

Oh, yeah. He still planned to check on them later tonight.

"You're right."

Zeke's smile brightened. "Of course I am. It's Ben who doesn't believe it."

"Ha! If you admit I'm smarter than you, I'll admit you're right ninety percent of the time," Ben quipped.

"One hundred percent of the time. And there's no way you're smarter than me," Zeke countered.

And back and forth they went. Newman could only smile because he had missed them. Missed this. The camaraderie. The working a case together. The companionship. Putting their minds together to solve a mystery.

They were leaving tomorrow morning. Their time was up.

"I'm going to miss you guys."

They both stopped and stared at him as if he had drool hanging from his lips.

Then a warm smile emerged on Ben's face. "It's not like you'll never see us again. We'll visit. You can visit. You still need to meet Corrine."

"I'd like that." He meant it. He might not get his old life back, but if he could have a small part of it, he'd take what he could get.

"Hey, we're still friends. Let's put the past behind us. Where it belongs," Zeke said, his stare intense, yet with kindness in the depths.

"I wish I could. You two make it sound so easy."

"It is," Ben said. "Even Captain Ganderson has no hard feelings. When we asked for some time off to help you out, he gave the A-okay right away. You're not an outsider, Newman. Even though you seem to have made yourself one. Nobody is perfect."

Yeah, he heard that a few times lately. Yet, he always had a deep desire to be perfect, even knowing it would be an impossible feat.

Which was why love and commitment wasn't something he'd ever achieve, because to make a relationship work, he had to be perfect.

As they finished looking around the area, Zeke and Ben wandering around inside the cabin, the last words from Ben festered in his mind. He joggled them back and forth, wondering if they were true.

Was he the only one who saw himself as an outsider? Because he figured the moment he lied to everyone was the moment he turned into an outsider.

Damn. Now he was going to miss his friends even more.

MEL LET the curtain fall back in place and walked away from the window. She was going to go insane looking out the window like a maniac every other second.

It was nothing.

It had to be nothing.

No one was driving by their house repeatedly watching them. Waiting for the perfect opportunity to strike. To take Adam once again.

Except it felt like it deep down in the pit of her stomach. That unease. That worry. That gut-churning sensation that someone was casing the place waiting for the perfect opportunity to force their way in.

Every time she looked out the window, moving the curtain in the slightest way, she never saw a thing. No car. No person. No new footprints in the snow. Nothing.

Every time she walked away, the anxiety, the apprehension, the strong gut instinct that someone was out there returned full force.

It had been a vicious cycle for the past hour. Checking outside, noting nothing, walking away, returning a few minutes later to double check again no one was outside.

If she was this agitated and concerned, she didn't even want to comprehend what Adam was feeling.

She had no clue. He wouldn't speak to her. Supper had passed about an hour ago. Although, in his defense, she had been nervous and anticipating...something. She had no idea what, but she sensed something was going to happen. To avoid the constant worry, she started cooking one of his favorite meals—lasagna—a bit earlier than normal. It was about six o'clock in the evening. He had to be hungry by now. She could heat up the lasagna for him.

Of course, he'd probably mumble go away, give her a signature glare that always told her she was annoying him, and then ignore her until she left the room. That's all they'd been doing today since they got home from the hospital. She'd go and check on him, he'd do his routine and she'd leave him alone feeling useless and so lost with what to do.

On a bright note, the plate of cookies she left in his room was all gone. He at least ate something.

Maybe he wasn't hungry.

Maybe lasagna was too heavy of a meal after how many days of starving and not eating or drinking anything.

She wanted to slap herself in the forehead for her idiocy.

Of course, he didn't want lasagna. That would upset his stomach.

Easily solved. She'd make him soup. Chicken noodle soup. Their mother's specialty. Although she didn't have the recipe handy, she was pretty confident she could make it by memory.

Before heading to the kitchen to start the new meal, one Adam would hopefully eat, she walked back to the curtain and ever so slowly inched it away.

The sun had already disappeared making it hard to see outside. But with the slight help from the moon and one street lamp not too far from the driveway, she had a good view of the front yard. Enough to feel somewhat confident nobody was out there.

Of course there wasn't. She was being silly. Utterly ridiculous.

Those men weren't coming back.

Except, why'd they take Adam in the first place? Why treat him as they had?

"Mel..."

Squealing, immediately feeling like an idiot for being startled, she let the curtain go and turned around. Adam stood near the opening of the living room with an odd expression. She couldn't quite decipher it. A cross between fear and concern?

"Hey, there you are. I was thinking I'd make some soup. How does soup sound?"

Forcing a smile, even though she knew she sounded like a complete imbecile, she waited for Adam to respond. Maybe even with a joyous tone he did want soup. Ha! Yeah, right. That was some serious wishful thinking on her part.

"It might sound strange," —he took a hurried step forward, determination in his features— "and I'm not acting like a baby or anything, but I swear someone is outside."

Her mouth dropped open. Literally fell open.

Maybe she wasn't so crazy after all if her brother was sensing it, too. Or did he actually see something?

"You don't believe me. I knew it. I should've—"

"Adam, wait!" She rushed forward a few steps. He

stopped his retreat. "Did you see something? Because..." She dropped all pretenses that everything was okay. No smile. No grin. Nothing appeared but the worry she'd been carrying around the entire afternoon that someone was outside watching the house. "Because I've had a weird feeling..."

What was she doing? She shouldn't be admitting this to her thirteen-year-old brother who just went through a traumatic experience. He wouldn't sleep well tonight, and he definitely wouldn't sleep well with her adding to his fear and agreeing with him someone was out there.

"I didn't see anything." He bit his bottom lip and turned his attention to the floor. "I can take it. You don't have to choose your words carefully or anything with me. Newman didn't. He didn't treat me like some useless, idiotic kid that got kidnapped."

Her heart broke into a million pieces at her brother's dejected, sad words. She didn't stop to think or worry about his reaction. With three long steps, she was standing in front of him and pulling him into a hug. A bone-crushing hug that said how much she loved him, how much she wanted to take his pain and fear away, how much she would protect him until she couldn't anymore.

"It was not your fault. Do you hear me? So you better stop thinking that right now."

"Mel, I can't breathe." A low chuckle muffled in between their bodies.

The fact he laughed made her want to press him even closer. Instead, since she *was* holding on to him pretty tightly, she loosened her grip but didn't fully let go. She kept a hold of him by the shoulders.

"You know I love you, right? I would do anything for you. If I could erase the last few days, take away your pain, beat the living shit out of every single person that hurt you, I would." She lightly squeezed his shoulders. "And I won't allow you to think you are responsible for the actions of those men."

He turned his gaze away. "Well, if I didn't act like a jerk and leave the house—"

"Stop. Please stop, Adam. It's not your fault. And I do believe you. I've had a weird feeling for the past few hours someone is outside."

He glanced back at her. "Really?"

Letting her hands drop and taking a step back, she nodded. "Yeah, and I've looked outside so many times I've lost count. I never see anything, though. I feel like I'm going crazy creating something that isn't really there."

A tiny grin formed. "That's..." Adam shrugged, his grin widening. "That's kind of how I've been feeling."

"Well, we both can't be crazy."

"Are you sure?" A teasing brow rose as he laughed a little.

"I'm positive." Tapping her chin, she matched his grin. "So, the question is what do we do about it? I'm not about to let anyone hurt you again."

"Oh, me either. I'm fighting back this time."

Her brother said it with such conviction and determination, she wanted to find a corner and bawl her eyes out. He should've never had to endure what he had.

But he was right.

They would fight back.

And she only knew one place where she felt safe enough to fight back.

Newman's cabin.

"Go pack a small bag. We're leaving."

Excitement and relief hit Adam's anxious-filled gaze. "Where are we going?"

She wasn't sure it was the best decision because she didn't want Adam to get used to relying on Newman, but it was the only place she felt safe.

"We're going to visit Newman. We could call and have him check everything out, but I prefer to ask him in person. What do you think?"

"Yeah, sure."

He said it nonchalantly like he didn't care either way, but the pleasure in his eyes told her exactly what he thought. He couldn't wait to leave.

Adam started to walk out of the room.

"And what sort of things did you and Newman talk about that you say he didn't treat you like a child? He didn't say anything inappropriate, did he?"

Adam looked like a deer in headlights for two seconds before putting on a stern face. "It was guy stuff, Mel. You're a girl, you wouldn't understand."

She chuckled, shaking her head as her brother walked out of the room to pack a bag.

Oh, her and Newman would be having a long chat tonight.

She couldn't wait to spar and get into a good argument with him.

Honestly, she couldn't wait to see his handsome, adoring face. If anything would calm her racing heart, the anxiety coursing through her veins, it'd be him.

17

Newman pulled into his driveway surprised to see Amelia's car. Nobody was in the car waiting for him, and nobody was lounging on the porch. Which meant they were inside his cabin. His cabin that he knew for a fact he locked before he left.

Chuckling as he exited his car, he wasn't shocked Amelia picked his lock, or that she even knew how to pick a lock.

His laughter died as he neared the door.

But why did she come to his cabin and break in?

He increased his pace and tried to whip open the door, but met with resistance. Well, at least she was smart enough to lock it.

Perhaps nothing terrible happened. She didn't call him telling him she was coming over to his place. That notion didn't calm down his racing heart or jittery nerves as he searched for the right key on his keyring. Unlocking the door, he swung it open, keeping his expression cool. He saw Adam chilling on his couch and Amelia digging in his cupboards.

"You're home," Amelia said with an upbeat smile.

Although, he heard the anxiety underneath the facade of happiness.

And her words. *You're home.* They nearly knocked him on his ass.

Because as he met her gaze, locking eyes with her, he wished they shared a home. He could get used to seeing her every day. Laughing with her. Joking around. Fighting about silly nonsense.

"Mel said it'd be okay if we came inside."

Newman jerked his attention away from Amelia's gorgeous, worried face and landed on Adam's even more agitated face. He looked ready to flee. Did Adam really think he was about to holler at him?

He produced a smile as he closed the door. "Of course, it's okay you came. I actually stopped by your place to check on you and saw you weren't home."

It had been a long day working alongside Ben and Zeke, meeting with the sketch artist and the guy from the hardware store. The sketch artist was taking a little longer than he anticipated, but it wasn't her fault. Their witness was having a hard time remembering distinctive features, so it was a slow process. Not to mention it took a few days to even find a decent sketch artist who could make the drive to the small town.

He figured it would be easier on Adam once the sketch artist was done. He'd show Adam and see how well the description matched instead of making Adam go through the terrifying process of describing the man. He didn't want to put more pressure on the kid. He was dealing with enough already. They couldn't do much else until the lab results came back from the evidence taken from the cabin. They could only hope some DNA matches came back with the names of suspects.

When he parted ways with Zeke and Ben, he thought it was the perfect time to check on Amelia and Adam, and he was dumbfounded when he found they weren't home. He didn't want to come off as overbearing, but he had planned to call her once he got home to find out where they went. This was even better they came here.

The question was why?

Amelia joined them in the living room. "I thought I'd make some soup."

He nodded, liking the idea very much. He was starving. "Sure."

But why were they here?

"Are you, like, waiting for me to leave the room or something to ask why we're here?" Adam muttered like a typical angsty teenager.

Newman arched a brow, giving the kid props for being so brave and bringing the problem out in the open. He *did* want to know why they were here. He just didn't want to have the conversation with Adam in the room, but hey, the kid was tough. And most likely, the reason they left had to do with him.

"No, buddy. You don't have to leave the room. You obviously missed me." Newman cracked a grin, hoping to ease some of the tension in Adam.

"Well, you are cool to talk to." Adam glanced around the room, a smile finally appearing. "But you have no TV. That's so lame."

Newman chuckled. Visiting his grandfather was always a nice break from reality. His grandfather had never owned a television since the day he purchased the cabin. Newman never bought one either when he moved in three months ago. He was lucky he got internet service for his phone and laptop.

"You get used to it. It's peaceful."

"Yeah, but what do you do?" Adam asked with the shock lacing his tone like he couldn't believe someone didn't own a TV.

"I like to work out," Newman said pointing to the punching bag in the corner. "I also read sometimes. My grandfather has a lot of great books here."

He also thought about his life and all the mistakes he made, even though he tried hard not to, but he didn't feel like sharing that part.

"He was also a fan of comic books. There are tons in the spare bedroom."

Adams face lit up with excitement. "I like comics."

"Perfect. You won't be too bored." Newman smiled, then turned to Amelia. "Is everything okay, or did you really miss me?"

Her eyes flashed with a small dose of desire at his teasing words before the fear slipped in. "We wanted to..."

"We thought someone was outside. But we didn't see anything. Mel thought you could check it out," Adam said when Amelia couldn't seem to finish her sentence.

He glanced back and forth between them before settling his attention on Amelia. "I was just there and I didn't see anything odd. I can go back and check more thoroughly if you want me to."

The relief was palpable in her eyes, her posture relaxing as if she were afraid he wouldn't do anything to help them. Of course he would. She should know that by now. He couldn't deny her anything. All she had to do was ask.

But perhaps she didn't quite know that yet.

That particular feeling was still new to him.

But right now, if she asked him to sleep with her again,

to simply lay down with her and comfort her, he wouldn't hesitate. He wouldn't deny her anything.

"That would be great. We'd both appreciate it. But we're most likely being silly," she said with a lackluster laugh.

"You're trusting your gut as you should. Don't ever ignore it. There's nothing silly about that." He meant it. Gut instinct had saved his ass many times.

Adam stood up. "Can I come with?"

"Absolutely not."

"Sure."

Amelia stared at him like he had horns sitting on the top of his head and suddenly wanted to gut him from his sternum straight to his nuts.

"I don't think Adam should go with you."

Well, if they thought someone was outside the house watching them, he didn't think leaving them alone, even in his cabin, was the best decision either. Adam would be safer with him. As would Amelia, but he didn't want to make it seem like she couldn't take care of herself. He had every faith in her that she could.

"He'll be safe with me, Amelia. I promise. You're more than welcome to come with, too."

"Fine. We'll all go," she snapped. But he saw the fear still lingering in her eyes.

She might think she was putting on a brave front, like she was only coming with because Adam was, but he saw the fright in her golden hazel eyes.

And damn it, he didn't like seeing it.

"Well, let's go. Now that you mentioned soup, I'm starving." He smiled extra wide to loosen the tension in the room. For Adam, it worked. Amelia still looked like she wanted to slice him into tiny little pieces.

They grabbed their jackets and all piled into his car. It

didn't take long to reach their house. When he pulled into the driveway, he turned the car off and twisted in his seat so he could see both of them as he spoke.

"We'll check the perimeter first, then inside."

"All of us?" Amelia asked, her voice kind of squeaking, betraying her bravado.

"Well, I can't protect you if I walk off and you're chilling in the car." Newman didn't bother to add he was carrying a gun in case they did come across the men who hurt Adam.

If they thought someone had been outside, it was highly probable. The entire case was odd. It mirrored the old cases of the missing boys from seven years ago, yet it didn't. They never once thought multiple suspects were involved in those cases. Right now, they figured at least three perps were involved in kidnapping Adam. The three men might not be finished with him. Maybe they even wanted to kill him so he couldn't identify them, or, at least, the one guy with the scar.

"These are good things to know, Mel. We should know how to check the perimeter of the house," Adam piped in, his voice filled with excitement.

Amelia didn't look convinced but nodded.

They all exited the car and started walking around the house, taking care to watch where they stepped and keeping their eye out for anything. There wasn't much involved checking the perimeter besides looking for anything amiss. Newman spoke quietly as they walked around looking for signs of anything, like footprints or scrapes or scratches around the windowsill. With snow on the ground, it was easy to determine the only footprints found were the ones they were creating.

After walking completely around the house, determining no one had ventured close to the property, they headed inside. Newman walked around each room, double checking every window was securely locked.

Everything looked good.

Nobody appeared to have approached the house.

Except they both thought someone had been outside. Maybe watching the house from a car. That was plausible.

They were scared. He couldn't stand it. He had to make everything better for them.

"Well, I guess we were being silly, then," Amelia said with a lightness in her tone, although the agitation was mingled in each word. He could also tell she was frightened by the way she hugged herself, trying to hide the tremors in her body.

"You were being cautious. There's nothing wrong with that. Why don't you guys spend the night at my place? I don't mind."

Except it'd be another uncomfortable night on the couch, aching to join Amelia in the bed. Which he obviously couldn't do with Adam in the cabin, especially since those two would have to share his bed. But if they were still wary to stay in this house alone, he didn't mind offering peace of mind for the night.

But what about tomorrow? And the day after? And the day after that?

"Cool. Let me grab my games. I'm not sure I can survive without a TV." Adam left the room.

"You don't have to do this, Newman. I think I'm…having Adam back is great, but I can't get out of my head what he went through. I'm probably—"

Her words were cut off as he pulled her into his arms, embracing her tightly. He couldn't have stopped himself if he tried. Hearing her anguish, the pain in her voice gutted him straight to the core. This vibrant, strong woman sounded so broken and it killed him. Because the Amelia he knew, the one who knocked on his door and refused to leave until he gave in and helped her, wasn't broken. She was tough and strong and full of grit. He refused to let her think, or even feel, she was losing her mind or that her worries were silly. Because they weren't.

"I never do anything I don't want to do. We haven't known each other that long, Amelia, but..." The words got stuck in his throat. Was this the best time to be telling her she meant something to him? Something more than friends?

Absolutely not.

He wasn't worthy of her anyway, not with his past, lying and cheating. She deserved a better man than he would ever be.

She lifted her head from his chest, wiping a tear away. "But?"

"But you and Adam are my friends and if you don't feel safe here, you're more than welcome to stay with me." That was the only answer he could give her. He couldn't confess how much she meant to him. "This case is odd, too. I can't be sure what these three guys plan to do. It's better to be safe than sorry."

"Three men?"

Maybe he shouldn't have confessed that part. But he didn't want to lie to her. Or Adam. If he asked, Newman would tell him the truth.

"We found evidence at the cabin that three men were likely involved."

"You found it?" she asked, amazed. Then her eyes turned into little slits. "It seems me and you need to have a conversation later when Adam can't hear."

"About what?" Oh, boy, but he loved the fire in her eyes.

The way she got all irritated with him. It shouldn't turn him on, but it did.

"About you not updating me about the case, and the things you talked about with Adam."

He had meant to update her about the case when he visited her earlier, and the things he and Adam talked about...well, he promised Adam he wouldn't tell her.

Damn. Not a conversation he wanted to have.

"Got my game. Are you two—"

Newman abruptly dropped his arms from around Amelia and they jumped apart like a hot iron torched their skin. Newman met Adam's puzzled expression. Like he was confused why Newman had been holding Amelia in his arms.

That wasn't a conversation he wanted to have either.

"Do you two need more time together alone?" Adam asked, a sly smile inching slowly on his face.

Did they? Of course they did.

But they couldn't.

Newman wouldn't go there.

Except if Amelia asked, he wouldn't be able to resist the temptation any longer.

Good thing Adam would be in the cabin with them.

A very good thing.

18

MEL CAREFULLY GRABBED the handheld gaming device that Adam had clutched in his hand, then pulled the covers up over him. He looked so peaceful sleeping. Like a thirteen-year-old boy with no worries in the world should. What a lie.

She had no idea where to even begin to help him heal.

Setting the device on the nightstand, she walked out quietly and closed the door behind her. She wasn't quite ready for bed herself because she and Newman had to talk. Especially since Adam interrupted their conversation back at her house.

Newman was sitting on the couch when she walked back into the living room. Just sitting. Staring at the wall. He looked very deep in thought where she didn't want to disturb him.

Too bad they couldn't avoid this conversation any longer. She kept her turmoil in the entire night as she cooked soup, ate it with a happy smile on her face. She even kept the smile as they played a few board games.

It felt nice forgetting about their worries and problems for a few hours. Acting like a family.

But they weren't a family. And Newman had no right to say whatever he wanted to Adam.

She plopped down on the couch right next to him. Her thigh touched his. It was a temptation she hadn't fully considered before she sat down. Having a serious conversation suddenly didn't sound so appealing.

Her body went on high alert, attuned to his. And by a mere touch.

It was amazing how much she wanted this man like she was dying for her next meal after starving for years. Craved him. This aggravating, arrogant, yet sweet, caring man.

He took his time looking away from the wall to meet her gaze. "How's Adam?"

"He fell asleep playing his game. Hopefully, he has a good night's sleep. He needs it."

"I hope so, too. I know I won't." He chuckled, as he patted the couch on his free side. "This isn't the most comfortable bed."

She was very aware of him. Too aware. She ached to grab his hands or even lay a hand on his thigh.

But no. She wanted to have a serious conversation. Where to start?

"Thank you for letting us spend the night. We should be able to go home tomorrow."

"Will you?"

This was a perfect time as any to say what she wanted to say.

"We can't rely on you, Newman."

His entire face shut down. The awareness she felt, that she swore she saw in his eyes as well, disappeared. He looked away from her, the disgust coated in his tone. "Yeah, you shouldn't. I'm nothing but a lying, cheating bastard."

Oh, dear. She hadn't meant for it to sound like that. She laid a hand on his thigh, unable to resist.

"That's not—"

"Stop. Don't touch me, Amelia."

The venom in his tone had her snatching her hand away without hesitation.

"You took my words the wrong way. I didn't mean it like that."

He snapped his head in her direction. "Oh, really. Then how did you mean it?"

"Adam looks up to you. He—"

"Yeah, sorry about that. I know I'm not the best role model. No need to rub it in."

"Stop interrupting me and putting words into my mouth. I didn't mean it like that either." She was so very tempted to slap some sense into him.

"Oh, do go on. I can't wait to hear what else you have to say."

She sighed, then powered on. "How long do you intend to stay here?"

He looked at her, puzzled and surprised she was changing the subject. Which she wasn't. "I don't know. I haven't thought about it."

"Well, I do. I have. I see a good man, an honorable one. Because I can't see you as anything else, not when you've been by my side this entire time. I don't care what anyone else thinks about that. I don't even care what you think about that." She poked him hard in the chest. "But you seem to want to push us away. Push me away. You don't want anything to do with me, so I can't have Adam getting close to you and then suddenly you're not there. He worships you. You're his savior. And when you leave, I'm the one here picking up the pieces. So, that's what I mean by I can't rely on you. I don't—"

Her voice broke. She paused to collect herself. "I don't know what to do. Adam hates me. He won't talk to me. He wants me to treat him like an adult like you apparently have. And I want to be so pissed at you for speaking to him like he's not a child. Because he is. And on the other hand, I want to hug you and say thank you for making him feel better. I'm so confused and pissed and...and..."

"Scared," Newman finished as his hand reached up and cupped her cheek.

The warmth from his hand, the comfort, was almost her undoing. She wanted to sink into his embrace and forget about everything. Lose herself inside him.

But she couldn't. She wouldn't. She steeled her spine and refused to move an inch. She didn't even smile at his soft, tender touch. Or that he knew her so well and finished her sentence with the one word she was too frightened to utter.

Yes, she was scared as hell.

"What was said between me and Adam was..." He groaned in pain. "I don't want to lie to you. I promised myself I wouldn't lie anymore. But I also promised Adam I wouldn't tell you anything. Trust me when I say I didn't say anything terrible. Yeah, I treated him like an adult. Maybe I shouldn't have, but I wasn't thinking. It's my specialty."

He still hadn't removed his hand from her cheek, his thumb moving slow and steady, rubbing, caressing, and enticing her. She was having a hard time concentrating.

"You told me not to touch you. I think you need to adhere to that rule as well. Don't touch me." The words left her mouth in a whisper because she didn't *want* him to let go. She didn't want to voice it at all.

"Damn. I did lie to you." His gaze turned intense, filled with desire. "I do want you to touch me. So much. Which is why I told you not to touch me. I can't...I'm not sure I can control myself."

His hand slipped away.

"What's going on here, Newman? You're confusing me left and right. You either want me or you don't. Adam's safe. You found him like you promised. We can have sex now." Well, not right now. But they could when Adam wasn't around. And, oh how she wanted that so much like she wanted to take her next breath.

She wouldn't throw subtle hints around either. She needed him to understand what she wanted. And she wanted him deep inside her for days. Talk about horny and needing some serious hot, sweaty sex.

A muscle twitched in his cheek, his jaw clenching. "I want you, Amelia. I've wanted you since you knocked on my door. You're a woman, so why wouldn't I?"

She wanted to slap him hard across the face, but she didn't believe in violence unless it was in self-defense. She knew why he was acting this way, saying the things he was. A defense mechanism. She wasn't the only one scared right now. He was scared, too. Of letting anyone close to him.

"Is that all I am to you, Newman? A warm body. Another woman to pass through your life."

"Yep." He immediately looked away, betraying how much that was a lie.

And he claimed he wouldn't lie to her.

He was lying right now.

"Where did you learn how to pick a lock?"

Oh, he wanted to change the subject, did he?

"I taught myself. My father loved to lock me in my room as punishment. I didn't like being caged in like an animal."

His eyes whipped to hers. "You speak so freely about your past."

She shrugged. "And I always will. That's your problem, Newman. You don't know how to leave the past in the past. My past doesn't define me. It might've shaped me into the person I am today, but it's not who I am. I am Amelia. I am strong. I am a survivor. But what I am not is a victim. My father did not win, nor break me. Why should I hide my past? I embrace it. It makes me stronger. Maybe you should try it."

They stared at each other for the longest time before he finally looked away.

The silence grew.

The tension thickened.

Then he spoke.

"Adam doesn't hate you. He loves you. But he doesn't always express it in the correct way."

She nodded, although he still wasn't looking at her. She figured there was some truth in those words. It didn't feel like Adam cared or respected her when he constantly pushed her away.

"Amelia, did you hear me?" Newman finally turned to her.

"I did. I don't know what to say."

"Give him time. And maybe stay here a few days."

This time she looked away. "I don't think that's a good idea. Coming over here tonight...wasn't a good idea."

His warm hand touched her cheek again, forcing her to look at him. "I don't trust those men. Give me a few days to find them."

"You're touching me again."

His eyes lowered to her mouth, his thumb gently caressing her cheek. "I can't help myself. Not when you say being with me is a bad idea. And damn it, it is. I just wished it wasn't true."

She decided to test him. His restraint. His true desire for her. She smoothed her hands onto his thighs. A shiver rippled throughout his body.

"Why do you think so badly about yourself?"

"Because everything said about me is true. I'm not a good man. Not like you keep saying I am."

She leaned closer, unable to resist the temptation, especially when he still cupped her cheek.

"Is that why you push me away? Is that why you lie to me? And yourself?"

"I haven't been lying to you."

"Admit it. You want me. Not because I'm just another woman. I mean something to you. I want to know from your lips how much."

His jaw clenched. His eyes flashed with maddening rage. She couldn't determine if that was with her or at himself.

"This is a bad idea, Amelia."

She leaned even closer. So did he. "What is?"

His lips were inches from hers. "Falling for you. I'm not the man you deserve."

Then his lips were on hers, caressing, touching, devouring her as if he would never get to kiss her again in his life.

Oh, boy. She wanted more kisses. Definitely way more kisses. Everywhere on her body. She knew if she asked, even begged, he'd kiss her wherever she wanted.

His hand fell away from her cheek and wrapped around her waist. He pulled her onto his lap, enveloping her in his embrace so she couldn't escape.

There wasn't anywhere else she'd rather be but in his arms.

His cock was pressed intimately in the perfect spot. She couldn't resist rubbing against it as the kiss deepened. His arms tightened, meeting her, thrusting his hips up.

All they needed right now was to lose their clothes and it would be perfect. She could melt into him, become as one, and forget everything that happened over the past week. She could make him see, make him feel how right they were together.

His kisses were tender even as they moved in a frenzy. Her pushing roughly into him and him meeting each touch with a thrust of his hips.

In this moment, this beautiful chaotic moment, she knew. She loved him. Every single little thing about him. His arrogance—thinking he knew what was best for them. His thoughtfulness—making sure they felt safe for the night. His tenderness—always touching her with sweet gentleness even when he was upset. His determination—never giving up when everyone else had.

Yes, she loved Newman.

She loved him enough to make him see the man he was, not who he thought he was based on his previous actions.

The kiss didn't stop, not even for a moment. His hands clutched her back with a strength that said he never wanted to let go. His hips kept thrusting upward, grinding against her, building her up past the point of no return. They might not be naked, but she was so close to the best orgasm of her life. She could feel it.

His hands slid up her back, colliding in her hair, grabbing a handful. He didn't quite pull, but he squeezed as his movements became faster. She met him pace for pace.

Then, like seeing a beautiful sunrise on a quiet morning on a deserted beach, she moaned and bit his lip as exquisite bliss hit her.

His hands tightened in her hair, his hips still grinding against her hot core. Then a low, sexy groan left his lips, his body tensing.

A trail of kisses made a path from her lips to her neck, his hot breath fanning across her heated skin. Their heavy breathing was the only sounds that filled the room.

Her body felt wonderful and tingly and so inflated with bliss she didn't know what to say or how to say it. She knew professing her love would be the wrong thing to do so she waited for him to speak first.

Another soft kiss touched her neck.

"I feel like I'm back in high school," Newman whispered, chuckling, as another sweet kiss touched her neck.

"Considering I didn't do anything like this in high school, I can't compare. But I thoroughly enjoyed it."

His hands slowly disengaged from her tangled hair, smoothing out the strands before he ran his soft, tender fingers down her back. "We shouldn't have done that. That was a mistake."

And there it was.

The self-destructive part of him she hated with a passion. Instead of embracing the moment, enjoying the intensity and passion they just shared, he had to say something that would push her away.

Well, fine. If he wanted to act that way, she'd play her part.

"You're right. We shouldn't have. So glad a stitch of clothing never came off. I'd hate to know what you'd say if we were naked right now. Probably that I have itchy, dry skin and one of the worst women you've ever slept with."

She scrambled off his lap before he could stop her. He looked at her, yet, she couldn't determine what he was thinking.

"Maybe this isn't worth it."

Then she walked out of the room, regretting her words the moment she said them.

19

AFTER REFILLING HIS MUG, he took a seat at the table, contemplating his next move.

Last night had been a disaster.

Somewhat.

Having Amelia in his arms had been...perfect. So perfect it was wrong. Which was why he opened his dumb mouth and ruined the moment, turning the nice night into a complete disaster.

Newman took a sip of coffee, burning his tongue a little.

He deserved the pain. No matter how he felt or the turmoil going on in his life, he should've never let her think what happened between them was a mistake.

It *was* a mistake. But telling her was a dick move.

And yet, he promised himself he wouldn't keep lying.

Of course, she was right. He was still lying. Constantly. He couldn't even be straight with her and tell her what she meant to him.

Definitely more than friends.

Definitely more than a woman to sleep with.

Girlfriend material?

He couldn't quite define what she meant to him, but she held a spot in his heart and that was enough for him. Enough for him to lie and pretend she meant nothing. Because nothing good would come from letting her completely in. He'd screw up and hurt her down the road. Something he had done to every person in his life. Why would she be any different?

"You look like shit."

Newman looked up to see Adam standing by the table, eyeing him funny.

"Language. We talked about this."

Adam glanced at the floor, a hint of red running up his neck and across his cheeks.

He hadn't meant to make the kid nervous, but he also didn't want him swearing. Amelia was right about quite a few things last night. Adam was only a kid. As much as he wanted to treat him like an adult, he couldn't forget at the end of the day he was a kid.

"There's cereal in the pantry. Or I can make you something. Eggs and toast?" He nodded toward the pantry, hoping to ease the sudden tension and embarrassment flooding his cheeks.

Adam's eyes gradually met his. "Cereal's cool."

Newman nodded again toward the pantry since he didn't see him do it the first time. He sat quietly while Adam grabbed a box of cereal, a bowl and spoon after he pointed where to grab it, and some milk from the fridge. Then he sat at the table across from him.

He still didn't say anything while Adam munched away, slurping the milk as he went. It didn't stop him from staring and observing. Adam looked better than the day before, which was a miracle, considering he didn't even sleep in his own bed. He actually looked like he got a good night's sleep.

How well did Amelia sleep?

He slept like shit. Which was why he looked like shit, as Adam so eloquently pointed out.

All night he tossed and turned on the uncomfortable, lumpy couch, thinking, turning the words he said to Amelia over and over in his head, aching for her sweet, delicate body next to his.

He didn't get much sleep with her on his mind all night.

It would only get worse the longer she was around.

Yet, he couldn't kick them out. No matter what happened between them, he had to make her see it was safer for them to stay with him while he, or the police, found these bastards.

His best offense at the moment would be to get Adam on his side.

"Sleep well?"

Adam looked up from his bowl, the spoon dangling in the air not far from his mouth. "Yeah. Mel likes to hog the bed, but it wasn't bad."

A tiny grin appeared. She hogged the bed, did she? He wouldn't mind that. More opportunities to put his hands on her. Roam around and enjoy her sweet, lithe body. And his hands had a mind of their own. They wouldn't push her back to her side. Oh no, they would entice her to the brinks of pleasure.

Yeah, he wouldn't mind finding out how much of a bed hog she was.

"You like Mel."

His grin disappeared in a flash.

Leave it to the kid to put him on the spot. He could play it off as if he had no idea what he was talking about, even though Adam didn't pose it as a question. He stated it as a fact.

"I like you, too."

Adam rolled his eyes as he dropped his spoon into the bowl, making a loud clanging sound.

"You like her. I'm thirteen, not five."

Newman leaned forward, resting his elbows on the table. It wasn't his fault he talked to Adam as an adult. It came easily. He couldn't find the strength to lie to the kid.

"I like her a little."

Adam chuckled, his eyebrow rising, not convinced.

"Okay. A little more than a little."

"Is that like a riddle? Are you trying to confuse me?" Adam laughed. "I'm cool with it."

Damn it. Maybe Amelia was right about too damn much last night. The kid just gave him an opening. He could tell him right now he shouldn't rely on him for anything because he wasn't sure how long he'd be sticking around.

But the words wouldn't come.

He couldn't say why exactly Adam trusted him so much so quickly. He couldn't say why they clicked so well and Adam felt comfortable around him, and vice versa.

But he couldn't hurt him. He couldn't deflate his sense of safety. If he said one little word about not being around in the near future, Adam might react in a way he wouldn't be able to fix. And he refused to fail now. Adam was safe and sound back at home, but this case wasn't officially closed until the suspects were in custody.

Well, he could give the kid a bit of the truth. He didn't want to completely string him along.

"I'm always here for you, Adam. I want you to know that." He grimaced, leaning back in his chair. "But don't count on me and your sister getting together."

"She's playing hard to get," Adam said with a silly smile as if he knew everything about girls.

But Adam didn't know anything, especially about the thing between him and Amelia. Because, nope. She wasn't playing hard to get. If anything, he was. But not really. He couldn't let her in because nothing good would come from it. He was doing the right thing by backing off and keeping her at a distance.

A brief flash of her exquisite moan as she came last night penetrated his mind and he wondered if he wasn't the biggest idiot on the planet.

"We're just friends, Adam."

His smile vanished. "But you like her."

Considering he didn't admit that with a confident yes, he liked her, he thought about ignoring it once again.

"It doesn't matter."

Adam shook his head. "I don't understand." He slapped his hand on the table. "And don't give me the I'm only thirteen shit."

Newman leveled a stern gaze in his direction for the swear word. If nothing else, he'd rein in that bad behavior for Amelia before he...well, he hadn't decided if he was leaving yet, but yeah, he'd fix that issue for her. If it was an issue. He didn't know since they never had the conversation, but he figured if Adam talked to him like that, then he did it with his sister as well. It wasn't acceptable. As much as she had done for him, she deserved his respect.

"Did you swear in front of your father?"

Adam's face paled like he had seen a ghost. Newman instantly felt like the world's biggest jackass. Nothing new there. He had already asked the dumb question when he first found him. He knew the answer.

And then it hit him. Like a brutal punch to the gut, knocking the wind right out of him.

"I'm sorry, Adam. Feel free to swear whenever you want."

Adam jerked in his seat as if he had been electrocuted, a form of torture to spill the truth from his lips. "Is this some kind of mind trick?"

Newman had the grace to wince, ashamed he didn't see it earlier. But in his defense, he'd never dealt with a kid this young with such a heartbreaking past.

"You were never allowed to swear in front of your father. Ever. Or do normal things a kid your age should be able to do. I don't need the details. I can figure it out on my own it wasn't pretty." Newman shrugged, communicating it was no big deal he swore anymore. "You now have the freedom you didn't have before. I get it. I won't tell you not to swear anymore."

Adam's shoulders slumped like he was just defeated in the last round with a rough uppercut to the jaw. "Mel always looks at me with disappointment when I do it, but she never says a word."

"Because she understands. I'm sorry I didn't see it right away."

"I don't mean to act like a brat. I..."

"Can't help it." Newman nodded as he finished the sentence with how he felt about his own life and his actions. He didn't want to act the way he did half the time, but he couldn't seem to help himself. It was like watching himself in a movie, in slow motion, shouting at the screen to stop, don't do it, make a better decision, and nothing. Because it was a movie and you couldn't do anything to change a movie. It just kept playing the same scenario over and over.

Adam looked up and met his gaze. They sat there staring

at each other, communicating with their eyes they understood what the other was going through.

Maybe that's why he couldn't seem to treat Adam like a kid. Because he didn't act like one. He'd been through so much in his short life, he was damn near close to being an adult.

"Mel jumped in the shower before I came in here."

Okay. That was a swift conversation change.

Newman wasn't going to argue. It was a heavy conversation to have with him.

"Do you think she'd like some eggs and—"

"She said we were going home today. That we didn't need to stay here any longer."

His heart took a nosedive, splintering into a tiny million pieces. Why? He shouldn't be surprised. He purposely shoved her away last night after a breathtaking moment between them, and damn, they hadn't even lost a shred of clothing.

Who was he kidding?

His heart hit rock bottom last night when she said he wasn't worth it. It shouldn't have astounded him to hear it from her sweet red lips. Because he'd been trying to tell her that from the beginning. But it hurt, nonetheless, hearing her actually voice it.

Now she was leaving. She was done. She wasn't even going to give him a chance to change her mind.

"She knows best, buddy."

"I don't want to leave. I don't feel safe at home."

He didn't think it was the best idea either, even though he just agreed with her decision.

He started to open his mouth in reply when Adam shocked the hell out of him.

"I don't feel safe here either."

He could only stare. How could he not feel safe? He would never let anyone hurt him or Amelia.

A shiver rippled throughout Adam's body, his skin turning a pasty white. "I don't feel safe in this town."

Now that, he could understand.

But how did he fix that particular problem when he had no idea where to begin to look for those men?

20

LEANING QUIETLY against the kitchen counter, he resisted the temptation to stop Amelia's pacing by crossing his arms and pretending her agitated movements didn't bother him.

"I don't know why I agreed to this. This is ridiculous."

Newman started to open his mouth to reassure her, but no words came forth. It was an odd decision, yes. He wouldn't deny it. But how did he explain it was the best decision for Adam?

Two hours ago, as they were finishing up the heavy conversation for a thirteen-year-old, Ben and Zeke knocked on the door to say good-bye. They were leaving town.

One minute they were chitchatting, trying hard to keep it light for Adam's sake, and in the next, he was asking Ben if Adam could join him and Rina for a few days.

It just popped out. Ben had mentioned his niece and nephew would be staying with them while his sister and brother-in-law went on a cruise. Newman knew his nephew was around Adam's age and it sounded like a great idea.

Adam had said he didn't feel safe in town. He knew Amelia would argue about staying with him, and he didn't feel comfortable with them being alone without his protection. Problem solved all around. If Adam wasn't in town, then he wouldn't feel frightened, and maybe being away from this town would help him.

Surprisingly, Adam had jumped at the idea, immediately agreeing. Ben also hadn't hesitated at the idea, offering his home with open arms. Which didn't surprise Newman. Ben was a friendly guy. Anyone could always count on him to help out.

Amelia, when she joined them after her shower, had not been as easy to convince. But Adam eventually persuaded her, most likely from the sour look on his face when she repeatedly said she wasn't sure it was the best idea.

Then he brought the hammer down on her by saying, "I don't want you to come with. You can totally stay here. This town sucks."

Before he could interject and give Adam a piece of his mind for speaking to her in such a nasty tone, Amelia finally said yes.

After that, they left his cabin and headed to Amelia's so Adam could pack more clothes than what he brought to his place. Ben and Zeke hung out in the living room while he followed Amelia to the kitchen. But when he saw her pacing back and forth, the angry, hurt look on her face, he didn't know what to say.

Adam's words wounded her. He thought about saying something to the kid but decided against it. He'd already said plenty concerning Amelia. When Adam was ready to tell his sister he was frightened and scared and didn't know how to properly express his feelings, he'd tell her. He couldn't keep badgering the kid about it.

He just wished he had the right words to make Amelia feel better. For her to understand that Adam didn't hate her or blame her for anything. Because he could see it in her expression, in her stooped posture, she thought Adam blamed her for a lot of things.

Back and forth she paced the kitchen. Back and forth he watched her anxious energy.

When she came back his way for what seemed like the twentieth time, he stood up straight and grabbed her arm, stalling her movements.

"This might be what he needs. Some space away—"

"Yeah, from me. I got that loud and clear." She jerked her arm away. "Seems like a lot of people need space from me."

Oh, that hurt. But nothing he didn't deserve. He pushed her away on purpose. What did he expect?

"I was going to say some space away from this town. He definitely needs you, but this town right now is the enemy. He's frightened. That's all."

"He hates me."

He was so tempted to pull her into his arms to comfort her, especially with the forlorn look on her face. But he didn't move an inch because she already pulled away once. The pain in his heart would increase tenfold if she did it again.

But didn't he deserve the pain for acting like an asshole?

"He's hurting. He's acting out. He doesn't hate you."

Her eyes blazed with fury, so strong and intense, like she wanted to burn a hole right through his forehead. "You're his new best friend. He doesn't treat you the way he's been treating me."

A soft knock interrupted the thick tension building between them. Newman looked away from Amelia to see Ben standing near the kitchen entryway with a bashful expression.

"I don't mean to interrupt. Adam's packed and ready to go." Ben smiled at Amelia. "You're more than welcome to come with."

"Oh, my brother doesn't want me to come with. It's fine, as long as it's okay with you and your wife. I can come down and pick him up in a few days."

"He's more than welcome to stay. My nephew Nicholas is fourteen. They should get along great. It'll be good for him."

"So Newman said."

He wanted to laugh at the way she said it so begrudgingly as if it pained her to admit he might actually be right.

"I'm not sure he'll get along with your nephew. He hasn't exactly been friendly with anyone here."

Ben nodded, understanding why. Amelia wasn't shy about her past. Everyone knew what Adam went through. Surviving a worthless father.

"If you don't want him to come with, it's okay. He's been through a lot. Maybe this isn't the right thing for him."

Wait, what? Why was Ben backtracking? Newman wanted to spout nasty words at him for confusing her. Except, when he glanced at Amelia, he didn't see confusion written all over her face. He saw what appeared to be acceptance.

"No, you are right. This will be good for him. I hope your nephew has thick skin, though," Amelia said with a chuckle that sounded forced.

Ben grinned. "Oh, he does. The men are completely outnumbered in my family. Way too many females."

Amelia laughed some more, this time more genuine. "Well, you have my number. I'll call to check on him, but call me if you need me. Please keep an eye on his ankle and make sure he doesn't walk too much on it."

"Will do." Ben met his gaze. "Don't be a stranger, Newman. Let's keep in touch."

Newman walked across the kitchen and shook hands with him, then leaned in when Ben didn't give him a choice as he gave him a hug. "I will. Thanks for all the help."

"Anytime."

They walked to the living room where Newman said good-bye to Zeke—a decent good-bye like he shared with Ben in the kitchen. Zeke had seemed to shed his attitude towards him. When he left three months ago, the annoyance and wariness had been plain as day in Zeke's eyes every time they shared a look. Now, it felt like old times before everything went to shit.

He also pulled Adam in for a short side hug and whispered, "Don't hesitate to call if you need me. Or your sister."

At the mention of Amelia, Adam immediately shielded his gaze. Oh, yeah. The kid knew he was acting like a jerk, but as Adam had explained earlier, he didn't know how to stop it. He couldn't fault the kid when he had the same lack of control in his own life.

Adam barely muttered a good-bye to Amelia, and before long, they were all out the door and gone. Only he and Amelia stood in the quiet house, the tension back with a vengeance.

Then she spoke.

"What are you doing the rest of the day?"

Whoa! Was she already forgetting how he treated her last night? The devastating words she said to him as she walked away?

Was she suggesting they have sex right now?

"Because if you're searching for the bastards that hurt Adam, I'm coming with."

Or not.

So sex wasn't on her mind. Only on his.

But he couldn't help himself. Every time he gazed into her gorgeous hazel eyes, saw her bright-red lips made for kissing, her vibrant pink hair that made him smile, he wanted her. It didn't take much but one look.

"Newman, ignoring me will not deter me."

Oh, he knew that.

"It was my plan for the day. But honestly," he said with a shrug, "I have no idea where to start. Without any evidence or DNA to lead the way, there's no place to start."

"You say Adam doesn't feel safe here. Well, you better figure out where to start because he's coming back home and I need him to feel safe."

And he needed her more than words could express. Even if they could never be together—correction—would never be together, he'd do everything in his power to make her happy.

If making sure her brother came back free from fear, then that's what he'd do.

Not a lot of weight on his shoulders at all. Just the whole entire world.

"I got this. You can trust me."

Her answer was silence.

He wasn't surprised by that either. Nobody trusted him. Why would she?

Newman's first stop had been the police station. That wasn't the first place Mel would've chosen to go, but she wasn't the expert, so she didn't argue.

The man wasn't easy to argue with either. It was like a damn tug-of-war. She was starting to get exhausted from all the arguing. And yet, she enjoyed it. Because when she argued with people, she always won. With Newman, it was a fight to the death to win an argument. It was fun. That wasn't something she had a lot in her life. She wanted to soak up a bit of fun when she could.

Not to mention, it might get her mind off Adam and the way he treated her. Newman said Adam needed her. She wasn't sure about that. He sure didn't act like it.

"How are you doing, Ms. Benedict?"

Mel jumped, not enough to embarrass herself that she had been lost in thought, but enough to be noticeable to the officer standing before her. She couldn't help but offer a smile in return to the polite one on his face, but for the life of her, she couldn't remember his name.

"I'm fine. Thanks for asking."

That sounded stupid the second she said it, but she didn't know what else to say. Newman had left her in the lobby while he went to have a chat with Chief Dodson, the prick. She was more than happy to stay in the lobby. Every time they shared a look, his slimy, judgmental gaze unnerved her to the point she felt the need to take a shower and wash off the disgusting feeling.

"Good. I know what happened hasn't been easy to deal with. I can't imagine what your brother is going through. How is he doing?"

Oh, boy. Not a question she wanted to answer, but the officer's question sounded so sincere. Not at all like he was mocking her or asking out of pity.

"He decided to visit a friend for a few days. I think getting some space from this town and away from the reminder of what happened is the best thing for him."

Wow. It was like a rapid slap to the face. One of the many things her father had delivered to her growing up. The memories swarmed her senses, so surreal she could feel the sting on her cheek.

Newman had been right. As soon as those words fell from her lips, she knew it had been the best thing for her brother. So caught up in her own hurt feelings at the treatment from him, she didn't even stop to consider how he felt.

"That's good to hear. It'll take time. My nephew, my sister's son, he was playing around in the quarry with his friends. He jumped off in the same spot he did a million times before and just that one time he hit the wrong spot in the water. He hit his head on some rocks and he...well, it's been a long road to recovery. He hasn't been the same since. But every day gets better and he gets stronger. It takes time."

How unfortunate for her because she wasn't a very patient person. But—whatever this nice officer's name was —he was absolutely right. She had to give Adam time. Eventually, he'd let her in. Let her comfort him. Console him. Let her be a big sister in some sort of way. That's all she asked. That's all she wanted.

"I'm so sorry to hear that he was hurt. I appreciate your kind words. You're right."

The officer laid a gentle hand on her arm as he smiled, lighting up his features. Bright smile. Kind blue eyes. Short, brown wavy hair that looked made for running hands through. Not that she wanted to.

"Let me know if you ever need anything. We're a small town, so we look out for each other."

She wasn't sure she'd completely agree with that, but he was kind, thoughtful, and made a point to talk to her when everyone else in the precinct ignored her as she waited by herself in the lobby.

Did everyone else share his opinion? Did they all look out for each other? Because while people were friendly enough, she hadn't seen anyone step out of their own little bubble to make her feel more welcome in town. Sure, they liked to gossip and spread news like wildfire, but they didn't treat her like one of them. She wasn't privy to every little whisper of gossip. Although, in their defense, Adam hadn't made a very good impression for both of them. And she did have pink hair. Some people took one look at her and decided she was bad news based off that one little thing.

Whatever.

She normally rolled her eyes at those condescending people and did something that really made their tongues wag. Like lower her shirt and show more cleavage. Or talk loudly using swear words. Or budging in front of them at the checkout line like she had every right to.

It always put a smile on her face to make those cruel, unkind people feel uncomfortable and show them she would not be treated like she was beneath their station.

"Thank you so much. I will keep that in mind."

The officer let her arm go and walked away with a sappy grin.

She couldn't seem to remove her own happy grin.

"What did Officer Dawson want?"

That was his name. Now she remembered. Even though it was a small town, she did not retain names very well. Considering Adam had been through the police station like a revolving door, she should know every single officer by name that worked here.

Turning to her right, she met the angry glare of Newman. Geez, what was his problem? Probably didn't have a pleasant conversation with Chief Dodson, which was why she didn't join the conversation in the first place. She was already having a shitty day and speaking with that man wouldn't help it any.

"He was saying hi and asked how Adam is doing."

Newman scowled even more.

"Is there a problem? What did Chief Dodson say?"

Newman's features relaxed a fraction. "He didn't say much. What little he did say, he begrudgingly gave me and only because I think he's afraid of the mayor. Sometimes, it pays that my grandfather was so loved around here."

"So no new leads?"

"They're still waiting for the DNA to come back, which, honestly, could take weeks. And the few prints they lifted, they're still going through it all and processing it. I guess the cabin has been abandoned a long time. Kids around town used to use it for parties and stuff. They pulled a lot of prints."

She sighed, yet refused to give in to the temptation of pity and misery. They would find these men. She had every faith in Newman. She might not have faith he'd see the light and how wonderful they could be together, but she had faith he'd find these men. The determination was clear as day in his eyes.

"What do we do now?"

He shrugged, which wasn't encouraging. "Check in with the sketch artist, I guess. She should have the composite done. I know a guy in the FBI. Maybe he'd be willing to do me a favor and run it through their database. If we're lucky, we'll get a facial recognition match before they find some viable prints."

"Okay. A plan. I like having a plan. That sounds good."

Newman nodded, then held out his hand for her to precede him. She didn't miss the way he glared at Officer Dawson as they passed by.

What was that all about?

Because the only conclusion she could come up with was that Newman was jealous.

Interesting.

Since he claimed he didn't care about her, why in the world was he jealous? Time to test a theory.

Just how jealous could she make him?

21

THE WOMAN WAS TORTURING him on purpose. He knew it.

Every time they came across a guy, and it didn't matter who—old, young, fat, bald, damn good-looking—she smiled a sexy, flirty smile that made every single man stop and return a smile.

Every single time she ignored him as she did it. Yet the distance between them was wired with tension; he knew she was doing it to drive him insane.

And oh, it was driving him to the point of madness. To the point he wanted to punch each man in the face and tell them to stop looking at her, to not even think about her.

Of course, letting her know it grated on his nerves would only fuel her fire that he was a damn liar and wanted her more than he could admit out loud. So he offered no expression, no acknowledgment, no indication with a twitch of his body that he cared she was flirting with any man who got near.

He almost threw her game back in her face when they stopped to talk with the sketch artist. She was a very attractive woman who would've had his interest before he met

Amelia. But he couldn't do it. Because a hint of pain for his actions in Amelia's expression would've broken him more than he already was. The last thing he wanted to do was hurt her, even if she was tempting the devil inside him.

They retrieved the sketch. Since Amelia barely saw his face, she couldn't confirm whether he was the man she saw in the white truck the day Adam disappeared. But he looked vaguely familiar. Newman took a picture of it and sent it to Ben, who showed it to Adam.

Ten minutes after sending the text, he got a response.

It was the same man who stopped the truck on the side of the road.

That's all he needed to know.

After getting permission from Chief Banner, since he approved the sketch artist, they faxed the photo to his friend Dax in the FBI, who lived in New York. Dax told him he'd get back to him as soon as he could.

Newman hoped the same day, but he didn't think it'd be that quick. Tomorrow would suffice.

After completing all those tasks, Amelia offered to make him what she called her famous Stromboli meal. She said she had to start it early because it was a process but so worth it in the end. Considering he wasn't ready to leave her side for the day, he agreed.

Here they were, walking through the grocery store picking up supplies and she was back at it, smiling at every guy who passed by.

He had to keep gritting his teeth to stop himself from saying something he'd regret.

"Are you okay, Newman?"

Forcing a grin to hide his annoyance at her ploy to make him jealous, he nodded. "I'm hungry. How long does it take to make?"

"Quite a few hours. The dough has to rise. Like I said, it's a process, but worth it. You'll be begging me to make it for you all the time."

He could also think of a few other things he wanted to beg for.

Like her sweet, delectable body naked next to his. Her red, luscious lips kissing a trail down the length of him. Her bright-pink hair fanned out across his bed.

Oh, yes, he wanted to beg until his voice disappeared from exertion.

He wanted her.

Oh, he wanted her, and not because she was the most beautiful woman he had ever seen with a body that enticed a man to the point of pain.

No. He wanted her because she was the only woman who could tie his gut in knots with aggravation and worry, then untangle it with a simple tender smile his way.

Not even Chrissy had held that kind of control and power over him. Yet, he had loved her. He had been prepared to marry her and spend the rest of his life with her.

When it got too serious, when he saw his life flash before his eyes, when he realized he'd never be the perfect husband she deserved, he destroyed his relationship with one irreversible mistake.

Most likely—because could a man like him change—he'd do the same to Amelia.

If he let her completely into his heart, let her know how he felt, he'd repeat the same mistakes. Because that's what he did time and again. Fail. Fail. Fail.

No matter how hard he tried to be the perfect son, the perfect student, the perfect cop, the perfect boyfriend, he failed. Quite accurately and miserably.

He'd always be second fiddle in everything.

Just once he wanted to be perfect and right and the first to succeed.

"Hey," Amelia said, stopping the cart and waving a hand in his face. "Did you hear me? Where did you disappear?"

Blinking, trying to remember what she said, he cracked a grin to mask the fact he let his mind wander into a territory he tried like hell to never get lost in.

Begging. That's right, she thought he'd beg for more.

In his past life, she would be right. He might've begged until his lips turned blue. But not now.

"It better taste damn good for all the trouble I'm going through here."

Then he stomped ahead, needing to get away and create some space between them. Maybe it wasn't such a great idea to let her come back to his cabin and cook.

Well, she had to come back anyway for her car since they had left together in his vehicle earlier this morning. But she didn't have to come inside. She could leave right away.

He heard a heavy sigh behind him and refused to acknowledge it. Good. Let her get annoyed. Because damn it, he was annoyed beyond belief. And so damn sexually frustrated he wanted to scream until his voice went raw and he couldn't speak for a week.

They grabbed the rest of the supplies she needed in silence. He brooded the entire time. She delivered right back with her games, smiling at any man who stepped into her pathway.

She even had the audacity to smile at the three boys ahead of them in line. They looked to be Adam's age. Why was she smiling at them?

When the cashier stood up from scanning something underneath the cart for the woman in front of them, he realized she hadn't been smiling at the boys. She had been smiling at the damn cashier. He couldn't have been older than twenty-one, yet he had a body ripped to the extreme that said he worked out and worked out well. Daily, for sure. Slicked back hair, not a strand out of place. And a cheesy-ass grin the entire time he scanned item after item.

As they waited for their turn, Amelia couldn't take her eyes off the guy—kid more like it—practically drooling at the sight.

Whatever.

She could look and drool over any man she wanted. He had no say.

He didn't care.

Because they were never going to be an item. It didn't matter to him.

The three boys were goofing off and joking around. The woman, who also couldn't take her eyes off the cashier, turned in the boys' direction to reprimand their loud behavior.

Her eyes connected with Amelia and she winced, a hint of red blushing across her cheeks.

"Oh, Ms. Benedict. How are you? I heard Adam was found safe and sound."

"He was. We're fine, thank you," Amelia replied politely, yet he saw the strain in her posture because it pained her to be polite.

"Loser had it coming," one of the boys muttered under his breath.

He knew Amelia heard it because he did. He started to step forward when Amelia grabbed his hand and squeezed hard, a clear indication she wanted him to back off.

The woman must've heard it, too, because she glared at

the boy, hushed him, and then turned her attention back to the cashier.

He stood rigid and tense the entire time as they waited for their turn. Not once did she let go of his hand, which was a very good thing. It was the only thing that kept him grounded and his lips zipped.

As soon as they paid for their groceries, something he insisted he pay for, and they were back in the car, he pounced.

"Why the hell didn't you want me to say anything? That damn woman should've said something at least. Rude-ass kids."

Amelia buckled her seatbelt as a long, heavy sigh released. "It doesn't matter. Berating them, losing your temper, it wouldn't make a difference. Do you even know who that woman was?"

He shook his head. He didn't know many people in town. Sure, he recognized faces since he had been in town a lot the last week interviewing people, but he didn't remember everyone's name. Was he supposed to know who that woman was?

"She was—is—one of Adam's teachers, Mrs. Portman. The boy that called him a loser wasn't her son, but he is her son's friend. She's nice, always very patient with Adam, but she has no backbone. Adam doesn't get along well with anyone here. I can't be sure if he tried at first, but the kids don't like him now. I do know that. I've already had to have a few talks with his teachers about bullying, and I even had a chat with the principal once. They all said they'd take care of it, but as you can see, whatever they said or did didn't change anything. Those kids are still mean. It's not worth it to get into an argument with a kid like that. I'm not sure I even want to send him back there. Maybe I should do home-schooling."

"It's not right."

"Yeah, well, there's a lot of things not right in the world. But some things you have to let go."

Let go?

Maybe she was right.

But he wasn't sure how he was going to let her go when this entire case was closed.

Having no answer, he started the car and headed home.

A home that really wasn't a home but a placeholder for him as he figured out where to go in life.

Some things you have to let go.

Damn. It hurt thinking about letting anything go. Especially her.

MEL SAT on the couch and watched as Newman attacked the punching bag in the corner of the room. He'd been at it for the past hour, taking a few breaks, but otherwise beating the bag like his life depended upon it. She sat on the couch the entire time, mesmerized by the sight of him shirtless, sweating, his muscles flexing and looking like they needed to be touched. She'd be more than happy to give him a massage. In other places that she couldn't see, too.

She only had to get up from the couch once to put the Stromboli in the oven. Otherwise, she hadn't moved an inch from the couch.

Newman was very aware of her. Not often, but a few times she caught him glancing at her. Every time he looked away quickly, his back going rigid that he was caught in the act.

She didn't care one bit that she was gawking. He was a fine-looking man. Why shouldn't she look?

It was cruel of her to tease him and make him jealous all day, smiling and talking a little too friendly to every man they came across. But she couldn't help herself. She had wanted to test him. Find his limit.

She hadn't found it yet. He barely reacted. A few times she saw his jaw clench, his fists tighten into fierce balls, but otherwise, he didn't say a word or do anything to indicate he cared.

But she knew he did. Those little signs couldn't be ignored. Why couldn't he admit he liked her?

What was he so damn afraid of?

That's all it had to be.

Last night, in this very room, they made out like rowdy teenagers and came from dry humping each other. If that didn't say they had chemistry and a strong connection, she didn't know what would.

He was trying to distance himself. Trying to ignore the pull between them, trying to push her away at every available opportunity. She didn't know how to get through to him.

After supper tonight, what would happen? Would he invite her to spend the night? Would he kick her out?

Her heart had been going crazy off and on all afternoon as she prepared supper. Newman had roamed the cabin like a coiled predator stalking his prey, walking back and forth waiting for the best time to pounce.

Yet, he never did anything. They barely even talked.

She didn't avert her gaze when he stopped punching and grabbed a small towel from the table and wiped the sweat from his face, then across his hair.

He turned in her direction, a brow cocked and a sexy-as-sin grin on his face. "Enjoy the show?"

Shifting in her spot, her body wired high and on full alert, she nodded. "Very much so."

He shook his head as he laughed, then he nodded toward the kitchen. "That smells good. I'm getting hungry."

"It should be almost done. I have to make some marinara sauce."

"I'm going to take a quick shower."

She stood up as he started to walk toward the bathroom. "Want some company?"

He stumbled, looking at her as if he couldn't believe she actually asked such a question. Then he got his bearings down, hid his surprise, and laughed. "I like marinara sauce."

"Chicken." Rolling her eyes as she rounded the couch to head to the kitchen, she pressed her lips into an irritated grin. "I don't know what you're afraid of happening between us, but it can be about sex if you want. I'm horny. You're horny. Why do you have to make things difficult?"

His eyes clouded over into sadness and despair so strong it broke her heart. "I guess because life's never been easy for me. Always fighting to be the better person."

"There's nothing wrong with being in second place. There's nothing wrong with being you, Newman."

She swore she saw a hint of arousal hit his eyes. Was he about to cave and give in? But then it disappeared as fast as it appeared.

"I can't do this with you, Amelia. I can't be anything but friends." His expression turned fierce. "It's not just sex between us. It never would be. Whatever you want to call the pull between us, it's deeper than sex and I..." He hung his head down, then popped up looking her straight in the eye. "And I'm not strong enough. I'll end up hurting you and it will kill me if I do."

With those parting words, he left the room.

The man was a certifiable idiot.

He wasn't strong enough? Ha! He was the strongest, most determined, most focused man she had ever met. He was letting his past and the fear eating him up inside win.

That was all.

But she was smart. She could think of a way to get him past everything. If only an idea would come to her. Because the longer it took to think of a solution, the more distance he'd put between them.

She started to prepare the sauce, mixing all the ingredients by memory. By the time it was finished, so was the Stromboli. She pulled it out of the oven and started to cut it into pieces. Scooping two portions for Newman and two for herself onto a plate, she grabbed two tiny bowls and added some marinara sauce, and set the table.

If she knew where Newman kept candles she would've dug some out and put them in the middle of the table. Show him a bit of romance, but sadly, she had no idea where any were.

Before she could interrupt him in the bathroom, find him naked and wet, he walked into the kitchen looking refreshed and delicious and so damn handsome she wanted to drop to her knees and beg him to realize how great they could be together.

Resisting that idiotic idea, she made a show with her hands toward the table and smiled. "Let's dig in."

He took a seat next to her and didn't stop to check the temperature and picked up a piece, taking a bite. He immediately dropped it. "Damn, that's hot."

"I just pulled it out of the oven." A small chuckle escaped.

"I burned my tongue. So glad you find that funny."

Sending him a saucy smile, she chuckled again. "I can kiss it and make it feel better."

"You have no idea how tempting that is." He sighed. "I'm not going to change my mind."

She enjoyed arguing with him. It got her blood pumping, her heart racing, her body ramped up and ready for anything. She liked the rush it gave her. Because she knew an argument with Newman would be just that. Words would be thrown back and forth, but nothing damaging. Nothing where he'd hit her and turn it into something brutal and savage. He was nothing like her father or any other man she had dated.

That's why she liked him so much. He was different.

But she didn't think she would ever win this argument with him.

Holding his gaze, she offered a smile meant to say she was calling a truce. Sort of. "Okay. I won't say another word about us ever again if you answer one question."

He looked at her warily, then nodded. "I feel like this is some sort of trick, but okay. You get one question."

"You have to answer it honestly."

"I'm always honest with you. I always will be."

She wanted to believe that. But she knew he wasn't always honest with her. He couldn't even admit how he truly felt about her, and she knew he felt something.

"You have this innate belief that you have to be perfect and excel and be the best at every single thing you do. And if you're not, then you're a failure. Why?"

He flinched as if she slapped him. He also had a look of

confusion glittering in his eyes. Then he shrugged. "I don't know."

"That's not an honest answer."

He looked down at his food. "That's the only answer I have."

She picked up her Stromboli. "Then I guess you better put on your armor, my dear Newman, because I'm not backing down. You're either going to answer the question honestly and then kick me out and I'll leave without an issue..." She cocked a brow. "Or invite me to stay and show me what those hands of yours can do. Because without answering it, we have no deal."

22

AMELIA'S QUESTION swirled around his brain all night. Why did he think he had to be perfect at everything otherwise he was a failure?

He had been honest with her. He had no clue. Since his childhood trying to one-up his older brother, he always felt like he had to be perfect.

His brother, being the smart, dashing, educated man he was, even as a child, he could never seem to be the better one. He always fell short. His parents always let him know in an overt, condescending way he'd never reach the same kind of perfection. Because of that, he always took it as a challenge.

The only time he ever felt like he could be himself, not have to worry about being the best he could be, was when he visited his grandfather. But even then, he still had that knee-jerk reaction to be perfect. His grandfather had never cared if he didn't do something as great as he should've. It was always the effort that counted.

What would his grandfather say about him now? His effort in everything failed colossally. He was a disgrace.

And yet, Amelia wanted him. Somehow, she saw past all his bullshit and to the real person inside. All through supper they made small talk, ignoring the huge gauntlet she threw down, but every time they made eye contact, he knew she wouldn't let it go until he answered her question.

What did it say about him that he didn't want to answer it because he didn't want to lose her. That he didn't want her to stop fighting for him. He was a jackass of great proportions for playing with her heart and mind like this. The situation would be easily solved if he told her how much he cared about her.

He could answer her question and kindly ask her to leave, and she would.

He didn't want that. The thought of her leaving had his body trembling with heartache.

They cleaned up the meal together, doing the dishes as a team. Before long, everything was picked up, put away, and back to normal.

He had no television. They couldn't just veg out on the couch and relax watching a show.

He could make some hot chocolate and they could sit in front of the fire.

He could suggest they play a game.

Or he could man up and either tell her how much he cared about her, or answer her question and tell her to leave.

None of those options sounded like a good idea. Even if he could admit he cared about her, he'd still want her to leave. He would destroy her because that's what he did to things, to people.

And he didn't know how to honestly answer the question.

"Well?" A silky brow rose as she pierced him with a sultry smile.

Leave it to her to put him right on the spot. All the time.

He shrugged. He didn't know how to respond.

Clucking her tongue in disappointment, she shook her head. "I'm actually exhausted. It's been a long-ass week. I'm going to give you a reprieve for the night." Her expression turned stringent. "Don't take this to mean you won or anything. I'll be in your face tomorrow."

He sure hoped so. Even though he couldn't admit how he felt, he didn't want to lose her from his life. He enjoyed talking to her. He wanted to be her friend, at least. It was amazing how fast he'd gotten used to her being in his life. How comfortable it felt to have her by his side.

"I always want to be friends."

By the flash of anger that flickered in her gaze, it was the wrong thing to say.

"You're such an idiot." Shaking her head, she grabbed her jacket and purse and headed for the door. "Hopefully, you gain some brain cells after a good night's rest."

He chuckled, unable to hide how much he enjoyed her brazen attitude. Oh, he was positive she meant that as an insult, but he couldn't help but laugh.

With another annoyed glare in his direction, she opened the door, walked out, and slammed it. He stalked to the closed door with hurried steps and opened it, watching as she climbed into her car. She might be upset, but he worried about her. She should've at least let him walk her to her car. He figured watching her from the porch would have to do.

She didn't wave back as he waved.

As soon as her car was out of sight, he closed the cabin door and looked around the room.

Emptiness stared back.

The loneliness immediately engulfed him.

He had been in this cabin for three months all by himself and not once did it ever bother him. He actually enjoyed the solitude.

Barely one week with Amelia and he suddenly hated the quiet. Hated being by himself.

She didn't just waltz into his life with a carefree attitude. She rammed into it, demanding he take notice.

Oh, and he noticed her. A little too much.

He had no idea one woman could turn him inside out. How come Chrissy never made him feel uneasy and chaotic and so full of confusion?

Because she was safe and familiar. They had dated during high school and broke up amicably right before they headed off to college. His parents had adored her. She was the one thing he did right for once in their eyes. When they broke up, the disappointment had been immediate and swift.

"You'll never find a girl sweeter than her and with a good head on her shoulders." His mother said it with disgust and then walked away shaking her head.

Well, he had found another girl sweeter than her. Amelia had her sweet moments. She was like a piece of candy, sweet on the outside but with a dose of sourness when you hit the middle. He loved that kind of candy.

Stumbling back from the door, he nearly tripped and fell on his ass.

Love?

Amelia?

Well, he loved that kind of candy, but was his mind trying to tell him he...he...loved her?

He was in lust with her. That was for damn sure. Every time he saw her, heard her delicate voice, gazed at her luscious red lips, pictured running his hands through her soft pink hair, he wanted her so much he almost begged for a small taste.

Taking a seat on the couch, he shoved his hands in his hair and pulled on the ends. What was she doing to him? Making him question everything in his life. Making him go through and ponder every single decision he ever made.

Why *had* he started to date Chrissy again when he ran into her? His high school sweetheart. One look and he had been mesmerized by her beauty—and by his mother's words. So he asked her out.

Because, at the time, he thought it would make his life more perfect, make him appear like the better son. And his parents had been happy to hear they were back together.

Chrissy had been a great woman. He had loved her.

Leaning back into the couch, he realized he still loved her.

As a friend.

Only a friend.

His actions, his behavior toward her was unacceptable. Instead of taking his fear and his pain out on her, cheating on her, he should've admitted the truth. She was a good woman, but she wasn't the right one for him.

He was such a damn coward.

He was still a damn coward.

Because he didn't think he'd ever be able to tell Amelia he loved her. She might be okay with second best, but she deserved perfection.

And he was nothing even close to perfect.

MEL TOSSED and turned all night. Her mind couldn't shut off thinking about Newman, contemplating what he might be thinking about.

Did he have a terrible night like her? Did he get any sleep?

She couldn't stand the politeness between them last night. His indifference to her ultimatum. She told him she wouldn't back down, but last night she had needed a breather. His determination to ignore her and how he felt grated on her nerves and she needed time to herself.

She wasn't sure if leaving had been the best option, but today was a new day.

After grabbing a quick breakfast, she showered and got ready, taking extra care to do her hair and makeup. Newman should want her for her, not how she looked, but enticing him a little more wouldn't hurt.

She even dressed a little sexier, wearing a white cashmere sweater that hugged her breasts and a pair of jeans that always made her butt look fabulous. She wanted to wear a pair of high heels that made her feel sexy, but she didn't want to break her neck walking in the snow. Nixing the idea, she put on a comfortable pair of tennis shoes that were sparkly and full of life.

Double checking her appearance, making sure her makeup hadn't smeared or smudged, her hair still perfect, she headed out the door to Newman's house.

The first time she tried to start her car, it roared and then sputtered out.

Oh, no.

Not now.

This couldn't be happening.

Her car wasn't that old, but it did have some age on it. Considering this was her first winter in Minnesota and her car wasn't used to the temperatures, maybe this was normal behavior for any kind of car. She hadn't checked the weather app before leaving, but the minute she stepped outside, her face had frozen like an icicle. It had to be in the single digits.

There wasn't much for her and Newman to do today but wait for his friend in the FBI to get back to him. They could cuddle up in front of the fireplace in his cabin and keep each other warm.

If he got his head out of his ass, anyway.

Rubbing her gloved hands together, she tried again. This time her car sputtered first, then roared to life.

Clapping gleefully, then rubbing the steering wheel, she whispered, "Stay with me, baby. Just make it to Newman's. He'll be stuck with me then if I can't get you to start."

Putting the car in reverse, she backed out of the driveway and headed for Newman's cabin. She had no idea if he was awake, although she figured he was. Hopefully, he hadn't decided to go anywhere this early in the morning. If he had, that was okay. She'd pick his locks again and make herself at home.

She could've called him to tell him she was coming over, but there was no need to give him warning. Throwing him off balance was much better.

She had high hopes today would go better with Newman than it had with her brother when she called him this morning. She called Ben asking to speak with Adam, who had been awake because she heard him in the background, but he refused to speak with her. Ben tried to ease her hurt feelings by saying Adam was into a video game with his nephew. Both were being quite competitive, but Mel knew Adam didn't want to talk to her.

The only thing that made her feel better was that Adam

was having a good time. According to Ben, Adam and his nephew hit it off immediately. They had been playing, chatting, and acting like they were the best of friends. That was such good news to hear. Adam needed that in his life, especially with how shitty it had been in this small town with the other kids.

Whatever. Her attempt to talk to Adam hadn't gone well. She refused to be defeated by Newman and his attitude. One of the men in her life had to give in, and she was expecting it to be Newman. She gave him space last night, for her own sanity, but today was definitely a new day. He better be prepared for her.

Halfway to his cabin, her car started rumbling and sputtering. She barely had time to pull over to the side of the road before it died.

Shit.

Her car wasn't on her side today. Which was so crazy since she never had an issue before.

Rubbing her hands together, she tried to determine what to do. She could call Newman to pick her up and he would, or she could attempt to look for the problem herself.

Well, she wasn't an idiot. It wouldn't hurt to look under the car herself.

Popping the hood release, she inhaled a deep breath and prepared to feel the brutal cold. Immediate shivers attacked her body as soon as she stepped outside. Opening the hood, her eyes roamed over everything, hoping the issue would jump out at her. Not that she was a car expert or anything, but maybe it would be easily noticeable.

"Having car trouble?"

Jumping back, she glanced at the man standing close to her, too close for comfort, especially since she didn't hear him walk up. Or even hear a vehicle come up behind her.

But darting her eyes behind her car she saw a truck sitting behind it.

She took a closer look at the man.

He had a scar running down his face.

Double shit.

She took a step back, going through the options in her head. She could start running and see how far she got before the man tackled her to the ground and she'd have to fight him off. Or she could make a move right now and kick his ass.

But whatever she decided to do, she needed to get away from him and to the phone in her car and call Newman.

"You do realize I'm going to kick your ass."

The man smiled, enhancing his menacing features and the scar running from his left eyebrow to the corner of his mouth. The evil in his eyes intensified. "We should've taken you from the beginning, not that dumb-ass kid. Him, we just wanted to get rid of." The malevolent smirk that appeared made goose bumps flush across her arms. "You, oh, we're going to have some fun with you."

Well, she was a good runner. And she wore her tennis shoes, thankfully. Maybe it would be better to try to outrun him.

Before she could make a decision, a strong arm swooped behind her and shoved a cloth over her mouth.

She tried to fight back, but it didn't take long for darkness to descend.

23

RUNNING a hand through his ragged hair, Newman cursed viciously, then swiped the keys from the counter.

He couldn't take it anymore.

He had to see her.

All night his mind had been on Amelia. Not just her beautiful face, but her words wouldn't stop pestering him to death. He didn't get a wink of sleep because they kept repeating over and over in his head.

Why was he fighting this? Why was he fighting his feelings for her? So what if he would be second best? So what if he wasn't perfect?

She didn't seem to mind.

But she deserved it. That was the problem he grappled with. Was he doing her any favors by letting her submit to the likes of him?

He had expected her to come by his cabin already, knocking on his door, demanding he answer her question.

Except it was nearly ten o'clock in the morning and nothing. Not even a phone call to ask what was on the agenda today.

She could still be sleeping. But he found that hard to believe. She wanted these guys caught as much as he did. Although, without more to go on, there wasn't much they could do at the moment.

Well, he was done waiting on her. He would bug her first this time. He wasn't sure he was ready to admit anything to her quite yet, but he refused to stay away from her any longer.

Rushing to his car like some randy teenager getting ready to leave for a hot date, he tried to slow down. He'd see her soon enough.

Maybe he should call his friend Dax to see if he had any updates.

He started the car instead. He was looking for excuses to delay his departure.

Heading toward her house, his heart exploded from the inside out when he caught sight of a car with its hood up sitting on the opposite side of the road. As he slowed down and got closer, his gut churned with unease.

It was Amelia's car.

Jerking to a stop, he barely took the time to put his vehicle in park before dashing out and across the street to hers. The car was empty, but her purse was still on the seat. Removing a glove, he touched the side of the vehicle near the raised hood. It felt cold to the touch. So it had been sitting here awhile. Or it hadn't been that long and with the cold temperatures, it cooled immediately.

"Keep calm, man. Just keep calm. She's a smart woman."

Maybe she started walking to find help.

He rejected that idea when he was able to open the car door and saw the keys in the ignition. After digging through her purse, he found her phone tucked inside. She would've never left her purse, phone, and the keys dangling in the ignition.

Slamming the door shut, he walked around the car. It was hard to tell, especially since he didn't take care to approach the vehicle, but he saw a few footprints around the car. The snow was disturbed. A struggle happened near the hood.

Best as he could figure, Amelia had car trouble. She stopped, popped the hood to check it out, and someone surprised her. She fought back, which was something he knew she'd do, and lost the fight.

Someone took her.

Like Adam.

Most likely, for whatever reason, the same men who took Adam.

Hating it, but having no choice, he called the police. The first person to arrive was Officer Dawson.

He checked over the vehicle as Newman had done. Newman even gave the officer his likely scenario of what happened.

"I agree with your assessment. She would've never left her phone and purse in the car if she went for help. Did she call you at all?" Officer Dawson asked.

The concern in his tone grated on his nerves. His concern didn't stem from a law enforcement point of view, but as a man infatuated. He was the same officer who flirted with her yesterday. It gnawed at his insides yesterday, eating him alive, just as it was right now.

But he didn't have time to be jealous. He had to find Amelia before something serious happened. They didn't hurt Adam too much, besides not giving him food and water, and they didn't beat him or brutally torture him. But that didn't mean they wouldn't hurt Amelia. He had to play nice.

"I haven't spoken with her since last night. I'm not sure where she was headed." He'd like to think it was his cabin. She did happen to be heading in that particular direction.

"I'll put out a missing person's report immediately. I'll also inform the chief. We'll get every available officer on this. Considering what happened to her brother, this probably isn't a coincidence."

Well, at least Dawson wasn't dumb. But would the chief of police take it seriously?

"I'd like to help in any way I can."

Dawson smiled. "Staying out of the way is the best help you can provide. No offense, but we can handle this."

The man was lucky he didn't want to be tossed in jail because it took all of his self-control not to knock him out. Not be offended? Like hell. His words were like a slap to the face.

"Right. You'll call me with any updates."

"Of course. Now, if you'll excuse me, this is a crime scene."

Bile coated his throat as those terrifying words washed over him. A crime scene. With Amelia's vehicle. How in the hell had he let this happen?

This was his fault.

He should've admitted his feelings last night. He should've begged her not to leave. Just because Adam left town didn't mean the threat was over. He should've gotten down on his hands and knees and groveled for her to stay. Because then she'd be warm and safe in his cabin right now. Not...wherever the hell she was.

Since Dawson dismissed him, something that irked him,

he got back in his car and drove home. As soon as he walked inside the cabin, he called Sauer.

Keeping the terror out of his tone, he told him everything.

"How can I help?"

He ran a trembling hand through his hair as his other hand squeezed the phone hard. "I have no idea." His voice hitched. "I'm scared, man. I got lucky when I found Adam. What am I going to tell him if I can't find her?"

"You'll find her. I'll come—"

"No. Stay home. Dee needs you."

Sauer sighed. "She's fine. She's stuck on bed rest, but she's fine. You need me, too."

"I was told to stay out of the way. I don't even know where to start looking. You don't have jurisdiction up here either."

"She's smart, Newman. She'll fight hard."

Yeah, he knew that. He saw the evidence in the snow she fought back, but she still lost. They still took her.

He tried to push the fear away and forced himself to sound confident and like he wasn't falling apart inside. "I wanted to tell you. I don't think I can call Ben with an update. I don't think I can tell Adam."

Damn. He was such a coward in every aspect.

"I'll do it for you. I mean, I'll call Ben and Zeke and let them know what's going on. But I don't think you should say anything to Adam yet."

So maybe he wasn't a complete coward. Maybe it was the right thing to do. Not tell Adam yet.

"Thanks, man."

"Of course. I'm always here for you."

He hung up with Sauer and paced back and forth in front of the fireplace.

He could call his friend Dax. But he didn't know what that would accomplish. As soon as his friend had any information, he'd call him. And if Dax was anything, it wasn't a liar. Not like him.

He should've told Amelia the truth. How much he cared about her.

That he loved her.

A sharp ring tore through the quiet cabin, startling him. Glancing at his phone, his heart started pounding when he saw Dax's name flash across the screen.

Was his luck finally shining?

"Hey, man. Tell me something good."

"Oh, I have so much information, I don't even know where to begin, buddy."

Well, Newman figured the best would be to start with what would help him find Amelia as fast as possible.

MEL BLINKED a few times before she found the energy to keep her eyes open. Taking her time, moving her head to glance at her surroundings, she tried to keep in a gasp. Because the slightest movement made her ache, considering it felt like someone was pounding on her head with a sledgehammer.

She was in a small bedroom with a window to her left. Although it didn't matter she had the means to escape like Adam had because she was tied to a chair. The ropes bound around her chest felt unyielding. Her hands were pulled behind her back and tied so tightly, the rope cut into her wrists. Her feet were also secured with what she assumed was rope as well. She couldn't exactly lean forward to check.

Her captors obviously weren't about to repeat their mistakes and let her get away.

She had no idea why they were doing this. Why they took her brother and now her. What had they done to deserve this?

Just like Adam, she saw the man with the scar, but she never saw the guy who came up behind her. Even though she tried to struggle out of his embrace, it didn't make a difference.

The sun was shining outside, a small light glistening in her direction.

So it told her the day hadn't passed by yet. How long had she been out?

Did Newman call her yet? Would he call her?

Well, she didn't doubt he'd call her. If nothing else but to give her an update about Adam's case. If there was an update. Perhaps his friend hadn't called yet. He could've decided not to bother her until his friend called.

How long would it take for him to contact her and realize something was wrong? Did the men take her car?

She sucked in a sharp breath.

Were they the reason she had car trouble? Most likely, now that she thought about it. Why didn't she figure it out sooner? She should've called Newman immediately this morning. She should've told him she was on her way to his cabin.

Would it have made a difference? Would she still be tied to a chair in a small room with freedom a few feet away?

Struggling against the ropes, hoping against hope they weren't as tight as they felt, she gave up after a few seconds. The pounding in her head hadn't decreased. If anything, it increased tenfold. And her struggling did nothing but further dig the ropes into her arms and chest. The bastards took off her winter coat, so the rope dug in quite easily. The pain was too much to bear to keep struggling. They tied it securely and efficiently.

The room was chilly as well. She couldn't feel much heat.

Were they going to try to kill her slowly with hypothermia?

She didn't want to think about what their plans were. What she needed to do was think of a way to escape. She would not go down without a fight.

The bastards had no idea who they were messing with.

24

NEWMAN WAITED SOMEWHAT PATIENTLY after he called Dawson and told him to meet him at his cabin. He had information about the case.

He refused to give it to him over the phone, insisting he had to see it with his own eyes.

Because, oh, did his friend Dax give him everything he needed.

When a knock sounded on his door, he opened it calmly, with a friendly smile. Honestly, he couldn't believe how calm he felt. Because when Dax told him everything, his anger and rage had spun to the surface so fast, he had been ready to kill anyone who crossed his path.

But now, after waiting and thinking it all through, he was as calm as could be.

Because he wasn't the one going to jail today.

Officer Dawson was.

"What did you find that was so important you couldn't tell me over the phone?"

Newman shut the door, then pointed toward the kitchen table. "Let's have a seat."

The second Dawson turned toward the kitchen, he pounced. He grabbed the man, twisting his arm behind his back, and brought him to his knees. Then he snatched Dawson's service weapon and pointed it behind his head.

"What the hell are you doing?"

He was about to get some answers. He wouldn't kill the guy and go to jail for the rest of his life, but that didn't mean he wouldn't make Dawson *think* he was going to kill him. Anything to find out where Amelia was. He was finished playing it by the book.

"We're going to have a chat, and you're going to tell me everything you know. Or this gun might accidentally go off."

"You're insane. No wonder you got fired. You're a loose cannon."

Newman shoved the gun harder in the back of his head. "I quit, asshole. I don't know why people can't get that straight." Then he let some of the pressure off. "You'll tell me where Amelia is right this minute or you're going to see how insane I can be."

"I have no—"

Newman twisted his arm some more. Dawson screamed in response.

"Lying to me is useless. I know everything. Well, I know everything besides why you targeted Adam and Amelia, but I figure we'll get that information later when I know she's safe."

"I don't know what you're talking about."

"The man with the scar on his face, his name is Earl Dawson." Newman tightened his hold, twisting his arm as he did. Dawson couldn't hold back a painful moan. "Does the name ring a bell? Because it should. He's your cousin."

"I don't—"

Newman twisted his arm some more. Dawson yelled

with agony. "Lying to me will get you nowhere. I'm through with my patience. I want to know where Amelia is right now. And I want to know who the third guy is. I'm thinking it's your other cousin Matthew. Because according to my friend in the FBI, he has quite the extensive record for robbery, assault, carjacking, and the list goes on."

"I had no idea what they did until after they took the kid. I swear. I had no idea they would grab Amelia. I like her. I honestly do."

Newman leaned closer, raising Dawson's arm as he did, making sure he felt every ounce of pain. "And when you did find out, what did you do? Nothing. Because Adam had to escape on his own. There was evidence of three people involved in that cabin in the woods, which means you did nothing."

He couldn't hold in his anger, shouting the words in his ear. Newman was tempted to keep twisting the asshole's arm until it broke. It pissed him off beyond reasoning that he allowed those men, even though they were family, to hurt Adam.

"You think I didn't want to turn them in. I did. I swear. They threatened my family. I have two kids of my own. A boy and a girl. I'm divorced, but they threatened my ex-wife, who they hate. We don't get along all the time, but I didn't want to see her get hurt, or my kids."

Oh, yeah. He knew he had kids. He had at least one son because he was one of the little jackasses from the store yesterday who thought Adam had what happened to him coming. Amelia told him what their names were. So he knew his son was one of those kids who bullied Adam.

"Your son bullied Adam. Is that why Earl and Matthew grabbed him and did what they did? For your son and his friends?"

Dawson sighed in between heavy breaths. "I don't know. Maybe. Earl didn't say. My son is a good kid. He just has a temper sometimes. The divorce wasn't easy on him."

"Your son is going to turn into your cousins Earl and Matthew if you don't straighten him out. I don't care about that right now. I want to know where Amelia is. I'm not going to ask again."

"I have no idea. I was as surprised as you when I found out. I told those two to leave town. I did not tell them to take her. I like her. I swear I'm not lying."

Newman didn't hesitate to twist his arm again and press the gun harder into the back of his head. "You even think dirty thoughts about her and I'll break your arm right this second."

"I got it. She's off-limits. But I swear I don't know where they took her. I tried calling them as soon as you left. They didn't answer."

"Where do you think they'd go?"

"I don't know."

Newman started to twist his arm some more.

"Stop! Okay, just stop. I don't know." He breathed heavily as he continued. "I have a cabin a few miles north of here. Maybe they took her there. I haven't been there since this past summer. That's the only place I can think of because they don't have a place around here. They barely have any money, always asking me for some."

"Stand up. Now."

Newman helped him stand up, making sure to keep a good grip on his arm. Shoving the weapon behind his waistband, he grabbed Dawson's handcuffs from his utility belt and handcuffed him. Then he dug out the keys to the handcuffs and turned him toward the door.

"What are you doing?"

Chuckling, because it was such a damn funny question, he opened the door, pushing him forward. "I'm locking you in the back of your patrol vehicle. I'm going to call the chief of police to let him know your roll in everything, and then I'm going to find Amelia before your cousins hurt her. And if they so much as scratched her in the slightest way, you'll be the sorriest man alive."

Dawson didn't fight him as he shoved him in the backseat of the car. He made sure to take the car keys and anything else away from him to prevent his escape before the cavalry could arrive. He didn't even bother to start the car for him and turn the heat on. He didn't care if he got cold waiting for anyone.

He removed the clip from the gun, opened the trunk of the patrol vehicle, and threw the gun inside. He had no desire to keep his weapon.

Then he hopped into his own vehicle and headed in the direction Dawson provided. He made a quick call to Chief Dodson about everything, hanging up before he could badger him with questions. But he didn't doubt for one second the chief probably thought he was lying, so he didn't care how rude it was when he hung up.

Pressing his foot on the gas pedal, he drove as fast as he could to get to Amelia before they hurt her.

Because as Dax's words rolled through his mind like a horror movie going in slow motion, he was afraid she was already hurt. Maybe even dead.

Matthew Dawson didn't just have a record for the things he mentioned earlier. He also had a few sexual assaults and one attempted rape on his rap sheet.

Thinking about what Amelia was going through was enough to press his foot even harder.

He wouldn't think about it. He couldn't. Not if he wanted to save her in time.

MEL WIGGLED IN THE CHAIR, not to attempt to escape because that was a useless endeavor with how tight the knots were, but to attempt to keep warm. The room wasn't freezing like it was outside, but the longer she sat here, the more the coldness seeped into her bones.

She couldn't feel her fingers anymore. If someone did walk into the room and untie her, she'd be useless to defend herself. She didn't even think she'd be able to move her body, she was so cold.

A loud crash echoed in the distance.

Stalling her movements, she listened. And waited.

What was that?

She hadn't heard much since she woke up. A few times she thought she heard voices, but never anything distinctive. And nobody had entered the room. She couldn't be sure how much time had passed. Maybe an hour. Maybe two.

Time seemed to stretch when one was tied to a chair with no means to escape.

Then loud popping sounds reverberated off the walls.

Pop! Pop! Pop!

She screamed, jerking violently as if she could run away. Because that sounded like gunshots.

But it was the wrong thing to do because when she jerked, she jerked too hard, making the chair wobble and topple backward.

She hit the floor with a rough blow, knocking her head against the hardwood floor. The air rushed out of her lungs like she had been sucker punched right in the gut. Trying to inhale a simple breath was difficult.

Concentrating on breathing, focusing on that task alone and not the sounds coming from the other part of the cabin, she finally gulped in a breath. She breathed deeply a few times, then went as silent as a mouse.

No sounds could be heard anymore.

What was going on out there? Who shot who, and why?

The door swung open.

Sucking in a sharp breath, she held it. Lying with her back to the floor tied to a chair, she was unable to see who opened the door, and she had no desire to see who walked in. Her eyes slammed shut.

"Oh, God, Amelia. Are you okay?"

At Newman's worried tone of voice, her eyes snapped open. He knelt beside her, his face twisted in agony.

"I'm fine. The sounds scared me and I fell backward. Can you untie me, please?"

"Of course." He gently raised the chair to a sitting position, jarring her teeth a little when it bounced back to all four. "Sorry. Hold on a sec while I undo these knots. Are you sure you're okay? Please tell me they didn't touch you."

Besides knocking her out, kidnapping her, and tying her to a chair, no. Thank God, no, they didn't touch her in any other manner, which was what he was asking.

"I'm better now. You're here. I knew you'd come."

He stalled in undoing the knots around her wrists to look at her. His expression was full of puzzlement. "Did you? Because I was afraid I'd never find you. Finding Adam was pure dumb luck."

"I've always had complete faith in you. Nothing's changed that. You're my hero, Newman. Didn't you realize that from the moment you agreed to help find Adam?"

He averted his gaze and went back to the ropes. "Well, you can thank my friend Dax. He called me after I found your car abandoned on the side of the road. I was about to go out of my mind with worry when he gave me everything I needed. These men will never hurt you or Adam again."

"Thank you."

The ropes around her wrists fell off. He started working on the ropes around her chest and had those off as easily as he did her wrists. Not a minute or two later he had her feet free as well.

Then he met her gaze. "You don't have to thank me. I would do anything for you."

And that was why he was her hero. Even when he didn't want to help her, he did.

Before she could protest, he scooped her up.

"I can walk."

"Can you? It's freezing in here. And I don't know how long they had you tied up."

Good point. Her entire body was tingling. She was starting to get feeling back in her joints after sitting in one position for so long, but she probably wouldn't have been able to take one step.

"What time is it?"

"A little after noon."

Her bottom lip started to tremble. "I left the house around 8:30."

Oh, God, she had been here far longer than she realized.

Kissing the side of her head, he squeezed her tighter in his arms. "It's okay. I got you now."

But for how long?

He didn't want anything to do with her besides be her friend. After the morning she had, she wasn't sure she had any energy left to fight him about it.

"Close your eyes," he whispered as he walked out of the room.

"Why?"

He inhaled deeply before kissing the side of her head again. "Because I don't want you to see a dead body. I had to shoot one of them."

Well, he did say he would never lie to her. In this instance, she wished he would've. But, not wanting to see a dead body, she closed her eyes as he recommended and didn't reopen them until they were outside and he was helping her into his car.

He rounded the car quickly and immediately started it. The heat felt wonderful on her frozen body.

"I'm taking you to the hospital. I have to call Chief Dodson on the way, so I don't want you to be alarmed at what I tell him."

She nodded but didn't respond otherwise. She knew he had to relay everything to the chief.

Shivering, as he started to back out of the poorly shoveled driveway, she wrapped her arms around her middle to stave off the cold.

He abruptly stopped the car, unbuckled his belt, and took off his coat, and then wrapped it around her. He smiled but said nothing as he buckled himself again and started driving.

She barely listened as Newman relayed everything. How he came up to the cabin and knocked on the door. She actually didn't believe that part of the story because with the loud bang she heard, it sounded more like a door being kicked in, not someone knocking. But she wasn't going to dispute his version of events since she wasn't able to see anything. Then he told the chief one of the men pulled out a gun and he had to fight him for it. The other man ran off as they struggled with each other. In the process of fighting, he managed to get the gun away and was forced to shoot.

He ended the conversation with they were heading to the hospital and that's where he could find both of them. He said the dead man was Earl Dawson and the man on the loose was Matthew Dawson. She immediately wondered how he knew their names, but then remembered his friend had called with information.

She jumped when he grabbed her hand.

"Sorry. I didn't mean to startle you." He started to remove his hand from hers, but she tightened the grip before he could.

"I'm just a little jumpy. I'm fine, though."

He didn't take his eyes off the road, but she heard his soft sigh. "You're tough, Amelia. But after everything that happened, I'd be surprised if you're fine. I'm still not fine after I was accused of murdering a woman I slept with once."

She almost held her breath waiting for him to continue but didn't as it hurt to hold in air so long after having the wind knocked out of her.

But he didn't continue.

"Why would they think that? You'd never murder anyone."

He glanced at her with a gentle smile. "I just killed a man."

"In self-defense. Not murder."

"Very true. I guess they thought so because I never told my partner or my captain that I knew the woman. I slept with her when I was dating Chrissy. She was the other woman." He sighed. "I didn't mean to keep it a secret. It was just...hard to confess. Hard to say that I made a mistake."

"I can see why you needed to take a breather and think

about things. But you're a good man. You can still do what you love. And you love being a detective."

"I'll never be a detective again, no matter how much I want it. I've burned my bridges there." He grasped her hand a little harder. "After knowing everything about me, I can't fathom why you still see me as a good man. You asked me why I always think I have to be perfect and if I'm not then I'm a failure. Because I've never been perfect. I've always been a failure. I've heard it so many times from my parents that I'm not sure what else I'm supposed to believe. I've heard it from teachers, although not in those exact words. More like, your brother always did this with flying colors, or he could ace a test with his eyes closed. I never measured to perfection when compared to my brother. And even in my job, I failed to be honest to my best friend and partner. What does that make me but a failure. There's your honest answer."

She thought she had been in pain, tortured, tied to a chair in a cold, empty room. That feeling didn't compare to how she felt sitting in a car, holding the hand of the man she loved, knowing this was the end. He was officially saying good-bye and throwing her out of his life.

She asked him to answer the question honestly and she believed he did.

In doing so she promised to walk away without arguing.

It was going to be the hardest thing she ever did.

Harder than seeing Adam again and getting through his stubbornness, and boy, she dreaded that.

She didn't release his hand as he continued to drive to the hospital. But she closed her eyes and tried to forget how much she'd miss him when he finally walked away and never returned.

25

NEWMAN RAN a tired hand through his hair. "Did Dawson say anything useful yet? Like where his cousin Matthew would run and hide."

Chief Dodson shook his head as he glanced down the hallway of the hospital, then back at him. "He gave us a list of places he might go, but we haven't tracked him down yet. I've got every available officer on it, and I've also notified the other surrounding agencies. He won't get far."

He wished he could help search, but he didn't want to leave Amelia's side. She was still acting like nothing bad happened, like none of this affected her, and he knew better. She was holding it in until she could break down alone. Well, he wasn't about to abandon her now. When he first got released, after being interrogated for murdering four women, he went home alone. Nobody was by his side, and it made the pain worse.

Amelia would never feel alone.

She was resting in one of the rooms while he spoke with Chief Dodson. She had already seen the doctor, who gave her the all clear to leave soon, having witnessed no serious injuries besides rope burn on her arms and wrists. Chief Dodson had also taken her statement. Not once did he use a condescending tone of voice like he didn't believe her. There was enough evidence and testimony from one of his own officers that what happened really happened.

"You'll let me know when you find him."

Chief Dodson nodded. "I will." Then he cleared his throat. "And I'd like to apologize for my attitude. For not believing them. I saw a juvenile delinquent in Adam when I should've seen a kid in need of help. Sounds like Officer Dawson's son and his friends were talking shit about Adam to Earl, who decided to teach Adam a lesson. At least, that's the story Officer Dawson's son is claiming. He said Earl swore he wouldn't hurt him."

Newman had to control himself and not ball his hands into fists. Those punks...

"They left him in that room with no food and water for more than four days. How is that teaching him any sort of lesson?"

Chief Dodson eyed his fists that he hadn't managed to control, but didn't say a word. "I'm charging Officer Dawson with accessory to kidnapping, and I'm thinking about charging those three kids with something, too. They were all aware of what happened to Adam, but none of them came forward."

He blew out a slow breath and relaxed his fists. "That should teach *them* a lesson."

"Yes, it should. Are you leaving town any time soon? We do need to conduct a full investigation into the shooting today."

Newman figured they would. It was a clean shooting. He didn't want to shoot the guy. But it was his life versus Earl's and he wasn't ready to die. He could've approached the cabin in a more stealth-like manner and caught them unaware, but honestly, he hadn't been in the right frame of mind. His only thought had been to get to Amelia.

He didn't knock on the door like he said either. It was more like he shoved it open and it swung so fiercely it smacked into the wall, which sounded like a knock. Close enough.

"I'm not sure. Adam left with my friends for a breather. Amelia might want to see him and I'm not sure I want her driving. She's still pretty shaken up." He paused, hating to ask, but he had to. "Am I not allowed to leave town?"

Chief Dodson looked deep in thought, then grinned. "You can. I don't doubt you had no choice. Just let me know as a courtesy if you do."

"I can do that."

Chief Dodson said good-bye and walked away. Newman joined Amelia in the room, careful to be quiet when it looked like she was sleeping. Yet, her eyes popped open as soon as he sat down next to her bed.

"I want to go home. I'm fine."

Every time she said she was fine, it grated on his nerves. She couldn't be fine. Because *he* wasn't fine. He could still picture her tied helplessly to the chair lying on her back. Her eyes filled with fright, her wrists bruised and deep-red marks from the ropes being too tight. He didn't think he'd ever get that image out of his head.

But if she wanted to go home, then that's what he'd make happen. He'd do anything for her.

He stood up. "I'll see what I can do."

She smiled and closed her eyes once again.

He managed to get her discharged about an hour later. She was more steady on her feet than when they first arrived, but he didn't care. He picked her up and walked her to his car and helped her inside, wrapping her back up in his coat. She closed her eyes as soon as he started driving.

She had to be exhausted. Some rest and relaxation was all she needed and she'd be back to her normal self.

Instead of heading to her house, he headed for his cabin. He passed her vehicle still sitting on the side of the road and made a mental reminder to get it towed to the local mechanic. The less she had to deal with, the better.

When they reached his cabin and he shut off the car, she finally opened her eyes. The question was in her gaze why he brought her here, but she didn't say anything. He took that as a good sign. Carrying her from the car to the cabin, he deposited her in the bathroom. "A nice warm shower should help you relax, and then you can take a nap in my room. You need to rest."

"I could've done all this at my own house."

"I'm sure you could've."

Then he walked out of the bathroom and closed the door. He had to leave her alone. Because if he stayed gazing into her battered, desolate eyes still full of terror, he wouldn't be able to resist helping her. Removing her clothes and all. Hell, even get in the shower with her.

He decided to make her a cup of hot chocolate while she showered. She claimed it was the best she ever had. He made a quick phone call regarding her car, and one call to Sauer to give him an update. Sauer said he'd call Ben and Zeke for him. Adam wasn't aware that anything even happened. For now, he was okay with that. He'd leave it up to Amelia whether she wanted Adam to know what happened to her.

He carried the hot mug to his bedroom and set it on the nightstand and then turned to leave the room.

He froze in place.

Amelia stood wrapped in a white fluffy towel, her pink hair a tangled wet mess, her eyes filled with agony. Yet she looked like an angel sent down from heaven. And she was. His angel. He found his redemption when he met her. She saved him from a life of misery and loneliness.

The question was how did he tell her?

"Feel better?"

She nodded. "I feel clean."

"Let me grab you a shirt."

Rummaging through his dresser, he grabbed a pair of boxers that wouldn't fit her well and snatched a T-shirt from the closet. Then he set it on the bed and smiled.

"I'll let you rest."

He started to walk past her when she grabbed his hand. "Rest with me."

She said it as a statement, yet it hung in the air as a question. As if she wasn't completely confident in what he would say. He had no problem resting with her. In fact, he was dying to hold her in his arms and make some of the pain disappear. Some of the terrible memories wither away.

"Of course."

She smiled, then walked to the bed and dropped the towel. He tried to keep his feet planted firmly in their place as her sweet, soft body from behind made him salivate. Damn, but it was going to be difficult keeping his hands to himself. But he would and not make a move until he knew she was ready. Now was not the time to be thinking of sex.

She put on the shirt and boxers, which slid down her hips. She kept a hold of them until she climbed into bed and scooted over to make room for him.

He took off his pants but kept his shirt on so he didn't make her worry or nervous that his mind was thinking in the wrong direction.

As soon as he slid into bed, she scooted closer to him. He let her fall into his arms and pulled her as close as he could get her. Then he ran a hand through her wet hair, untangling a few strands and kissed her forehead.

"I made you some hot chocolate. Do you want a sip?"

Her head shook against his chest as her hand gripped his side. "Not right now, but that was thoughtful of you."

"Okay. Close your eyes and rest."

"You'll stay with me the entire time?"

He kissed her forehead once more. "I won't leave your side for anything. You're safe now. I promise."

She clutched him tighter. "I feel safer." A tiny cry slipped from her lips. "I was so terrified. You're right. I'm not fine. I feel like I'm still tied to that chair."

"It'll take time, but those memories will fade. You're safe. I will never let anyone hurt you like that again."

Never again.

He loved her so much. This morning, the fear and panic he experienced when she went missing confirmed it even more how much he loved her. How much he needed her in his life.

Now, he had to tell her. Confess his feelings.

He was a coward. His actions three months ago proved that as a fact.

Was he still a coward? Could he profess his love?

If so, would she believe him? Would she trust that he would never hurt her as he had with Chrissy? Because as long as he lived, he vowed to be a better man than he was before.

NEWMAN OPENED HIS EYES, surprised to find he fell asleep quite easily. The events of the day hadn't just wiped Amelia out, but him as well. A quick glance toward his window said they slept the afternoon away. Night had descended. Twisting to catch a glance at his clock on the nightstand said they slept heavily for a long time.

"What time is it?"

Shifting his gaze to Amelia, he kissed her forehead before responding. "A little after midnight. I didn't mean to wake you up. How do you feel?"

"Like I could sleep another whole day."

"Then you can."

She smiled. With the moonlight pouring into the room, it gave him enough light to see the happiness in her eyes. He could've shouted for joy seeing that emotion and not the fear that had held her captive earlier in the day.

"And what do you plan to do?"

His hand slid down her back. She shivered in response. "Whatever you're doing."

"Thank you."

"You don't have to thank me for anything. I'd do anything for you."

"Because that's the kind of friend you are?"

A dose of pain entered her golden hazel eyes as she asked. This was his chance to confess. His heart started to pound. With her body wrapped perfectly in his arms, she most likely felt the change of pace.

"No, because I..." He dipped his head and kissed her lightly on the lips. Only long enough to tell her without words what he was trying to say. He didn't think he could actually voice those three little words yet.

He willed his heart to slow down and not give his nervousness away. It had been a long time since he felt nervous with a woman, to the point he didn't want to screw up one little thing and ruin the moment.

"Are you going to finish your sentence?" She had a sweet smile brimming on her face, with teasing laughter in her eyes, as if she knew what he wanted to say but couldn't.

"You should rest."

Her brows rose. "You're changing the subject. How interesting. We slept the day away. I feel rested."

He drew his hand back up her body, relishing in the delightful way she trembled in his arms. He should stop this maddening torture because the only thing he was doing was teasing them both. "Then I should feed you."

Her lips connected with his. "Or maybe you should finish your sentence."

"You deserve better than me."

Her brows drew together in puzzlement. "Are you trying to convince me to stay, or push me away? I can't tell. With you, I wouldn't be surprised if you're trying to push me away. You want me well rested. You want to feed me. You're comforting me and making sure I feel safe. Yet, what you're really doing is pushing me away. Why?"

"I don't know. I..." He closed his eyes, berating himself for not telling her the truth. He met her worried look. "You do deserve better than me."

"Don't we all deserve a second chance? Or are you the only one who doesn't get it? Is it written in some rule book I know nothing about?"

God, he loved her saucy attitude. Giving him hell for trying to hide behind his fear. Because that was what he was doing. Hiding. Being a damn scaredy cat and not admitting his feelings.

"I cheated on my ex. I'm ashamed of my actions. Don't you think you deserve a better man than that?"

Amelia's lips pressed into a thin, raging line. "I once added cayenne pepper to my father's coffee when he wasn't looking. I thoroughly enjoyed watching him sputter and cough when he took a big gulp. I regretted it the moment he started beating me for it. We all make mistakes we shouldn't have done."

Newman made a mental note to always sip his coffee carefully when Amelia was around, especially if they argued beforehand. How couldn't he love this fierce, unapologetic woman who constantly made him see he wasn't a bad person. Just a man who made mistakes. Something every person did once or twice in life.

That didn't mean he could get three simple words out. What happened if she didn't return the sentiment? Sure, she didn't see him as a lying, cheating bastard, but that didn't mean she loved him back.

"How did we get on this topic again? Shouldn't we grab a bite to eat? I'm famished."

"You're such an idiot." Then her lips connected with his. Strong and intense, kissing him like it would be her last breath she'd ever take. She let go as fast as she started. "I love you. Right now, I'm questioning why and how long it's going to take you to realize I don't care what you did in the past. I want to look to the future. Nothing good ever comes from living in the past. I should know. I had a real shitty one."

Damn.

He was an idiot.

But hearing her confession first, knowing it wasn't one-sided, made his heart that was beating rapidly slow down to a steady rhythm.

"So, I ask again. Are we just friends here? Finish your sentence from before. Is that all we're ever going to be?"

He swallowed hard, the words still lodged deep in his throat.

"I..." He swallowed again. "I don't want to be just friends."

"No? Why?"

Well, he knew he would never have it easy with Amelia in his life, and oddly, he was okay with that. One more reason he loved her. Her strength and in-your-face attitude. It would definitely keep him in his place when he needed to be re-directed.

"Because I love you, too." His words floated out in a whisper.

The way her eyes lit up with glee and happiness, he knew she heard what he said. He was such a coward, he couldn't even say them loud and proud.

"Because I want you to get used to saying it, I insist you repeat it all the time." A sinfully sexy brow rose as she twisted her lips into a devilish smile. "And you did say you'd do anything for me."

Laughter burst free. Oh, he did say that. What his Amelia wanted, she got. "If you insist, sweetheart."

Then he kissed her before she could insist he say it again so soon. Baby steps. He needed quite a few baby steps.

The kiss turned from sweet and tender to rough and frantic. He pulled her closer, then twisted so he was lying on top of her. Her hands roamed up and down his back, her nails digging in, urging the kiss higher and higher and higher.

Pressing into her, letting her feel how hard he was, how much he wanted to dive deep inside, he kept rocking and rocking as the kiss didn't stop.

They paused a brief moment when he brought her shirt up and over her head. His shirt disappeared just as quickly.

Then they were right back to the intense kiss. Her soft, warm hands running across his body was the sweetest, most erotic sensation he had ever felt. He had to tell her later to touch him more often.

"I want to feel you this time..." He grinned deviously. "Without the clothes on." His expression turned fierce. "I need to feel you. I need to be deep inside of you. I can't wait any longer."

"It's your own fault. I wanted sex days ago."

He chuckled, snatching a kiss before reaching over to his nightstand to grab a condom from the drawer. Tossing off his boxers at the same time she did, he sheathed his rock hard cock and positioned himself over her delicate, gorgeous body.

"I still don't feel like I deserve you." He brushed a tender hand across her cheek, soaking up the softness in every corner of her body.

"I'm far from perfect, Newman. I never asked for perfect, and you're the only man I want."

Her words hit his heart with a loud bang. They were starting to actually make a dent and make him believe they were true. He didn't wait any longer, easing himself inside her. He didn't take his time because he was unsure how long it had been since she last had sex, but because he wanted to savor and appreciate how beautiful she felt.

She wrapped her slender arms around him and pulled his head closer, kissing him with such warmth, he knew she was savoring the moment as much as him.

When he was fully inside her, he waited a moment, kissing her passionately and delightfully, tangling tongues and speaking without words how much she meant to him. Then he started moving. In and out. Lightly, yet blissfully. Making each thrust a sign of how much he loved her.

She answered in return. Meeting him every time with abandoned pleasure.

This was nothing like the other night on the couch. That had been filled with fun loving.

This, right here, was exquisitely beautiful lovemaking that he had never experienced with a woman. He felt connected with her, not just with their bodies, but also with their souls. Like she was the missing puzzle piece that he had always searched for in life. The piece that finally made him perfect in a small way.

The heat and fervency grew to epic proportions. Their pace increased, yet moving as one powerful couple.

He could feel his body tensing, the ecstasy rising to the surface. By her low, gentle moans as they kissed, she was rising right with him.

Breaking the kiss, he lifted himself up, pumping harder. Her head went back as her eyes closed, her nails dragging a brutal path down his back.

The pleasure and pain hit him directly in the heart. He wanted more. More of her. More of her love. More of her beauty. More of her acceptance.

Getting closer, dipping his mouth toward her neck, he pressed a few tender kisses, then bit her ear. Maybe he told her in an unspoken gesture what he wanted because her lips found his shoulder and teeth sunk in.

The feeling shot right through his body like a loose firecracker going out of control. He tensed, holding her like he never wanted to let her go as his orgasm hit. Her hands and nails seared into his back as a low, throaty moan escaped her luscious red lips as she flew with him into bliss.

"I love you, Amelia."

A sweet trail of kisses brushed across his shoulder and neck and up to his lips. "I love you, too."

Rolling to her side so he didn't crush her, he smiled wickedly. "Are you hungry now? Can I feed you?"

She licked her lips as a saucy smile wouldn't disappear. "Depends what's on the menu. Will you be feeding me in bed?"

"Your wish is my command." He kissed her once before sliding off the bed and taking the condom off to dispose of it. "Keep the bed warm and I'll be right back with food."

He walked out of the room with her gorgeous body and the things he planned to do with her all night long on his mind. It was a very good thing they slept so long because she wouldn't be getting a wink of sleep for the rest of the night.

26

Mel shifted in the seat and folded her hands. Then she shifted again, unfolding her hands. Twisting her legs to curl slightly toward the left, she smoothed her hands across her thighs.

Then she decided she'd rather have her legs toward the right and shifted once more.

"Stop."

Newman grabbed her hand before she could fold them once again and linked it with his and set it on his lap.

He smiled at her before turning his attention back to the road.

"I'm antsy. It's been a long drive."

He brought her hand up to his mouth and kissed the back of it before placing it on his lap. "It's going to be okay. He'll be happy to see you."

She wasn't as positive about the prospect as Newman appeared to be. Adam hadn't spoken to her once since he ventured to St. Cloud with Ben. She knew he was doing well and enjoying his time, but she only knew that from updates from Ben, not from Adam.

The past two days had been wonderful. She and Newman didn't leave the cabin for anything. They barely left the bed. Although, for meals, they did eat in the kitchen, and a few times they worked out with the punching bag. Newman insisted. He said it would be good for her, to banish the negative memories. He told her for every punch she delivered, bring a bad memory with it, release it from her system. And it helped her. She always felt rejuvenated and ready to take on any obstacle in her path afterward.

Other than that, they enjoyed each other in bed. Sometimes not even making love, but holding each other, letting the quiet surround them.

Chief Dodson stopped by the cabin and informed Newman he had been cleared from any wrongdoing in the shooting. He also said they found Matthew Dawson attempting to leave town with help from an old friend. He had been found hiding in the back of a pickup truck underneath a blue tarp.

That made her feel safer. None of those men could hurt her or Adam again. Last night, Newman suggested they visit Adam and tell him everything that happened and what was about to happen.

But the longer they drove, the more the worry dug deeper inside. She wondered if maybe Newman should tell Adam everything. He seemed to like Newman more anyway. Adam never wanted to talk to her about anything, no matter how hard she tried.

"I can feel the words churning in your mind. Stop worrying, sweetheart." He brought her hand up again and kissed it. "Please, you're going to make yourself sick."

That wasn't a lie. She woke up once frightened from a nightmare so terrible it sent her rushing to the bathroom to throw up. She'd like to say the last two days had been the best because they had been beautiful and pleasant, but she couldn't. But what made the days wonderful was Newman and his support and his tender love that he let peek through more and more every second of every day.

He kept her grounded a lot more than he realized. Especially when he called her sweetheart. No man had ever used silly endearments with her, and she found she actually liked it. At least, when Newman said it, she liked it.

"I don't want him to hate me."

He squeezed her hand. "He doesn't hate you. I know he doesn't express himself well, but he loves you. Trust me on this."

No matter how many times Newman said he was the wrong guy for her, a lying cheating bastard, she trusted him. In everything.

She blew out a slow breath to calm her erratic emotions. "You're right. I do trust you, and you're right. You're terrible with expressing yourself, and I know you love me, so I have to remember that when it comes to Adam."

A low chuckle drifted her way and then another soft kiss hit her hand.

"I love how you remind me all the time about my shortcomings. I've been trying to express myself better."

She smiled at him with the love shining in her eyes. Oh, he had been trying so hard. She had to be strong and in his face the past two days to get childhood memories and stories out of him, but he started to open up a little more. Anytime she insisted he say three little words because she adored hearing he loved her—and to annoy him because she knew it was difficult for him to say—her heart did a little happy dance every time he caved in. He didn't like to do those things, but he did. Because he loved her. Truly and unconditionally loved her.

She had to remember that regarding Adam.

Twenty minutes later, the ride finally came to an end. It felt like the longest three hours of her life. She took her time getting out of the vehicle and walking to the front door of Ben's house to get all the kinks out of her body from sitting so long. Definitely not because she was nervous to see her brother.

"It's going to be fine." Newman kissed her softly on the lips, then knocked on the door.

A beautiful woman with auburn hair and a gentle smile opened the door. "Hi, Newman. Come on in. You must be Amelia. It's so nice to meet you. I'm Rina, Ben's wife."

Rina offered her hand after they stepped inside and shut the door. Mel shook her hand and tried to make sure her smile didn't display her nerves.

"It's nice to meet you, too. Thank you for watching Adam these past few days. I appreciate it. Oh, and you can call me Mel."

It was silly of her, but she kind of liked how Newman said her full name Amelia. People usually called her Mel, and she wanted to reserve Amelia just for Newman. She wouldn't be a bitch about it if they insisted on using Amelia, but hey, it wouldn't hurt to throw it out there what they should call her.

"He's been great. He and Nicholas get along so well. They're inseparable."

Her erratic heartbeat started to slow down a tiny fraction. That was great to hear. Maybe her news wouldn't be so bad after all.

"Hey, man. You guys made it," Ben said jovially as he joined them in the foyer, sliding an arm around his wife.

"Yeah, it wasn't a bad drive. Did you guys eat yet? I

should've called and told you to wait. We thought we'd take Adam out to eat before we head to my place."

That was the plan Newman told her they should do before they left and she didn't argue. When it came to Adam, she was trusting Newman to know what was best, which was crazy, considering he barely knew her brother. Yet they had a strong connection, so she trusted his judgment.

"We didn't. Rina has lasagna cooking. We thought we'd invite you to stay," Ben replied, looking back and forth between them.

That was nice of them, but Mel was slightly disappointed. Not that she wasn't grateful for their kindness, but she wanted to get the conversation over with.

"Yeah, of course. We'd love that. We don't want to impose or anything," Newman said as he grabbed her hand in reassurance. Something she desperately needed. Because how was Adam going to act with her in front of others? Would he still have the I-don't-care-about-you attitude?

"You're not. We'd love to have you stay. Honestly, it might be hard to pry Adam away from the gaming system with Nicholas." Rina chuckled.

Nothing but dread filled her up. Great. Adam would cause a scene and make her look like a bitch.

"Hey, Aunt Rina, I don't mean to interrupt, but I hear Corrine crying. I swear we were being quiet," a tall, handsome teenager with brown wavy hair said with a pinched expression as if he waited for them to holler for waking the baby. She assumed he was Ben's nephew Nicholas.

"It's fine. She's ready for a bottle," Rina replied in a soft, sweet tone, belaying without much effort that she wasn't upset.

"Hey, you finish up what you were doing in the kitchen

and Nicholas and I will feed Corrine," Ben suggested, glancing between Rina and Nicholas as he did.

"Do I have to help?" Nicholas mumbled.

"Yes, you do." Ben's tone of voice brooked no argument. Then he looked at her and Newman. "Adam's in the last room on the right. We turned it into a playroom of sorts. Corrine's not old enough to play with her toys yet, but when she is, it's all ready for her. We set up the gaming system there, too."

"Thanks, man." Newman squeezed her hand, obviously knowing she still needed his strength.

They all went their separate ways. Newman walked down the hallway and entered the room first. Adam's face lit up when he saw Newman, yet his features dimmed when his eyes landed on her.

Newman smiled as he pointed to the television. "I don't have that game, but I have this sweet racing game. I'll kick your butt at my house. We can play that later if you want."

"Your house?" Adam asked as he stood up from the pink bean bag he had been sitting on.

Mel wanted to smile at seeing her cranky, moody brother sitting on anything pink, but she held it in. She didn't want him to think she was laughing at him for any reason.

"Yeah, my house. If that's cool?"

"Yeah, totally cool," Adam said with a shrug, as if it weren't a big deal, but she could tell it was a huge deal.

Newman pulled her closer, wrapping an arm around her shoulder. "I'll let you and Amelia have a chat. She'll explain. She's much better at words than I am."

She couldn't hold back a glare when Newman met her gaze, a silly grin on his face. What was he doing? She didn't want to have this talk with Adam here. The man just officially put himself in the doghouse for the first time. She doubted it would be the last.

He winked, pulled her in for a hug and whispered in her ear, "You got this. Get it over with. He'll be fine." Then he kissed her on the lips and left the room.

She watched until Newman was out of view, then turned toward her brother. His expression definitely said he didn't want to be in the room with her.

"He kissed you." Adam shrugged. "Does that, like, mean you're a couple or something?"

She shrugged as well. "Yeah, a couple, I guess. If that's cool?"

Maybe if she used the same kind of words as Newman she'd get a better reception from Adam.

Another tilt of his shoulder went up. "Yeah, I guess. He's cool."

"Cool."

Geez, how many times were they going to say cool? Was that an in thing these days? She didn't even know.

"So, how long are we staying with him? I didn't see a gaming system at his place. He doesn't even have a TV."

"He has a house here. We're going to stay there tonight." The rest of her words stalled.

Although, the conversation was going pretty well so far. She had to admit that.

"How come he has two places?"

"Well, he lives here. He was just staying at his cabin for a while to sort things out in his head."

"So he's moving back here?"

Mel nodded.

Adam's lower lip started to wobble, then he sniffed and it stopped. "When are we going back to that shitty-ass town? We might as well go right now."

A lone tear slid down her cheek. She wiped it away before Adam witnessed it, but she didn't think she was fast enough.

"I thought maybe we wouldn't go back to that shitty-ass town. Maybe we'd stay with Newman instead."

"Here? In this town?"

"Yeah. If that's cool with you? I know all this moving hasn't been ideal. I know the things that happened to you sucked, but I'm here for you. I want what's best for you. I'm trying, Adam. I've been trying."

His bottom lip started to tremble again. Then he was moving and his arms were wrapping around her body so tight she couldn't breathe at first. And she didn't even care. This was the first time her brother had ever initiated a hug with her. She wrapped her arms around him, and she'd hang on for as long as he'd let her.

"I'm sorry, Mel. I don't mean to be a brat. I don't. I like it here. I want to stay. I like Newman. I'm cool with it."

"Cool."

She had no other eloquent words. Her brother was speaking to her, sharing his feelings, and hugging her, and she had no brilliant words other than cool. Because, damn, it *was* cool.

Adam started to pull away, swiping at his eyes. She pretended not to notice that he shed a few tears.

"If you ever want to talk about...whatever. I'm here. Or, you know, Newman is, too." She thought she'd throw that out there. She needed her brother to know she'd always be there for him.

"Yeah, I know. Ditto." He looked away, averting his eyes to the ground. "I might've overheard Ben and Rina talking the other night. I heard what happened to you. I'm glad you're okay."

She sucked in a sharp breath. That was the last thing she wanted her brother to know. "I'm fine. But thank you. It's nice to know you're there for me if I need a shoulder to cry on."

He looked panicked for a second until she started to laugh. Then he joined her.

"I don't mean literally cry. Like, to talk."

"Yeah, of course." He shrugged as if he knew that's what she had meant. "I also heard they got the guys. I knew Newman would."

She smiled. "I did, too."

A slow smile crept up until his face was filled with nothing but happiness. "I have a good feeling about this place. I swear I won't be as much trouble as I was before. I'll try harder this time."

"Me, too. This is a new beginning for both of us." She chuckled. "Hell, it's a new beginning for all three of us."

She gestured toward the hallway. "Food smells great. Should we see if it's done?"

"Yeah. Rina's a great cook."

"Better than me?" Mel said as she followed him out of the room.

He gave her an innocent look but laughed. "I mean, yeah. Sorry, Mel. Your meals are okay, but you could use some practice."

"Ouch. Don't be gentle on my feelings, geez." She grabbed him in a playful headlock and ruffled his hair.

He laughed as he pushed her away. "Your soup is amazing. I'll give you that."

They joined Rina and Newman in the kitchen. Rina immediately asked Adam to set the table. He complied without complaint. Maybe she'd send Adam over to their house more often.

Before joining Adam to help, Newman grabbed her around the waist and kissed her. "So, how did it go?"

"You're a smart man. He took it well."

"I'm glad you think so. And of course he did. Because he knows you love him." He kissed her again. "And I love you."

Oh, she would never tire of hearing those three little words coming out of his mouth.

Although he didn't say it often, unless she dragged it out of him, she knew it without any words spoken. She saw it in his eyes when he looked at her with heated desire. In his hands, when they caressed her from top to bottom in slow, delicious torture. In his actions, when he made sure everything in her life went as smoothly as possible.

Like today.

For a man who didn't think he was worthy enough. Well, she didn't think any other man would ever live up to his love.

EPILOGUE

Two months later

MEL NODDED her thanks to Zoe as she poured her some more red wine, filling it to the rim.

"I'm no lush, but I'll take it," she said with a giggle.

Zoe proceeded to fill her wineglass up and added some to Susan's as well. "Well, we have to pick up the slack for Rina and Dee who can't have a drink."

"Yes, you might need to drink another glass after that, Mel. I'm craving a glass so badly, you have no idea," Dee said, cocking a brow like she meant some serious business.

It hadn't taken her long to like Dee once she got past the rough exterior. She was a fierce and loyal friend behind all the talk. If Dee wanted something, she did it. If she said something, she meant it. But she had never seen her get downright nasty. Although, there were a few times she saw evil daggers in Newman's direction. She usually glared a few back in retaliation and Dee calmed herself down.

She was blessed to have found such wonderful friends.

All four of these ladies—Zoe, Rina, Dee, and Susan— she would've never met if not for Newman.

The move to St. Cloud had been painless and easy to settle in. It also helped Newman's friends banded around her and Adam and helped move things along. When they unpacked their things, Susan mentioned they always went out for drinks on Friday nights and asked if she wanted to join them. She hesitated, but then said sure.

That had been the start of entering their small-knit group. She wouldn't trade those nights for the world.

"We'll be having a glass in no time. It goes so fast. My sweet Corrine is four months old. Time flies," Rina said in her soft tone. And Mel had come to find that Rina never talked in any other tone of voice. Mad, sad, happy, annoyed, she always used the same soft tone, yet a person could decipher quite easily how she was feeling. It was amazing. It fascinated her.

"Yeah, I know. My sweet Brock smiled today. Sauer thinks it was gas because he's only two weeks old, but I'm telling you, he smiled at me." Dee nodded, her lips pressed together, daring anyone to argue with her.

"Isn't it wonderful? Zabrina is already walking. Like, I have a zooming toddler on my hands." Zoe laughed with the happiness shining brightly in her eyes.

"We haven't started trying yet for kids, but Stitch swears we're only having one after being around your kids lately." Susan rolled her eyes. They landed on the man himself sitting across the room with the other guys drinking beer and chatting amongst themselves.

Rina laughed. "That silly man. Corrine accidentally spit up once when he was holding her. Yes, it's common, but he'll get over it when it's his own child."

"Oh, I know. All I have to do is mention sex and he's all

about the baby making stage in the moment. It's when he's holding the actual baby he gets all nervous like he's going to break it or something," Susan said with a chuckle.

"How about you, Mel? You want kids anytime soon?"

Mel met Dee's intense stare. Leave it to her to put her on the spot about something kind of personal. Some people might take offense to such a question. She and Newman weren't even engaged. Yes, they were a couple. Yes, they had been living together for the past two months. Yes, things had been going well. But it didn't mean they were ready for kids.

Hell, she wanted a ring on her finger before kids even came into the equation. And she was ready to say yes whenever he was ready to ask. But it had been like pulling teeth to get him to admit his feelings. She didn't expect a proposal so soon in their relationship. It would be crazy if he did.

"I'll pass for right now. I have one kid, and he's a lot to handle." Adam might not be her kid, but she was raising him like he was, so it kind of counted.

Although, since leaving the small town filled with bad memories and haunting events, he'd been much better. They got along well. He actually talked to her with respect, and when she asked how school went, most days he responded with a kind answer. He didn't hesitate to ask for help with his homework anymore either. Such a huge step in the right direction. It helped Newman was there to guide him along and teach him things their dad never bothered to teach him. Like how to respect others, how to be responsible, and how to own one's actions. He taught those three things in spades.

Having a best friend for the first time, Ben's nephew Nicholas, also helped. Those two were inseparable, hanging out every weekend playing video games. Baseball season was coming soon and Nicholas played, insisting Adam had to join as well. She already paid the registration fee and equipment he needed. She was excited to watch him get involved in something for once.

"He's such a great kid, Mel. You're doing a great job with him," Zoe said with a gentle smile. "He's great with Zabrina."

He *was* great with the little kids. Such a good thing, too, since he was dubbed the babysitter in the playroom while all the adults hung out, talking and enjoying a few cocktails. Nicholas was over as well, so the two boys didn't mind.

"So..." Susan smiled wickedly as she met her gaze. "I think it's time we talked."

"Oh, girl, you have no idea. I've been waiting all night for this." Dee nodded, clapping her hands with a glee that made her nervous.

Even Rina and Zoe started to smile deviously at her.

Oh, dear.

"About what?"

Susan cleared her throat. "About Aurora Lockheart."

Mel's face instantly flamed with heat. She dropped her head to the table to shield herself. Oh, no. They didn't.

Laughter filled the table, making her cringe with embarrassment.

They totally did.

"Mel, stop. Look at us," Zoe said gently as she tugged on her arm. "Why didn't you tell us you're an author? A romance author."

Mel lifted her head, knowing quite well she was still red in the face. Then she shrugged helplessly. "I don't know. I don't like to talk about it much. It's no big deal."

"You talk about your asshole dad like you're talking about the damn weather, but you don't want to talk about the fact you write amazing stories. No big deal? Um,

Locked in Love was flipping amazing. I couldn't put it down."

Her mouth actually dropped open at Dee's ecstatic words. Because it was always such a huge thrill to hear someone enjoyed her stories. She tried to be active on social media as best as she could, although her presence had declined quite drastically since meeting Newman. She enjoyed spending time with him and Adam more than chatting it up with people on the internet. But she always loved when a reader reached out to her.

"We all read that book. It's great," Susan agreed when she didn't respond to Dee's loud outburst. "You know you can tell us anything. We don't judge here." Susan chuckled as she rolled her eyes a little. "Dee might judge, but we won't."

Dee scoffed and slapped Susan on the shoulder playfully. "Hey, I take offense to that even though it's true."

They all laughed.

"I started writing when I was a little girl. It kept me out of trouble sometimes with my dad. Other times, I couldn't help but be a little terror and piss him off, even though I knew the consequences. I guess when I decided to publish my stuff, I didn't think people would love it as much as they do. Part of the reason I write is to get out the part of myself that feels trapped sometimes. It's a release I need. I guess admitting I'm an author is sharing a part of myself that needs to be hidden. It's kind of why I use a pen name."

"Does Newman know?" Rina asked quietly.

It was a fair question. She kept it a secret from these ladies for over two months, and she was dying to know how they found out.

"I had to confess shortly after we moved in together. He finally asked me what I did for a living, realizing I never had to quit a job or anything when we moved." She laughed remembering the awkward conversation. Or maybe it was only awkward on her part because she had been so embarrassed to admit the truth.

"And what does he think?" Zoe leveled a motherly stare in her direction, her eyes zooming to Newman, a slight glare in her eyes. "Not that his opinion is the end all of everything. But I hope he supports you."

"Oh, he does. He's all about helping with the research when it comes to sex scenes."

The entire table roared with laughter. And it was the truth. Most of the time he joked around about it, but it always led to the bedroom and fun times between the sheets.

"Now I'm going to be picturing you and Newman every time I read a sex scene in one of your books. Thanks a lot," Dee groaned mercifully.

She laughed so hard tears started to form in the corner of her eyes. "Please don't. He likes to joke with me."

"I could give you some good stories about some interesting scenes to use." Susan bounced her eyebrows up and down. "Stitch is always wanting to try new things. The man is certifiable sometimes."

"And you love every minute of it, you dirty girl," Dee said a little too loudly. Then she turned to Rina. "I bet you get really loud in bed, don't you, Rina?"

Rina looked shocked, her cheeks blooming a bright red. "I do not. I'm very quiet."

"Oh my gosh, you ladies are crazy." Mel started laughing hard once again. She seriously loved these women. Loved how easily they accepted her into their lives, into their wonderful circle.

"Well, I guess what we're all saying is, if you need any

help writing a sex scene, we're all for helping with the fun details," Zoe said with a huge smile.

"Honestly, my favorite part was when Drake took Nora to the carnival and spent every last dime he had until he won her that teddy bear. And he didn't have the money to spare. But seeing that smile on her face, he couldn't help but do it until he won," Rina said with the sappiest, sweetest smile.

"Or when he surprised her with the picnic in the back-yard in the middle of winter when she was feeling sick and missing summer. They froze their butts off, but they had so much fun." Susan sighed as a wistful smile touched her lips. "Stitch actually made me hot chocolate the other night and suggested we sit outside on the porch. I might've mentioned the scene to him, and I thought it was so sweet we tried to replicate it a little bit. I did freeze my butt off, though."

Mel joined the laughter as they all chuckled at Susan's touching story.

"You made me cry at the end when he proposed in the middle of the auditorium in front of all the students and teachers. Something so terrifying for him, yet he did it because he knew she'd see how much he wasn't afraid of loving her." Zoe swiped a hand underneath her eye as if a tear had slid down, but Mel didn't see one. "That book is definitely not just about sex, it's so full of...everything. It was a beautiful story."

She looked at each woman, taking her time to connect eyes before moving on to the next. She saw nothing but love and acceptance, and maybe a bit of awe that she wrote something so powerful and raw and filled with emotion.

"Thank you. I'm glad you guys started with that story. The other four stories aren't as emotional as that one."

"Well, when does the next one come out? I'll be caught up with the other ones within the week," Dee said.

Considering the crazy things that happened, settling in a new town, working hard to get her mother out of prison, although it wasn't looking promising, she was way behind on her deadline.

"Soon. If I get my butt in gear. At least a first rough draft that I can let you guys have a sneak peek at."

All four of them squealed with excitement.

Wow. She should've told her friends her little secret two months ago. It was such a wonderful feeling to know her friends were excited for her.

Even Newman. He never once laughed or teased her or called her silly for writing the stories she did. Because she dated one guy who thought she was a loser for wasting her time on silly nonsense, as he called it.

Newman accepted her flaws and all, and supported her writing that meant the world to her.

Yeah, she was ready for the man to ask her to marry him.

She'd totally say yes.

EPILOGUE

(YES, ANOTHER ONE. LOL)

5 Minutes Later

"What do you think they're laughing about? They've been laughing so hard for, like, the past ten minutes." Newman couldn't tear his gaze away as all five women continued to laugh and smile. He couldn't help but watch Amelia as her face lit up with such delight. Her smile always made him want to smile.

"It actually worries me. Especially when Dee leans in like she's whispering some secret they plan to enact," Zeke replied, eyeing the women with a funny expression.

"I wouldn't doubt it. Dee's hormones and craziness have been much better since Brock was born, but she is still my same crazy Dee." Sauer nodded, then took a sip of beer.

Stitch slapped his knee and leaned back into the couch. "She's probably planning Susan's bachelorette party. Deena hasn't stopped bugging Susan about having a stripper. And they're always talking about these fun party favors, like dick shaped suckers and shit. I had to leave the room when they were talking about it, but I told her in no uncertain terms there would not be a stripper involved." He shook his head, reaffirming he meant business. "You say she's toned down her craziness. I don't know about that, man."

Sauer shrugged. "In my house she has. She definitely doesn't worry as much that she's going to be a terrible mother, although it was hard to tear her away from the hospital. But she needed a break, and my mom and dad are up there with Brock right now."

"When does Brock get to come home?" Ben asked. "He's a handsome fellow. He's a strong one, too, even though he came a little earlier than expected."

"The doctor thinks in the next few days. He's got all his organs and he's breathing on his own. He sucks down a bottle like it's nothing. It shouldn't be too much longer." Sauer sighed, although had a smile on his face.

Since moving back, Newman had been keeping in contact with Sauer regularly. Not as often since they didn't work together anymore, but they talked to each other on the phone and grabbed a beer at least once a week. It was nice. When Dee went into labor a month earlier than expected, he and Amelia had been the first people to arrive at the hospital. He spent the entire day in the waiting room with everyone else until Sauer came out of the room and announced Dee delivered a healthy baby boy. But because he came a little early, they hadn't released him yet. They needed his weight to increase and to make sure his breathing stayed normal. Because for the first few days he had a breathing tube that brought tears to his eyes. He had felt so bad for the little guy, and for Dee and Sauer, although they had taken it all in stride and did what they had to do for their son.

"Let us know if you need anything. We're here for you." Newman couldn't resist adding that one more time, even though he said it quite a few times in the last two weeks since Brock was born. He wanted his best friend to know he was there for him. Always. He was trying to be a better friend and a better man. And with Amelia by his side, it helped. She made him want to be better in every aspect of his life. Seeing a tiny look of disappointment on her face always made him sick to his stomach.

"I appreciate it. It means a lot." Sauer smiled.

"Did you solve that theft case you got last week?" Zeke asked as he crossed his leg over his knee.

"I did. His brother took all of his jewelry and pawned it at a pawn shop three blocks from his house. He definitely isn't the sharpest tool in the shed," Newman said with a laugh. "I picked up a new case today. A mother looking for her son. So a missing person, sort of. She thinks he ran off with his girlfriend, who happens to be a drug addict. She's worried about him. But I don't think I'll have to rely on dumb luck like I did with Adam. There's an actual paper trail to follow this time."

"That's good to hear. I mean, not that her son ran off with a druggie, but that your business seems to be doing well," Ben said.

"Yeah, it's not doing too bad at all."

Thankfully.

He had been nervous as hell when Amelia suggested he apply for a private investigator license. After about two hours of her on his case about it, he finally caved and agreed. He also made the decision because he needed to find a job. He couldn't live on his savings forever. Another two weeks later, he had everything squared away. It took another week to land a case. A sweet elderly lady who lost her cat. He managed to find it at a nearby shelter, although it helped her cat had a microchip to identify her. But, of course, the sweet lady thought he did it all on his own and recommended him to her friend.

His caseloads had been somewhat steady and he took almost any case that came along. He always drew the line at any case where the person wanted to know if their significant other was cheating. Having a constant reminder of his one mistake he'd always regret wasn't something he wanted to deal with. He always politely declined and referred the person to another guy he had become friends with, who happened to be a pretty decent PI. His friend appreciated the work, and *he* appreciated the fact he didn't have to deal with cheaters of any variety.

That was a chapter in his life he wished to forget and move on from.

"So, Stitch," Newman said, twisting his lips into a devious smirk, "when are we going to plan your bachelor party?"

"Oh, yeah. We need to do something amazing. Like Vegas or something," Zeke said with excitement, clapping his hands together gleefully.

"That seems a little over the top. I don't need any of that shit. I'd marry Susan right now here in this living room if she'd let me," Stitch said with a laugh.

"We should all be lucky he's sitting here with us right now," Sauer said as he and Stitch shared an intense look.

Newman was going to stay away from that comment. But he'd back Sauer up if need be. Not that he figured he'd need any backup. Although, Sauer was right in one regard. It was surprising Stitch was here tonight. He generally didn't come around because he liked to keep his distance since they were cops. Susan probably made him come.

"Three more months to go. It'll be here before you know

it, and you'll be a happily married man," Ben said cheerfully to reduce the sudden tension between the two men.

Stitch suddenly whacked him on the shoulder. "When are you becoming a happily married man?"

He glared at him. The asshole did that on purpose, taking the attention off himself and directing the spotlight right on him.

"Yeah, how is it going with Mel? She and Adam seem to be settling in," Zeke said, taking the bait of the topic change. Probably because he knew if Sauer and Stitch kept at it, punches could be thrown. It had been known to happen in the past.

"Amelia's great. Adam's doing good in school and making friends. He's doing much better here than he did up in Napleton. It helps that he's such good friends with Nicholas. Thanks, Ben, for that."

Ben nodded. "Those two are like two peas in a pod. I didn't do anything but introduce them. I'm glad it's working out. It's nice to have you back, Newman."

He said it with such sincerity, Newman didn't doubt him even a little bit.

It was nice to be back. Nice to have a semblance of his old life. He might not ever be a cop again, but being a PI was just as good. He still helped people and tried to make a difference in their lives, and that's all that mattered.

"Are you gonna pop the question any time soon or not?" Stitch asked, obviously not deterred.

Newman sighed as he stared at him. Then he lifted up his butt and dug for his wallet. Two seconds later, he produced a small one-carat diamond ring he had been carrying around in his pocket for the last month. Yes, he wanted to marry Amelia. But no, asking was not that easy.

He was terrified she'd say no, and right now life was good. He didn't want to lose that.

"Well, hot damn. Look at you." Zeke chuckled. "What are you waiting for?"

He blew out a nervous breath. "My nerves to stop going haywire. What if she says no? Things are good right now and..." He looked at the ring, twisting it in his hand. He made sure to keep it hidden in case the ladies caught a glimpse.

"She's not going to say no. Not with the way I've seen her look at you," Sauer said.

Yeah, he couldn't deny he didn't see the love in her eyes, but what if she wasn't thinking marriage? What if he wasn't the right guy for her?

"Go do it," Ben said.

Newman averted his gaze from the ring to Ben. "What? Like, right now? Right here? In front of everyone?"

He was pretty sure he had a completely panicked look in his eyes because all four men started laughing.

"Yeah, dude. Right now. Get it over with. And the sex tonight will be amazing." Stitch smiled, his eyes twinkling with merriment and delight.

Fisting his hand closed with the ring snug in his palm, he stood up. Why the hell not? "Okay. Wish me luck. And I will beat the living shit out of every one of you if she says no."

Zeke gave him a thumbs up as he chuckled. Ben also laughed, nodding in the ladies' direction. Sauer and Stitch joined the laughter, sitting up straighter in their seat.

He took a deep breath and headed toward Amelia. She smiled a sweet, brilliant smile. Her red, luscious lips curved into a delicious grin that made him want to drop down to his knees. Not just to ask her to marry him, but to give her a kiss that said how much he loved her.

"Hey, you okay?" Her smile didn't disappear, but her brows puckered in confusion.

Probably because the terror was written all over his face.

"I'm fine. Are you okay?"

"Stop acting weird, Newman. Go back to your side of the room," Dee piped in.

Yeah, he had to agree with Dee on that one. That *was* weird of him. Geez, he needed to get a grip.

He needed to get it over with.

Ignoring Dee, figuring what was the point of responding, he dropped to one knee.

He jerked in surprise when not only did Amelia gasp, but so did every other woman sitting around the table.

"What...are you doing?" Amelia said with a shaky voice.

His palm opened, revealing the ring. "Putting my heart on the line right now. I have to admit, because I promised never to lie to you, that I've had this in my wallet for about a month now. I've been, well, quite frankly, scared shitless to ask."

Her hand popped to her mouth as her eyes widened in surprise.

He blew out a deep breath as he picked up the ring.

"Amelia, my beautiful sweetheart, will you be my wife? I promise to do my best not to piss you off, but we both know I will. I can be stubborn. I promise to never lie to you and to prove to you that I can be the man you deserve. I want to be the man you deserve." Another breath escaped. "So, will you marry me?"

Her hand lowered from her mouth, then paused in the air near his hand holding the ring. "Of course I will. I thought you'd never ask."

He slid the ring on her finger and pulled her closer for a kiss. Then he whispered gently near her lips, "I almost didn't. I was scared you'd say no. Thank God for good friends."

Those same friends started clapping and cheering all around them. Newman stood up, bringing Amelia into his arms and hugging her as he continued to kiss her like he never wanted to stop. And he didn't. He wished he could whisk her out of the house and love her until the sun decided to say good morning.

Congratulations went around the room. They received hugs from everyone, a few cheers with their drinks, and even Adam and the other kids came out to see what all the ruckus was about. Adam smiled and hugged them both, rolling his eyes that it was about time.

Well, okay. Apparently, he was the only one worried she'd say no. It wasn't a strange thing to worry about; he did have a dubious past concerning women, and they hadn't been together that long.

But he couldn't imagine his life with anyone else.

Amelia was the perfect woman for him. She made him a better man, especially at times when he didn't think he was worthy of anything.

He never thought he'd redeem himself after the mess he made of his life.

But he found his redemption in the form of one feisty, strong, fierce woman who always put him in his place when he needed it the most.

He might not be the perfect man, but he was the best version of himself he could possibly be.

In the end, that's all that mattered.

For Zeke and Zoe's Story
Won't Let You Go
A Slaying Love Novel, #1

A determined detective. A woman refusing to bend. A killer who will make sure there are no second chances.

One night of passion became Zoe Sullivan's worst nightmare when Detective Zeke Chance mistook her for a prostitute. Now she wants nothing more than to forget the humiliation —and the man who caused it. But when her boss is brutally murdered, fate throws them together again as Zeke becomes the lead detective on the case.

Zeke knows he screwed up royally, and he's determined to make amends while keeping Zoe safe. But as the investigation deepens, it becomes clear that someone wants Zoe silenced permanently. With a killer closing in and their undeniable attraction reigniting, Zeke must overcome Zoe's distrust before they both become the next victims.

As danger escalates and passion burns hotter than ever, they'll discover that some mistakes are worth making twice —if they survive long enough to get their second chance.

Get ready for steamy romance, heart-pounding suspense, and a detective who'll risk everything to earn back the woman he wronged.

For Ben & Rina's Story
Doomed Love
A Slaying Love Novel, #2

A protective detective. A woman with dangerous secrets. A killer who will stop at nothing to have his way.

Detective Ben Stoyer has wanted Rina Chastain for far too long, but she keeps turning him down with sweet excuses he's tired of hearing. When the victim in his latest murder case looks exactly like her, Ben's protective instincts kick into overdrive—and this time, he won't take no for an answer.

Rina wants to give in to Ben's relentless charm, but her controlling father has destroyed every relationship she's ever tried to have. Now, with a serial killer targeting women who look like her, she's caught between the detective who's determined to protect her and the man who's determined to control her.

As the body count rises and Ben's investigation intensifies, they'll discover that some dangers come from within, and the deadliest enemy might be the one you trust most.

Get ready for pulse-pounding suspense, sizzling chemistry, and a detective who'll defy everyone—including the woman he loves—to keep her safe.

A sassy woman who doesn't believe in love. A shy detective who'll die to protect her. A killer who picked the wrong target.

Dee O'Malley has learned the hard way that men don't stick around, so she's not about to risk her heart on sweet, shy Detective Sauer—even if his kisses make her believe in impossible things. When she's brutally attacked, Dee's determined to find the bastard herself, even if it drives her would-be protector crazy. After all, he's adorable when he's worried.

Detective Sauer might be tongue-tied around most women, but loud, fearless Dee O'Malley turns him into a stammering mess for all the right reasons. The moment she's hurt, his shyness vanishes and his protective instincts take over. But when the attack connects to one of his murder cases, Sauer realizes keeping Dee safe means keeping her close—and his biggest obstacle might be Dee herself.

As the threat escalates and Dee refuses to back down, they'll learn that sometimes the most dangerous thing you can do is fall in love with someone who's willing to die for you.

Get ready for sharp-tongued banter, explosive chemistry, and a shy detective who transforms into a fierce protector when the woman he loves is threatened.

For Stitch & Susan's Story
Evidence of Sin
A Slaying Love Novel, #4

A tattooed bad boy with a record. A police department analyst who should know better. A killer who's making it personal.

One night of scorching passion with straight-laced Susan left tattoo artist Stitch running scared—straight out of her life. But now he's back, and everything about the woman he can't forget terrifies him in the best possible way. She's law enforcement, he's got a record—they'll never work, but when she's in his arms, none of it matters.

Susan knew getting involved with Stitch wouldn't end well, but she can't resist the way he makes her feel alive with just one heated look. She should be focusing on the latest string of brutal murders—no evidence, no leads, no time to waste —but Stitch keeps dragging her into dangerous territory, and she has no idea how close the killer is to making her his final victim.

As the killer's obsession with Susan escalates, Stitch realizes his criminal past might be exactly what she needs to survive. Because sometimes the only way to protect what you love is to embrace the darkness inside.

Get ready for sizzling chemistry, heart-stopping suspense, and a bad boy who'll risk everything—including his freedom—to save the woman who owns his soul.

For Rory & Brooke's story
Obsessed Hope
A Slaying Love Novel, #6

A detective with lethal instincts. A woman who attracts danger. An obsession that could destroy them both.

Detective Rory Walker's latest murder case should be simple —kinky sex gone wrong. Until he meets his prime suspect. Sweet, adorable Brooke Duncan with her terrifying cat and hidden depths is everything he never knew he needed. One look, one touch, and he's a goner. But as he digs deeper into the case, he realizes the dead man had enemies everywhere, and Brooke might be next on someone's list.

Brooke knows she should stay away from the intense detective who looks at her like she's both his salvation and his downfall. But when the investigation takes a deadly turn, Rory becomes her only protection against a killer who's growing more obsessed by the day. Now she must decide whether to trust the man whose obsession matches the killer's intensity...or face a predator alone.

As the case spirals out of control and the killer closes in, Rory will discover that sometimes love and obsession are separated by the thinnest of lines—and crossing it might be the only way to keep them both alive.

Get ready for possessive passion, heart-stopping suspense, and a detective whose protective instincts know no boundaries when the woman he loves is threatened.

ABOUT THE AUTHOR

I'm a *USA Today* Bestselling Author that loves to write contemporary romance and romantic suspense novels, although I am partial to romantic suspense. I even dabble in paranormal. Honestly, I love anything that has to do with romance. As long as there's a happy ending, I'm a happy camper. And insta-love...yes, please! I love baseball (Go Twins!) and creating awesome crafts. I graduated with a Bachelor's Degree in Criminal Justice, working in that field for several years before I became a stay-at-home mom. I have a few more amazing stories in the works. If you would like to learn more about me and my books, head to my website by scanning the QR code. Thanks for reading!

Scan me